P9-CPV-060

The
English Breakfast Murder

Laura Childs

BERKLEY PRIME CRIME, NEW YORK

THE BERKLEY PUBLISHING GROUP
Published by the Penguin Group
Penguin Group (USA) Inc.
375 Hudson Street, New York, New York 10014, USA

USA | Canada | UK | Ireland | Australia | New Zealand | India | South Africa | China

Penguin Books Ltd., Registered Offices: 80 Strand, London WC2R 0RL, England
For more information about the Penguin Group, visit penguin.com.

THE ENGLISH BREAKFAST MURDER

A Berkley Prime Crime Book / published by arrangement with the author

Berkley Prime Crime Books are published by The Berkley Publishing Group.
BERKLEY® PRIME CRIME and the PRIME CRIME logo are trademarks of
Penguin Group (USA) Inc.

For information, address: The Berkley Publishing Group,
a division of Penguin Group (USA) Inc.,
375 Hudson Street, New York, New York 10014.

ISBN: 978-0-425-19129-3

PUBLISHING HISTORY
Berkley Prime Crime mass-market edition / August 2003

PRINTED IN THE UNITED STATES OF AMERICA

25   24   23   22   21   20   19   18   17   16

Cover illustration by Stephanie Thompson Henderson.
Cover design by Lesley Worrell.
Interior text design by Kristin del Rosario.

ALWAYS LEARNING   **PEARSON**

ACKNOWLEDGMENTS

Once again, heartfelt thank-yous to some very special people: My husband, Robert Poor; agent extraordinaire, Sam Pinkus, and his very capable assistant, Christina Schoen; mystery great Mary Higgins Clark, who seems to have become my guardian angel; Jim Smith, world-class illustrator and world-class friend; Dawn Glaser-Falk, who taught me so much about assistance dogs; my sister, Jennie, who is always my first reader and critic; my mother, who loves every word I write, no matter what; fellow author R. D. Zimmerman, who's helped me learn the ropes; Kim Waltemyer, my marvelous editor, and everyone at Berkley Publishing; all the many tea shop owners who work so tirelessly to promote and foster the gentle art of tea; all the Tea Shop Mystery readers who have been so enthusiastic in their comments about Theodosia and her cast of characters; and all the writers and reviewers who have been so generous with their words. Bless you all.

This book is dedicated to all the hardworking volunteers who raise and train service dogs, then unselfishly give those dogs up to people who are truly in need.

**Find out more about the author,
her Tea Shop Mysteries,
and her Scrapbooking Mysteries
at www.laurachilds.com**

CHAPTER I

STARS TWINKLED IN the indigo sky as dusk settled over South Carolina's Halliehurst Beach like a blanket of spun silk. Waves lapped and burbled on the sandy shore and sawgrass whispered in the gentle breeze. In the western sky, Venus, that enigmatic planet known as the evening star, was just beginning to emerge. To the east, far out over the vast Atlantic, a satellite spun its way across the night sky, beeping and blipping telemetry signals to far-flung microwave towers.

"Quick," came the soft voice of Theodosia Browning as she crouched in sand still toasty from the afternoon sun. "Over here. I think this clutch is ready to pop!"

Alerted by Theodosia's cry, a half-dozen anxious volunteers from Charleston's Sea Turtle Protection League picked their way stealthily around a dozen carefully staked out turtle nests.

Louis Crowell, the Sea Turtle Protection League's resident naturalist and volunteer coordinator, knelt down next to

Theodosia. "Shhh," he said, putting a finger to his lips and looking, in his T-shirt and swim trunks, more like a youthful surfer than a professional naturalist. Slowly, carefully, like a grad student on an archaeology dig, Louis gently scraped away the top layer of sand that covered the turtle eggs.

Then the volunteers watched in collective amazement as the nest of approximately one hundred Ping-Pong-ball-sized turtle eggs began to pulsate and jiggle. Some eggs actually rolled and yawed in the sand as their determined contents struggled to mastermind their breakout. Finally, tiny logger-head turtles began to peck and nip their way out of the paper-thin shells that had served as their incubators, then cautiously emerge into their strange new world.

This was the beginning of the sea turtle hatch on Hallie-hurst Beach. Eggs that had been laid by giant, thousand-pound female turtles some two months earlier, many of whom had swum thousands of miles to return to these long-remembered shores, were finally yielding their miniature treasures.

Theodosia pushed back windblown strands of auburn hair and grinned as one tiny hatchling emerged from his shell by heaving himself up mightily with his tiny flippers. The tiny gray-black turtle, wearing a thumbnail-sized piece of shell on his head like a miniature cap, seemed to blink in surprise at the human reception committee that greeted him. Then, with a sudden burst of energy, the little turtle jetti-soned himself into the sand, and landed with a soundless plop. Instinctively, the hatchling scuttled toward the water, where the bright moon shone its sparkling path, a powerful biological cue that beckoned the tiny turtles toward their ul-timate home.

This was a far cry from Theodosia's usual day-to-day

activity of running the Indigo Tea Shop. In fact, this "turtle crawl," her very first, was enthralling.

Up until now, Theodosia's volunteer activities had been limited to taking Earl Grey, her certified therapy dog, on visits to children's hospitals and nursing homes. But Haley Parker, the young baker who magically turned eggs, flour, butter, and cream into the extraordinary pastries, scones, and cakes served at Theodosia's tea shop, had asked her to volunteer. Had assured Theodosia that *this* turtle hatch would be an amazing sight to behold. And pleaded that, *please please please,* they were in desperate need of volunteers.

Theodosia had been delighted to oblige Haley. In fact, she'd been utterly delighted as, every twenty minutes or so, another clutch of eggs virtually exploded with tiny loggerheads. It really *was* a remarkable sight.

Haley pushed a hank of straight blond hair behind one ear. "Didn't I *tell* you this was gonna be great?" she exclaimed. With an oversized T-shirt pulled over her bathing suit, Haley padded silently from one nest to another, thrilled by the activity going on around them. Theodosia followed in her wake.

At a second nest, the two of them giggled as another three dozen turtles stared unblinking at the humans hovering over them, then confidently pushed themselves out of their nests. Hurtling down the sandy beach, flippers moving like rotors, the turtles propelled themselves toward the roiling sea.

The Charleston Sea Turtle Protection League was the official "guardian angel" of sea turtles, particularly of the endangered loggerhead. This was Haley's second season as a volunteer with the Sea Turtle Protection League and she was utterly convinced that it was a *good thing* to help shepherd these helpless little hatchlings into the sea. After all, there were nasty, hungry predators just waiting to ingest the help-less little creatures as they made their perilous journey from nest to sea. Gulls, ghost crabs, even cats came prowling around these turtle nesting sites, looking for easy pickings.

Luckily there are three or four more shifts of volunteers scheduled to show up, thought Theodosia as she watched more loggerhead hatchlings tumble toward the ocean. She knew that hatching was likely to go on all night, and maybe even all day tomorrow. She and Haley had drawn assign-ments for the first shift, the 6:00 P.M. to 10:00 P.M. shift, and they'd been incredibly lucky to witness the very first wave of turtles emerge from their shells.

Now it was almost ten o'clock. Time for the dozen or so volunteers who'd been on watch for the past four hours to relax and take it easy, let the newly arriving volunteers take over.

Theodosia picked her way up the beach to a grassy spot where the embers of a small fire glowed. Not enough light to discombobulate the little turtles, but just enough to heat a steaming pot of Lung Ching tea and a simmering pot of gumbo. Inhaling the slightly floral tea and the spicy melee of duck and chicken, Theodosia figured these two steaming pots would be just the ticket to fortify spirits and chase away any night chills.

Stacking a few pieces of driftwood onto the embers, Theodosia was rewarded by a gunshot-sharp pop as the dry wood immediately caught fire and red and gold flames danced.

"This is mighty nice of you, Miz Browning."

Stirring the pot of gumbo, Theodosia gazed up into the eager face of Louis Crowell illuminated slightly pink by the fire. Louis had been a tireless worker tonight, gently school-ing all the volunteers on the exact techniques they should use to shepherd the tiny turtles down to the sea. No touching, he'd advised, just a kind of benevolent baby-sitting.

"I mean it," said Louis, indicating the two bubbling pots. "Bringing this tea and soup has turned the turtle crawl into a real nice event. Makes it easier to solicit volunteers for next time."

"It seems I had all this tea just sitting around," laughed Theodosia. "And Haley had this great recipe for gumbo . . ."

Theodosia plucked a paper cup from her large wicker picnic basket and ladled tea into it for Louis. This was the story of her life. Ever since she'd opened the Indigo Tea Shop some three years ago, she'd been a woman on a mission. Drayton, her right-hand man and master tea blender, had told her that, when it came to converting people into tea drinkers, she had the zeal of a Calvinist minister.

Maybe so. But ever since she'd opened the little tea shop on Church Street in Charleston's Historic District, her life had been wonderfully fulfilled.

Not that she hadn't been happy before. Oh no, that wasn't the case at all. It's just that . . . well, life had been *different* then. She'd been an account executive for a major Charleston marketing firm, busily pitching new business, servicing accounts, trying to help clients figure out *the next big trend*. That finely honed trend-spotting instinct of hers had, in fact, been what paved the way for her new career and provided her with an exit strategy from the marketing rat race.

The next big trend. *Tea.*

Tea was on the cusp of an enormous renaissance. Next to water, tea was already the number one beverage in the world. And here in the United States, people were drinking tea in droves. They were sipping hot tea, iced tea, bubble tea, and flavored teas in bottles, and suddenly ordering tea lattes at their favorite coffeehouses. High teas, cream teas, garden teas, and bridal teas were back in vogue, and ladies were once again staging lavish tea parties where they could break out their white gloves, best dresses, and rakish hats.

Fancy hotels, upscale restaurants, and cozy B and B's had all brought their silver tea services out of storage, polished them to a high shine, and were offering afternoon tea. Why, the Red Hat Society, a marvelous women's tea group, already boasted more than two thousand chapters across the United States! And the thousands of tea shops, tea salons, and tea rooms that had popped up like errant mushrooms were catering to their tea-hungry audience with everything from specialty teas and tea boutiques to tea etiquette lessons and book clubs.

And just like that, a dusty little tea room in Charleston's historic district, which had been boarded up for years, had suddenly looked very intriguing to Theodosia.

She'd spent one sleepless night pondering her new venture, then took the plunge. She quit her job, said *adios* to job security and her 401k, mustering up every ounce of entrepreneurial spirit. Using part of a small inheritance to finance the removal of several layers of grime and neglect, Theodosia set about "cozying" the place up. Cork tile was ripped from ceilings only to reveal original pressed tin. A dingy, pegged wooden floor, when buffed and oiled, shone richly. Forays to antique shops and county flea markets resulted in a marvelous collection of wooden tables and chairs as well as a kaleidoscopic assortment of fine china teacups, saucers, and plates.

Laying in her inventory of tea had been the most fun of all. Thanks to Drayton's know-how and smarts, the floor-to-ceiling shelves behind her counter were now stacked with gleaming tins of tea that yielded aromatherapy-type scents.

Buttery Darjeelings from India, malty Assams, aromatic Pouchongs that hinted of tropical fruit and flowers, orchid-flavored Keemans from China. And there were wonderful teas from Nepal and Kenya and toasty green teas from Japan, too. Plus the rich black tea that was grown at the Charleston Tea Plantation, located just twenty-five miles southwest of Charleston on the subtropical island of Wad-malow.

Theodosia couldn't afford to hire a large staff so she went for the best. She wooed Drayton Conneley away from his job as hospitality director at a major Charleston hotel with the promise of all the tea he could consume and a free reign at serving as master tea blender. Drayton's parents had been missionaries in China, so he'd grown up around tea and tea plantations, and had even apprenticed for a while at the world's major tea auction site in Amsterdam. The whistle and chirp of a tea kettle were music to his ears.

Finding Haley Parker had been pure luck. Haley was two years into college, undecided, bored, and forever changing majors. She was also a free spirit and a remarkably gifted baker. Now, Haley baked to her heart's content each morning and attended college classes a couple evenings a week. So far, Haley had switched her major from English literature to women's studies to history. Now Haley had vowed with a white-hot fervor that she would earn an MBA and eventually head her own small business.

The way Haley ran their kitchen operation, with the autocratic precision of a Prussian general, there was no doubt in Theodosia's mind that Haley would someday preside as CEO of her own company.

With the advent of the Indigo Tea Shop, Theodosia's life had taken on a new rhythm and a far saner pace. There was no more working 24/7 for the *other* guy. Now, when she burned the midnight oil or rose sleepily at four in the morning to prepare for a big catering job, it was for *her* benefit. For the Indigo Tea Shop and her hard-won dream.

Theodosia poured a steaming cup of Lung Ching tea for Louis. Lung Ching was a hearty, flavorful tea. Big on aroma with far less briskness than a morning tea would offer. Lung Ching was the kind of tea you could sip and relax with at night, a tea that easily held its own alongside Haley's gumbo.

"Anyone else for tea and gumbo?" Theodosia asked the group of volunteers and was pleasantly surprised when at least a dozen people grabbed for cups and held them out to be served.

Helping Theodosia pour tea and ladle out gumbo, Haley was beginning to worry. More tea could always be brewed, but their bubbling pot of gumbo was disappearing at an alarming rate.

"I should have brought *both* pots," Haley fretted. "I had no idea so many volunteers would show up!" Haley's concern was not unfounded. Volunteers who'd already completed their shift were still hanging around, enjoying the afterglow of the event. Newly arriving volunteers were also clamoring for tea and gumbo.

As she peered over Theodosia's shoulder into the dark of the parking lot some forty feet away, Haley's face assumed a glum look. "Rats," she said, "here comes somebody else. Bet they'll be hungry, too."

"Could anybody use another pot of gumbo?" called a familiar voice.

Theodosia jerked her head up from the fire. She was pretty sure she recognized that voice. "Drayton?" she called.

Drayton Conneley came stumbling across the sand dunes lugging another pot of gumbo. "Now I know I've completely lost my mind," he announced with his traditional gusto. "I was happily sprawled in a leather armchair in my perfectly cozy little house reading Victor Hugo. And I suddenly got this crazy *vibe*."

"That was *me*," exclaimed Haley, pleased.

"Well, no thanks to you, then, missy," said Drayton with mock sternness. "Anyway, since I'd already been psychically *summoned*, I figured you turtle wranglers could probably do with some extra gumbo."

"Drayton, you're a lifesaver," exclaimed Theodosia. "We were scraping the bottom of the pot, wondering what to do."

As Drayton swung his blue crackle glaze pot onto the grate that was propped above the fire, there was a crack and a pop, then a loud hiss issued forth. "Ah," he said appreciatively, a smile tugging at his lined sixty-three-year-old face, "nothing like the lure of a fine shore dinner."

"Or snack," said Haley. "Thanks, Drayton. You really are a lifesaver. Hey, you want to see the turtles?" she asked eagerly. "The little guys are absolutely *adorable*."

"Pass," said Drayton with a tolerant smile. "I fear the heart of a true city dweller beats within my breast. Not that I don't have a deep and abiding love for all God's wee creatures, because I do. But I simply don't feel the necessity to *interact* with them on an up-close-and-personal basis."

Several of the volunteers just stared at Drayton, but Theodosia shook her head knowingly. It wasn't a bit out of character for Drayton to speechify, even standing on a beach with baby turtles streaming everywhere.

Besides serving as Theodosia's right-hand man and majordomo at the Indigo Tea Shop, Drayton sat on the board of directors of the Charleston Heritage Society as parliamentarian. And besides having a left-brain outlook, he enjoyed a wicked command of the King's English. Drayton was also known for his love of history and for having a discerning eye when it came to antiques, art goods, and collectibles. He'd plucked more than one discarded object from a jumbled flea market table and found it to be a real treasure. In fact, a rather homely little green ceramic pot that he'd discovered at a rummage sale over in Goose Creek had turned out to be a piece of Edgewood art pottery worth several thousand dollars!

"Theodosia," whispered a young volunteer named Jennifer, "there's another nest about to hatch."

"Come on, Drayton," said Theodosia, plucking at the sleeve of Drayton's shirt. "One quick peek. Watch the baby turtles pop out."

Ever one for theatrics, Drayton rolled his eyes. "Do I have to?"

"Yes, you do," Theodosia insisted. "Every once in a while, a tiny dose of nature is good for the soul. Keeps one connected with life's greater mysteries."

Drayton handed the soup ladle to Haley. "Will you do the honors while I indulge Theodosia with her turtle rodeo?"

"Drayton, try to have fun, okay?" cajoled Haley. "Helping sea turtles is worthwhile."

"So everyone keeps telling me," said Drayton as he followed Theodosia somewhat stiffly down the beach.

Theodosia stopped and pointed at Drayton's loafers. "You'd better take your shoes off." She herself was barefoot, with just a T-shirt pulled over her maillot swimsuit. Drayton, of course, wore a linen shirt and dress slacks. Theodosia was surprised he hadn't shown up wearing his jacket and customary bow tie.

"You want me to stroll around Halliehurst Beach in my good silk socks?" Drayton asked somewhat peevishly.

"No," said Theodosia, trying to remain patient, "I assumed you'd remove your socks as well."

"Honestly," pouted Drayton. "I really must draw the line. What if some particularly ill-tempered blue crab suddenly charged out of the surf and took a nasty pinch at my big toe?"

"Then you'll either be walking with a limp," Theodosia told him as they stepped closer to the lapping water, "or if you're quick and clever, be noshing crab cakes for lunch tomorrow."

Theodosia nudged Drayton with an elbow as a group of tiny turtles struggled past them. Their tiny flippers worked like mad, the back edges of their shells left a fine trailing line in the wet sand as they made a beeline for the bubbling surf.

"Aren't they cute?" she asked.

"Adorable," he said in his overly serious parliamentarian voice. But Theodosia could tell from the look of delight on Drayton's face that he was really quite taken by the spectacle of baby loggerheads. In fact, Drayton was tiptoeing behind the little squad of turtles right now, staying a judicious distance behind them so as not to frighten or disturb them.

"Imagine," Drayton said with a tinge of reverence in his voice. "These tiny turtles must weigh . . . what? An ounce or two at the most? And yet, without hesitation, they plunge right into the vast Atlantic. Plucky little devils, aren't they?"

Theodosia stood next to Drayton and gazed out to sea. It really *was* amazing when you thought about it, she decided. With only their instinct to guide them, the tiny turtles hurled themselves into the seething Atlantic and immediately set off on a long, perilous journey. Louis Crowell had told them during their earlier training session that, once sea-borne, the little loggerheads would float offshore for several years.

They'd take refuge in floating seaweed and just drift along in the ocean currents, often floating for thousands of miles. In fact, new scientific research had confirmed that the baby turtles were carefully attuned to the subtle signals of the earth's magnetic field. And they used these finely honed instincts to stay within a zone known as the Atlantic gyre, a wide current of exceptionally warm water.

"What a mystery the ocean is," murmured Drayton. "Think of all the amazingly diverse life-forms that live within, how the moon exerts its magnetic pull on the tides, how so many shipwrecks lie silently at its bottom. The sea is a metaphor for poetry and peril."

The rising moon had turned into an enormous bright orb that bobbed overhead like a ripe round of Camembert. Theodosia thought about how the turtles keyed off the moon. And how moonlight rippling across water was the critical visual cue that told the little hatchlings which direction to head.

Theodosia dropped her gaze from the moon to its wide glimmering path that shone atop the sea. *It's a turtle beacon,* she thought to herself. *The moon and the big blue beckon these creatures to a rich nourishing home.*

As she gazed out at the peaceful sea, Theodosia slowly became aware of something floating there, some forty yards out. She pointed to it. "What's that, Drayton?" she asked.

He shifted his gaze and stared at the dark mass. "Driftwood?"

Theodosia squinted. With the moonlight dappling the water, it was difficult to see, like staring into a bright light. "Or maybe a clump of seaweed?" she offered.

Drayton frowned. "It doesn't *look* like seaweed." There was a sharp note in his voice. Mere observation seemed to have crossed over into curiosity. "It's fairly good sized."

"It is, isn't it," agreed Theodosia, peering out into the

darkness. Wiggling her toes in the still-warm sand, she wondered what on earth could possibly be floating out there. Looking around for other volunteers, so she could perhaps elicit some reaction or even consensus, Theodosia saw that most of them had moved farther down the beach where the majority of turtle nests were located.

"Do you suppose it's some sort of marine animal?" asked Drayton. "A dead whale or something?"

"Oh no!" said Haley, who had just walked down to the surf line to join them. "Please don't say that." Haley had a soft spot in her heart for all living creatures, and the thought of a dead whale practically traumatized her. "On the other hand," she said, "if it *is* a whale . . . maybe it's sick or injured." She glanced at Theodosia. "Do you think we should . . . um . . . check?"

"Whatever it is doesn't seem all *that* far out," said Theodosia, staring out to sea and mentally gauging the distance.

"You're not thinking of . . ." began Drayton.

But Theodosia had already pulled her T-shirt over her head to reveal a sleek navy swimsuit with a bright yellow racing stripe down the side. "I think I'll swim out and have a look," she told them.

"Oh no," protested Drayton, shaking his head. "Bad idea. *Very* bad idea. Whatever is out there is probably just a glob of seaweed or something."

Theodosia stuck her feet into her swim fins and pulled the straps up over her heels. "Really, Drayton, whatever it is, I don't think it's more than forty yards out," she told him.

"She'll be okay," Haley assured Drayton. "Don't you know, Theo's been certified as a senior lifesaver. She used to work summers as a lifeguard."

"Used to," snorted Drayton. "What if there's a nasty riptide that carries her off?" He hesitated, gazing out across the dark waters. "Or *something else* is out there? Something we don't . . ." His voice trailed off. "No, I say you don't go." Drayton folded his arms across his chest as Theodosia duck-walked toward the water, her flippers making little *splats* against the sand.

"But if a whale or dolphin needs help . . ." pleaded Haley.

"Then we shall phone the Coast Guard station and let *them* handle it," pronounced Drayton. "Sea creatures are their bailiwick, after all."

Theodosia waded in up to her waist and pulled on her goggles. Now *she* was getting a strange vibe. Which meant she just *had* to swim out and see what was going on. "See, no riptide," she assured Drayton, trying to keep her voice lighthearted and reassuring. "And the water's extremely warm. Soft as silk."

"Not too far now," cautioned Drayton as a wave rose up and Theodosia promptly dove into it. "Oh, this is just awful," he fretted. "We never should have let her go."

But thirty seconds later Theodosia bobbed to the surface. She gave a quick wave to the two of them, then turned and set out with strong strokes toward the floating mass.

The water really was warm tonight, Theodosia decided as she moved steadily through the water. And there was nothing about this late-night swim that worried her unduly. She'd grown up in and around the waters of South Carolina, swimming and snorkeling to her heart's content. She'd sailed boats through the Intercoastal Waterway and on the Atlantic Ocean, and even explored the reefs off some of the beaches on Kiawah Island and Hilton Head. She also knew there hadn't been a shark sighting off Halliehurst Beach since lord knows when, so she felt pretty confident on that front, too.

But the strange vibe remained with her. There *was* something out there. Something that warranted attention.

Theodosia was ten feet from the floating blob when she felt the first little ping of nervousness grab inside her chest. *What if it is an injured marine animal?* she wondered. *Will it bite? Or thrash around and get more entangled if the poor thing is already hung up on some sort of fishing line or treble hook?*

No, she told herself, *now you're just keying off Drayton's paranoia.* Rationally, Theodosia knew that everything was going to be fine. If she just kept swimming, she could satisfy her voracious curiosity and then head home. After all, tomorrow was a big day at work. The Indigo Tea Shop had reservations up the wazoo, with some sixty-five people slated to show up for a 10:00 A.M. cream tea and a 2:00 P.M. high tea. And the notion of fulfilling the expectations of *that* many paying customers was positively frightening!

As Theodosia approached the floating mass, she was initially disappointed. The gob was dark and dank and tangled. *Just junk,* she thought. *Fishing nets and line and . . . what else? Maybe old rags that fell off some fishing boat and got tangled in a hunk of seaweed?*

She relaxed a bit, slid her goggles up onto her forehead. *See, silly,* she told herself, *it's nothing at all.* She prodded at the mass of rags, and her finger connected with a soft, spongy mass. At the same time a whiff of something briny and noxious prickled her nose. Theodosia frowned. The odor wasn't particularly nice. Like something putrid or overly ripe.

What is this thing? she wondered as she poked at it again.

This time her fingertips detected something slimy and cold.

Ohmygosh! What is it?

Her eyes flew open, her breath suddenly came in short gasps, and she stopped treading water for just a moment.

Did I just touch dead fish? Or dead flesh?

Flailing about in the water, momentarily caught in a panic, Theodosia sucked in a great gulp of brackish seawater. Choking, spitting, hating the overly salty taste, she willed herself to calm down.

Stop this! she admonished herself. Calm down!

And why am I suddenly shivering uncontrollably? she asked herself. *The water didn't feel a bit cold before, and now I'm shaking like crazy.*

That's adrenaline kicking in, she decided. The body's inner defense mechanism. Fight or flight.

Flight. Definitely flight.

Theodosia tried to reason with herself. Tried to calm down and figure out exactly what this was. She didn't want to flail her way back to shore and cry wolf for no reason at all. She'd look like an absolute ninny, especially with two dozen volunteers standing around on the beach. She'd never hear the end of it.

Only one way to tell, came her own response.

Eeeyuh.

Theodosia slipped around the floating thing until she was on the other side of it. Now the bright full moon was at her back, shining down upon the water like a giant floodlight. And the *thing,* whatever it was, was between her and the shore.

Theodosia took a deep breath. Then, scissor-kicking hard with her legs so she'd remain upright and buoyant, she grasped the floating thing with her hands, pulled it toward her.

Lifeless, half-open eyes stared into hers. A mouth gaped wide, locked in a silent scream. Rubbery, white skin, like the underbelly of a nasty swamp thing, seemed leached of all life.

Dead body, oh yes it's a dead body!

Horrified, Theodosia thrust the body from her grasp and struggled away from it.

Darn, she thought. *Why did I have to be so nosy?* She tried to collect herself, but the neurons in her brain seemed to be firing all at once. *Who was it? What happened to him? Boating accident? Drifted in on a current?*

The pounding in her ears was matched by the timpani solo in her chest as her heart beat overtime.

"What is it?" Haley's faint call echoed across the water. "A dead dolphin?"

Theodosia paddled a few feet toward shore and waved at her, hoping she could be seen, praying she could be heard. "Get a boat!" she cried. "Get a boat out here right now!"

"Theodosia!" called Drayton. "Is everything okay?"

"Get a boat!" she called again.

No, everything was definitely not okay.

CHAPTER 2

*T*HE AROMA OF fresh-baked scones, *croissants aux pignons*, lemon poppyseed cake, and freshly brewed Assam tea perfumed the air at the Indigo Tea Shop. Tables were impeccably set with white linen tablecloths, embroidered napkins, and cups and saucers by Limoges, Spode, and Royal Doulton. Teapot warmers were at the ready. Tiny silver spoons stuck upright in cut-glass bowls filled with swirls of sweet Devonshire cream. A small fire crackled cheerily in the tiny stone fireplace.

But Theodosia, Drayton, and Haley felt anything but cheery. Last night had been a nightmare for all of them. Soon after they called for help, the Recovery Unit of the Sheriff's Water Patrol arrived to collect the floating remains.

And even though the evening had been warm, Theodosia hadn't been able to stop shivering as she stood on shore, watching the actual recovery. Haley had been hysterical once she found out her sick dolphin was really a dead body, and blamed herself for Theodosia's erratic state of mind.

But Drayton had ended up in the worst shape of any of them.

It had taken forever for the sheriff's men to float the tangled mass of nets, seaweed, and dead body back to shore. Then, of course, the police and paramedics had arrived with blazing lights and bleating sirens. That's when Drayton made a terrible mistake. In a pique of curiosity, he'd crouched down alongside the dead body to see if he could possibly identify the drowning victim.

Unfortunately for Drayton, he'd been able to. The poor drowned man turned out to be Harper Fisk, a local antique dealer and an old friend.

"I still can't believe he's dead," Drayton whispered harshly as he stared out across the empty tea room, shaking his grizzled head. His normally authoritative voice was choked, his whole manner, usually ebullient and upbeat, was incredibly subdued.

The three of them were seated at the small table nearest the kitchen, trying to relax, trying to pull it together emotionally before their eager customers descended upon them for the morning cream tea.

"He was an antique dealer?" asked Haley. She'd covered this same territory with Drayton last night, but she appeared to have forgotten. Or maybe she'd simply blocked it from her memory.

"Art and antiquities, really," said Drayton. He dropped a lump of sugar into his cup of Assam and stirred it absently. "Harper Fisk was nearly seventy but he still ran a little shop down on King Street. The Legacy Gallery. Harper carried a wide range of merchandise, but he specialized in architectural pieces and eighteenth- and nineteenth-century oil paintings. You know, Jarvis, Nathaniel Russel, Hesselius, that sort of thing. Very tasty stuff."

Theodosia nodded. She'd been fortunate enough to purchase a Russel for herself a few years ago. Now it hung in her small but elegantly appointed apartment just upstairs from the tea shop, where her dog, Earl Grey, lay snoozing after their early-morning walk.

"Harper Fisk was also a real Civil War buff," added Drayton. "Always had a nice collection of muskets and coins and brass uniform buttons for sale."

"Aren't those objects awfully difficult to come by these days?" asked Theodosia.

"Somewhat," said Drayton slowly, "but you have to understand, Harper Fisk was also an amateur treasure hunter. He was always dropping by the Heritage Society to study old journals and historic records. Then he'd try to plot the whereabouts of ancient shipwrecks and such."

"Do you think that's what he was doing when he drowned?" asked Haley. "Scouting for a shipwreck?"

Drayton shook his head sadly. "I have no idea."

"Did Harper Fisk own a boat?" asked Theodosia.

"Don't know," said Drayton. "Maybe. I guess I just assumed poor Harper fell off a dock or something. Or maybe he was clambering around on that old seawall down by the Battery." The Battery was the wedge of park land at the very tip of the historic peninsula. A popular tourist attraction, it boasted a Victorian bandstand, the very beautiful White Point Gardens, and a collection of antique cannons.

"You think Harper Fisk maybe slipped off the seawall and fell in?" asked Theodosia.

"Got pulled out by the current," said Drayton, sounding forlorn.

Theodosia nodded. It sounded like a plausible theory. Harper Fisk was an old man. He could have had some kind of cardiac incident, fell and hit his head on the seawall, then pitched into the ocean. If so, it was likely he'd have drowned right away. Those were dangerous waters, after all. The Ashley and Cooper Rivers surrounded the city of Charleston, and the confluence of those strong currents and eddies could have carried his body out. Which would account for Harper Fisk's body showing up near Halliehurst Beach.

"Harper Fisk lived near the Battery, right?" said Theodosia. "In the historic district?" Graced with block after elegant block of Italianate, Victorian, and Federal-style mansions, the historic district was the oldest part of Charleston. The neighborhood was drop-dead gorgeous with cobblestone streets and walkways, hidden gardens, and ancient live oaks dripping with Spanish moss.

Drayton nodded. "Yes, he lived in a carriage house off Archdale Street."

"Near Timothy Neville?" asked Theodosia. Timothy Neville was the octogenarian president of Charleston's Heritage Society, which served as a repository for important Charleston antiquities such as old paintings, drawings and maps, period furnishings, and historic documents and records.

"Actually, Harper occupied that little Gothic-looking carriage house behind Marianne Petigru's house," said Drayton. "You know, the woman who's one of the partners in Popple Creek Design."

"Oh sure," responded Theodosia. "I've jogged by there lots of times. Cute place."

Haley stood up and stretched, glanced at her watch. "You know," she said, "our guests are going to begin arriving in about ten minutes." She tied a long white French waiter's apron over her black T-shirt and slacks.

Drayton turned sad eyes to Theodosia and Haley. "I wish we didn't have to do this," he said. "My heart's just not in it."

Theodosia put a hand on Drayton's arm. "None of our hearts are in this," she told him. "But it was your good idea to offer our customers these special-event teas."

"Yeah," grumped Haley, "a Saturday cream tea and a high tea. And it's just our luck that everybody absolutely loved the idea and jumped on it. Do you know, people were *still* calling yesterday to see if they could reserve a table and I had to tell them both teas were completely filled!"

"We're lucky to have the business," said Theodosia quietly. "Not everyone is so fortunate these days." Even with the steady influx of tourists into Charleston, she knew that not all the small businesses up and down picturesque Church Street were as lucky as they were. The Antiquarian Bookstore just down the block seemed to be holding its own, but the ladies who ran the Cabbage Patch Needlepoint Shop had complained about business falling off. Times were tough right now. And Theodosia knew that during tough times, you were thankful for every drip and drop of business that came your way.

"Oh my *goodness*!" announced a loud voice. "This tea shop is absolutely *adorable*! Like something out of *Alice in Wonderland*!"

Theodosia blinked. She knew that voice. Or *thought* she knew that voice. On the other hand, she really didn't recognize the woman in the bright fuchsia suit and matching wide-brimmed hat who stood poised in the doorway, oohing and aahing so loudly.

Then when the woman in the fuchsia suit moved a few steps forward, Theodosia recognized the woman in the canary yellow suit who followed a few steps behind. It was Delaine Dish. Owner of the Cotton Duck Clothing Store, volunteer at the Heritage Society, good friend, and outrageous flirt. Not necessarily in that order.

"Theodosia!" came Delaine's excited cry. "How *are* you?" She extended her arms in anticipation of a huge embrace, propelled herself across the room, and administered a profusion of air kisses.

"And dear Drayton!" Now Delaine executed a tight spin on her teetery yet fashionable high heels and focused her complete and utter attention upon Drayton. Clutching his lapels and putting a gloved hand on his shoulder, she conferred a variety of air kisses upon him that looked very cozy and smoochy but never really did seem to make direct contact.

Bright-eyed with excitement, Delaine extended an arm toward the woman wearing the fuchsia suit. "And *this*," she pronounced, as though she were introducing visiting royalty to the Court of Saint James, "is my dear, dear *sister*! Everyone, meet Nadine DesLauriers. She's come all the way from New York City just to visit us!"

Now that she'd been properly introduced, Nadine of the fuchsia suit and matching hat came bustling over. "I've heard *so* much about you-all," she gushed. Her soft doe eyes darted around the Indigo Tea Shop, taking in the shelves filled with tea tins and jars of sourwood honey, the old wooden counter piled high with sweetgrass baskets, the T-Bath products with their elegant celadon green packaging displayed in an old wooden secretary. "And I meant what I said," Nadine enunciated carefully. "This is *exactly* like tumbling through the looking glass to attend a wonderful tea party!"

"What's all the commotion about?" demanded Haley as she stuck her head out from the kitchen.

Nadine arched an arm and pointed a finger at Haley. "Look at the long hair! You must be Alice," she declared.

Haley shook her head vigorously. "Nope, Haley," she said and immediately disappeared back into the kitchen.

Nadine turned toward Drayton and clapped her hands with delight. "You've got to be the Cheshire Cat," she declared.

Drayton favored her with a slight bow. "At your service," he said, playing along.

Wow, thought Theodosia, *and I thought Delaine was a little off-kilter. She looks like a straightlaced member of the Franz Kafka Book Club compared to her sister.*

Nadine turned bright eyes on Theodosia. "And you're . . ."

"The red queen," grinned Theodosia, figuring the best defense was a good offense. "Off with her head."

Nadine stared wide-eyed at Theodosia, a trifle unsure if she was joking or not. Then she collapsed into giggles. "Theo*do*sia," said Nadine, accenting the middle syllable and wangling a finger at her. "I've *heard* about you. You are reputed to possess a *wicked* sense of humor."

Theodosia smiled good-naturedly as Drayton proceeded to seat the two sisters, then she scurried off to begin readying pots of tea.

Hey, this is Delaine's sister who's down for a visit, she told herself. Would it kill me to be a little playful?

Measuring out six rounded teaspoons of Darjeeling, Theodosia dumped them into a Royal Winton floral teapot as Nadine's laugh suddenly exploded loudly throughout the tea shop.

Hmm . . . on the other hand . . .

Success came easily this morning. Every table was filled and each guest appeared to be having a rousing good time. Drayton poured tea and dispensed charm as though last night's tragic occurrence had never taken place. But Theodosia knew that, for all his gentlemanly manners and good cheer, Drayton was secretly brokenhearted.

Haley outdid herself once again, overcoming cramped and crowded conditions in their small kitchen at the back of the tea shop. Counter space was always at a premium and how they'd managed to cram an oversized commercial oven into that small space still amazed them all.

Today's cream tea started off with cranberry walnut scones, Devonshire cream, and Assam and Darjeeling tea. The cranberries, imparting just a hint of tartness, were beautifully complimented by the mellow, slightly malty flavor of the Assam tea and the muscatel flavor of the Darjeeling. The Devonshire cream, rich and sinfully sweet, was applied to the scones in great swirling mounds.

Haley's second course consisted of tiny tea sandwiches. A sliver of fresh roasted chicken nestled with the thinnest slice of garden-ripe tomato atop a thin piece of dark bread spread with cream cheese and chives. A second sandwich choice was a mound of crab salad on a tiny croissant rolled in pine nuts and accented with a slice of roasted red pepper. Heavenly.

The third course was a slice of Haley's famous broccoli and cheese quiche. To assure maximum quality, Haley had personally journeyed down to the Farmer's Market yesterday and bought a case of fresh brown eggs. The farmer, just in from the low-country for the day with his produce, had sworn to Haley that the eggs had been laid by eager hens just that morning.

Haley's dessert course consisted of a lemon poppy seed cake chopped into small squares, then drizzled with a light lemon custard sauce and served in tall, stemmed glasses.

As Theodosia circulated among the tables, pouring a

final cup of Assam here, a taste of Darjeeling there, Delaine waved her over.

"Theodosia, your presentation is so *elegant*," drawled Delaine. "It's not often we get so royally treated to tea," she hastily explained to Nadine. "Usually us tea shop regulars just run in for a bite of pastry and a quick cuppa to go."

"Thank you, Delaine, I'm glad you're enjoying everything," responded Theodosia. She was pleased to see that Nadine also seemed to be having a rollicking good time. Nadine had already downed three cups of Darjeeling, although Theodosia wasn't sure if Nadine was a real tea lover or she simply enjoyed flirting with Drayton every time he drifted by with a fresh pot of tea.

Oh, well, doesn't matter. She's here and she's happy and that's all that really counts.

"Theodosia," said Delaine, "you're still coming to Fashion Bash next Saturday, aren't you?" Fashion Bash was Delaine's big brainstorm to raise much-needed funds for the Heritage Society. The sixty-dollar-a-ticket luncheon, tea, and fashion show was scheduled to take place next Saturday at the rather elegant Garden Gate Restaurant down on Meeting Street. Coincidentally, clothes from Delaine's store would be modeled by friends and featured in the fashion show. Theodosia knew the whole event could probably be construed as a trifle self-serving. After all, Delaine would end up selling a ton of clothes since clothing worn by models always looked far better than simply suspended from hangers. On the other hand, Delaine *was* shouldering the brunt of the work and every penny of the proceeds was earmarked for the Heritage Society.

"I wouldn't miss it for the world, Delaine," said Theodosia, topping off Delaine's cup of Assam.

Nadine flashed Theodosia a wide grin. "Is your tea shop

doing the catering?" she asked. "You've done such a splendid job with *this* little tea. And your food is almost as elegant as the Four Seasons in New York."

"Thank you," said Theodosia, wondering why Nadine had referred to this as a *little* tea. "Actually, I'll just be a guest at Fashion Bash like everyone else," she explained. "Your sister is very capably handling all the luncheon arrangements."

And thank goodness, thought Theodosia, that Delaine hadn't tried to rope her in as caterer. It would be a delightful change to just sit and enjoy a nice summer event, no strings attached.

"Are you modeling, then?" asked Nadine, gazing at Theodosia in her maddening appraising way. "You've got the figure for it, even if you're not all that tall."

Theodosia gritted her teeth and smiled. *The customer is always right,* she told herself. *Even when they're amazingly rude.* "No, I'm afraid my modeling days are over," she told Nadine.

"Nadine will be modeling," offered Delaine, much to her sister's delight. "We're just not sure whether she'll be wearing the silver cocktail dress or the scoop-necked fuchsia crop top and pants."

"Fuchsia's my signature color," explained Nadine. "I have one closet devoted entirely to fuchsia. Fuchsia sweaters, fuchsia blouses, fuchsia—"

"You seem to be staying in Charleston for quite a long visit," said Theodosia, trying to gently steer the conversation. "I hope your husband was able to accompany you."

A frown flickered across Nadine's face. "No," she said quietly. "I'm no longer married."

Delaine leaned forward. "The big D," she said in a stage whisper.

"Dumped?" The word tumbled out of Theodosia's mouth before she even had time to think. *Oops.*

Nadine suddenly looked uncomfortable. "Divorced," she said, glancing away, her hands suddenly very busy with the cream and sugar.

"Well, it's nice you can manage such an extended visit," purred Theodosia as she moved on with her pot of tea to the next table.

Theodosia was standing behind the counter, tallying up checks, when Drayton slipped in beside her. "What on earth did you say to Delaine's sister?" he asked. "She's been throwing you dagger-like looks for the past five minutes."

"Has she?" said Theodosia innocently. "I really hadn't noticed."

CHAPTER 3

✧✧✧

$\mathcal{B}$Y TWELVE-THIRTY the last guest had departed and Theodosia, Drayton, and Haley suddenly shifted into overdrive. There were dishes to be cleared and washed, wooden floors to be swept, chairs to be straightened. Then, of course, the tables had to be made gorgeous again with flower arrangements, freshly filled cream pitchers and sugar bowls, and newly washed teacups, saucers, plates, and silverware.

"Déjà vu!" sighed Haley. "Now we have to repeat everything all over again. Staging one of these special teas is really a colossal amount of *work*."

"It's certainly not like Monday through Friday when our regular customers just drop by, is it?" said Theodosia. "Still, when we offer a special-event tea, we can charge a good deal more." In fact, their morning cream tea guests had gladly paid twenty-two dollars each and their high tea guests would be paying twenty-four dollars each.

"Hear, hear," said Haley. "I'm all for making money."

Like all of them, Haley was aware that running a tea shop was not always a wildly prosperous venture. Even though it was a delight and a labor of love, being the proprietor of a tea room was hands-on hard work. And profits were earned one cup at a time.

"How are you holding up, Drayton?" asked Theodosia. Drayton had seemed to revert to his old self as he mingled with customers, pouring tea and dispensing interesting tidbits of tea lore. Most customers were delighted when he took time to carefully explain the difference between oolong and Pouchon, or fascinated them with details on how he created his own blends of tea, then personalized them even more by adding dried currants, bits of citrus, and spices.

Drayton turned a sad face toward Theodosia. "I'm doing as well as could be expected. Wouldn't you know, I was just in a meeting with poor Harper Fisk two nights ago. We were discussing the possibility of the Heritage Society creating some sort of map display that highlighted all our local shipwreck sites. Most folks don't realize it, but there are almost forty shipwrecks strewn across the bottom of Charleston Harbor."

"Really?" squealed Haley. "I had no idea."

"Oh, yes," Drayton assured her. "We're talking three-masted schooners that were sunk doing the American Revolution, clipper ships that were torpedoed as they tried to run Civil War blockades, and various merchant ships sunk by pirates over the years."

"There were pirates around Charleston?" asked Haley, clearly fascinated by the idea.

"Still are," said Theodosia with a sly grin as she folded a stack of monogrammed linen napkins.

Drayton favored Theodosia with a small smile. He'd been around the block. He knew exactly what she meant.

"Anyway," Drayton continued, "it's just tremendously difficult to accept the fact that I won't be seeing Harper Fisk again. He was practically a fixture at the Heritage Society." Drayton wiped a finger at one eye. "Harper Fisk was certainly a fine old fellow."

"Does he have family here?" asked Theodosia. She'd didn't want to keep pressing Drayton about Harper Fisk's death. On the other hand, she knew it was often highly therapeutic to talk through your grief.

Drayton grimaced. "No family. That's what makes his death doubly tragic. He was the last of the Fisks. I'm afraid when Harper died, his family line died, too."

"That's *so* sad," said Haley, who was blessed with brothers and sisters and dozens of cousins. Now it was her turn to swipe at her eyes with the corner of her apron.

"The closest Harper had to family was the English Breakfast Club," said Drayton."

"What's that?" asked Haley.

"Bunch of older guys, mostly antique store owners and history buffs. They generally got together a couple mornings a week in Harper Fisk's shop to drink tea, reminisce, and talk a little history."

"A bull session," said Haley. "That's sweet. At least he had *somebody*. Families don't always have to be blood relatives, you know."

"I know," murmured Theodosia. As far as she was concerned, Drayton and Haley were family, too. Along with dear Aunt Libby, who lived out in the low-country. "What will happen to Harper Fisk's antique store?" Theodosia asked Drayton. She recalled that the Legacy Gallery was a fairly tasty little shop located in a fashionable brick building down on King Street.

"Oh," said Drayton. "He has a partner. A nice young

woman by the name of Summer Sullivan. I imagine she'll keep the shop going. As far as Harper's personal effects go, however, most will probably revert to the Heritage Society. I know for a fact that Harper's last will and testament specifically stated that the Heritage Society would inherit everything *outside* the realm of his shop. Stocks, bonds, personal collectibles, the whole ball of wax."

"What about that darling little carriage house where he lived?" asked Haley.

Drayton shrugged. "No idea. I don't know if Harper owned or rented."

"Well," said Haley, "I suppose it doesn't matter now." She gazed at Theodosia and Drayton sadly, as if recalling the incident of last night. Then she brightened. "Is anyone hungry? I made extra sandwiches. Figured we'd need to keep our energy up since we've got a second group scheduled to arrive in"—Haley fumbled for the antique watch she wore around her neck on a gold chain—"gosh, just under an hour!"

"Sandwiches sound great," said Theodosia. She for one was beginning to feel like she was running on empty.

"Bring them out," agreed Drayton. "I'll pour us each a nice cup of Yunnan. Nothing like a good Chinese black tea to keep us grounded."

"And pack a wallop of caffeine to keep us energized," added Theodosia.

The three of them were nibbling sandwiches when the door to the tea shop suddenly swung open and the little bell that hung above it tinkled merrily.

Theodosia turned toward the door, ready to inform their early-bird guest that they were a full *fifty minutes early* and that the Indigo Tea Shop wasn't properly set up yet. And killing time down the street at the Antiquarian Book Shop might be a good idea.

But the figure that filled the doorway wasn't a guest for high tea after all. It was Burt Tidwell, homicide detective *extraordinaire* of the Charleston Police Department.

"Detective Tidwell," said Theodosia, leaping from her chair. She was clearly surprised. She hadn't seen Tidwell in a number of months. Not since a certain cat burglar, who'd managed to snatch a number of precious jewels from residents of the neighborhood, had been apprehended. Thanks in part to her dog, Earl Grey.

In fact, Theodosia had thought that maybe Detective Tidwell had finally opted for retirement. Had decided to pack it in and spend his days tending the tiny eight-by-ten-foot garden that he seemed to dote on in his backyard.

But no, here was Burt Tidwell, standing in front of her, clearly larger than life.

"Detective Tidwell," said Drayton, "care to join us for a spot of tea?"

Tidwell swiveled his giant head around the tea room, taking in the fancy tea *accouterment*. Then his nose began to wiggle and twitch, just like a bunny rabbit. "Are those fresh-baked scones I smell?" he asked in his booming voice.

"Scones, gingerbread, tea cookies, and lord knows what else Haley has prepared," said Drayton. "We're entertaining thirty-five people for high tea in less than an hour."

What a smooth way to let Tidwell know we're busy, thought Theodosia. She, on the other hand, had been about to ask Tidwell flat out exactly what it was he wanted. Of course, it was doubtful she would have received a direct answer. Detective Tidwell liked his games, especially when they involved verbal jousts.

Tidwell lumbered over to the table to join them. He was

a big man with a strange bullet-shaped head that seemed to rest directly on his broad shoulders. His large, flat eyes missed nothing. While some of his police department colleagues thought him plodding, his superiors found him textbook methodical as well as supremely capable of sifting through evidence then making lightning-fast connections. Tidwell was a king cobra. He hissed, spat, and stalled his prey until they grew weary of his posturing and dropped their guard. Then, in a heartbeat, Tidwell would strike.

In Tidwell's younger days, he'd been an FBI agent. But it hadn't taken long before he'd grown disenchanted with the FBI's bureaucratic focus on process and information gathering. Tidwell had always been a strong believer in putting one's best efforts into fieldwork.

Now, at an age when many homicide detectives yearned for retirement, Tidwell hadn't given his exit strategy a passing thought. Crime solving was what he knew, crime solving was what he excelled at. There was no Mrs. Tidwell, no younger Tidwells clamoring for his time or attention. For him there existed only the thrill of the hunt. Even at his age, Tidwell still found police work an exhilarating experience. Not many people can still boast that of their life's work.

Tidwell allowed Theodosia to place a cranberry and walnut scone on a small pastel pink plate. He gazed at it hungrily, but broke it open gently.

"Jelly?" asked Theodosia, passing a cut-glass bowl of strawberry jelly to him. "And Devonshire cream?" She handed him a tiny glass slipper mounded with cream.

Theodosia was pretty sure Tidwell's visit today wasn't a random social call. *He must be here because of poor Harper Fisk,* she decided. *But Burt Tidwell is a homicide detective. And Harper Fisk drowned, didn't he?*

Wielding a tiny butter knife like a skilled surgeon, Tidwell lathered sweet delights onto his scone.

"And some Yunnan tea," said Drayton, pouring a cup for Tidwell, then a cup for Theodosia and himself. Haley was nowhere to be seen. She disliked and distrusted Burt Tidwell and made herself scarce whenever he came around.

Tidwell took a sip of tea, then smacked his lips with pleasure. "This is excellent," he declared. "A nice hint of spiciness."

"Some might say peppery," said Drayton.

Tidwell took another sip, rolled his eyes upward as he considered for a moment. Then a smile broke across his broad face. "As always, you're quite correct and precise, Mr. Conneley. Peppery is a very apt description. Delightfuly so."

For some reason Theodosia perceived Burt Tidwell's tea tasting as stalling. So she decided to jump right in.

"You're here because of Harper Fisk," she said to him.

Tidwell's teacup settled into its saucer with a tiny *clink*. "A fine man, as I understand it."

"A true gentleman," said Drayton. "He gave much of his time and energy to the Heritage Society."

Tidwell patted his lips with a linen napkin, settled it back into his ample lap. He gazed across the table at Theodosia. "And you, Miss Browning, once again find yourself smack dab at the scene of a crime."

"I certainly didn't *plan* it that way," said Theodosia, meeting his gaze evenly. A couple moments went by before she fully comprehended the weight of Tidwell's words. "You said *crime*," said Theodosia. "Are you implying that Harper Fisk might have been *murdered*?"

"Stranger things have happened," said Tidwell non-committally.

"I thought it was obvious," said Drayton, "that Harper Fisk drowned."

"With a net wrapped around him?" said Tidwell, dead-pan.

"The net was intentionally *wrapped*?" asked Drayton. "I hadn't realized that." He paused, swallowed hard. "Then again, I didn't study him all that carefully. Just seeing poor Harper lying there on the beach . . . lifeless . . . was terribly upsetting."

Tidwell focused his gaze back on Theodosia. "You swam out to get him," he said.

"I swam out because we thought we saw"—she faltered—"well, I'm not sure *what* we thought it was. Maybe an injured dolphin or something?" The theory that seemed to hold water last night sounded weak today. Theodosia wondered why that was.

"Never mind why you swam out," said Tidwell, waving a hand. "The important thing is that you were the first person to reach the crime scene."

There's that word again, thought Theodosia. *Crime.*

"And," continued Tidwell, "since it is virtually impossible to *secure* a crime scene such as that, the next best thing is to interview the nearest witness." He paused. "That's you."

"Gulp," said Theodosia. She meant her remark to be humorous but it didn't come off that way.

"So tell me exactly what happened," said Tidwell. "Exactly what you saw."

Theodosia went through her story with Tidwell, telling him of her sudden sense of nervousness, relating how she grasped at the floating mass, pulled it toward her, and came face to face with the dead Harper Fisk.

Drayton's face blanched white as she went over this part.

Last night, Theodosia had brushed over her encounter with the corpse when she'd seen how upset Drayton had been at having Harper Fisk's body finally hauled up on the beach.

"So you could see that Harper Fisk was wrapped in something?" asked Tidwell.

"Not really," said Theodosia. "First of all it was pitch dark. And then there were big hunks of seaweed clinging everywhere. And"—she closed her eyes, trying to remember—"I think there were . . . like . . . rags?"

She looked at Tidwell questioningly.

"If you say so," he said. "Tell me, was anything else encumbering the body?"

"What do you mean by encumbering?" asked Theodosia. She had a pretty good idea what Tidwell was asking, but she wanted to be sure.

"Were there lines attached to this floating mass?" asked Tidwell. "Part of a ship's propeller, an oar, anything?"

"I don't think so," said Theodosia. "At least I don't remember anything." She paused. "But the police must have the body in custody, correct?"

"Correct," responded Tidwell.

"Detective Tidwell," said Drayton, "do you think Harper Fisk fell from a boat?"

"We don't know," said Tidwell briskly. "Right now we're just beginning our investigation." Finishing the last bits of his scone, Tidwell scrutinized the platter of goodies that sat in the center of the table, then helped himself to a large piece of gingerbread. As an afterthought, he daubed on an enormous pouf of Devonshire cream. "From what I understand," said Tidwell, "Harper Fisk engaged in what folks around here might call *treasure* hunting. Am I right, Mr. Conneley?"

Drayton cocked his head to one side, thinking. "Yes, but

I'd have to say his hobby was more *theoretical* than anything. Harper Fisk was always rhapsodizing about the use of
magnetometers or global positioning to plot Civil War shipwrecks. I know he was quite passionate about locating the
Cotillion, a boat that was sunk during the Civil War. But I
don't think the man ever actually *dove* for treasure. I mean,
he was almost seventy years old, for goodness' sake."

"Is it possible Harper Fisk was out on a boat yesterday?"
Theodosia asked Tidwell.

Tidwell shrugged. "Anything is possible, my dear Miss
Browning. We checked Harper Fisk's name against South
Carolina watercraft registration records and he does, in fact,
own a boat. As to where that boat was moored still remains
a mystery. Obviously we're checking area marinas and such,
but it's fairly slow going. With the hot weather here to stay,
most marinas are virtually deserted."

Theodosia knew Tidwell was right. Summer temperatures in Charleston were nudging up into the mid-nineties,
with the humidity packing a real whollop as well. Was it any
wonder most folks had jumped on their boats and taken off
for the great sea islands or the resort towns and beaches
along the Intercoastal Waterway?

Drayton looked thoughtful. "A boating accident would
certainly account for his drowning," he said. "Perhaps
Harper Fisk was piloting a boat and a sudden lurch caused
him to take a nasty header. Or poor Harper could have
tripped on something, struck his head, and been thrown
overboard."

Theodosia looked at Drayton sharply. This was a far cry
from Drayton's original theory that Harper Fisk suffered a
heart attack and pitched off the seawall down at the Battery.
On the other hand, Drayton hadn't been privy to the fact that
Harper Fisk owned a boat.

"Detective Tidwell," said Theodosia, "if Harper Fisk had some sort of heart attack and then fell overboard, he would theoretically be dead first, right?"

"Theoretically," said Tidwell, his eyes gleaming dangerously.

"So his lungs would *not* be filled with water," said Theodosia. She was aware that Drayton was looking at her sharply. "On the other hand," she said, "if Harper Fisk had been intentionally drowned, his lungs *would* be filled with water."

"How ghastly!" exclaimed Drayton.

"Ah, forensics," said Tidwell. "A little knowledge is always a dangerous thing." He rocked back in his chair. "You watch too much television, Miss Browning."

"Detective Tidwell, is this an official investigation?" asked Theodosia.

Tidwell shifted his bulk in the wooden captain's chair. "Let's just say it's headed that way."

CHAPTER 4

T IDWELL'S IMPROMPTU VISIT seemed to leave a bad taste in everyone's mouth. Drayton stumbled about the tea room, distributing linen napkins and lighting tiny candles in the tea warmers. Haley rattled pots and pans in the kitchen. Theodosia perched on the stool behind the counter and puzzled over the possibility that Harper Fisk might have been murdered.

"Drayton," called Theodosia, "sunken treasure and gold bullion *have* been salvaged from shipwrecks around Charleston, right?"

Drayton straightened up. Born with a love for all things historical, antiquities and data relating to them were Drayton's passion. "Indeed yes. The *Emory* was found laden with Confederate gold. Same with the *Jessica Belle*. And then, of course, there's the *Hunley*. That was just salvaged, even though it wasn't laden with treasure." The *Hunley* was a Civil War–era submarine that had been recently located and excavated. There was now a major brouhaha going on as to which city should play host to the little prototype sub. The city of Charleston or the adjacent city of North Charleston, which, until recently, had been host to a major U.S. Naval Base for almost one hundred years.

"So maybe Harper Fisk *had* been out treasure hunting," suggested Theodosia. "He was in a boat and—"

"Alone?" cut in Drayton. "That hardly seems likely. And if Harper had a crew with him, wouldn't they have reported him missing?"

Unless his crew were the ones who tossed him overboard, thought Theodosia, though she decided not to verbalize that nasty supposition to Drayton.

Haley came bustling out from behind the green velvet curtain that separated the tea room from the kitchen and Theodosia's small back office.

"Everything's almost ready," she exclaimed, glancing about the empty tea room, where lights blazed, white linen napkins gleamed, and just-washed china sparkled. "So where the heck are our guests?"

As if to punctuate Haley's sentence, the door burst open and Angie Congdon from the Featherbed House came barreling through the door with three of her friends in tow.

"Angela!" declared Drayton. "How *is* the lovely proprietor of the historic district's premier bed-and-breakfast?" Located at the tip of the historic Battery, the Featherbed House *was* one of the nicer B and B's. Their elegantly furnished rooms boasted mounds of featherbeds piled on four-poster canopied beds, cypress paneling, and twelve-foot-high hand-molded plaster ceilings. A second-floor open-air bridge spanned the backyard and its picturesque, secluded garden, and led guests to a dining room that had been carved out of a renovated hayloft above the carriage house.

"Can you believe it?" chirped Angie. "We're celebrating our fifth anniversary! And I hope you-all are still planning to attend our barbecue this Wednesday. Mark guarantees it's going to be quite a bash!" In their past lives, Angie and her husband, Mark, had been commodity brokers in Chicago. To say they no longer missed the frantic, pulse-pounding pace of the windy city would be an understatement.

"We're all planning to be there with bells on," Drayton assured Angie as he escorted her group to a table, then spun on his heels to seat the next group of customers coming through the door.

"Drayton's a charmer, isn't he," said Haley, standing next to Theodosia.

"He's gold," murmured Theodosia as she watched him seat more guests. "Pure gold." She smiled at Haley. "Everything set?"

Haley nodded. She seemed to have regained her energy as well as the sparkle in her eye. "This is going to be a high tea to end all high teas," she bragged. "We've got cream scones with sourwood honey, tiny tea sandwiches with rare roast beef, cream cheese and cranberry chutney, crab Wellington, strawberries dipped in white chocolate, and miniature Napoleon pastries."

"Napoleon and Wellington together again," mused Theodosia. "You have a very poetic streak, Haley."

Haley wrinkled her nose. "Nah, I'm just an ex-history major with a warped sense of humor."

With so many different courses to serve, Theodosia, Drayton, and Haley barely had more than a few moments to chitchat with their guests. Haley was pretty much bottled up in the kitchen the entire time, plating the various courses and dispensing with dirty dishes as each delightful tidbit was gobbled up and the dirty plates quickly trucked back to th

kitchen. Theodosia and Drayton were like roadrunners—zipping from kitchen to tea room and back again, delivering food, accepting compliments, and pouring tea.

"Theodosia." Brooke Carter Crocket, Theodosia's dear friend and regular customer at the Indigo Tea Shop, put her hand on Theodosia's arm. "I haven't had a minute to talk to you!"

"I'm sorry, I haven't had a minute to say hello to *anyone*," said Theodosia. Her cheeks were pink and flushed, her hair, always full to begin with, was rapidly expanding about her in an auburn halo, thanks to the summer heat as well as the extra humidity that seemed to be generated by all those steaming tea kettles. With her clear, flawless complexion and soft smile, Theodosia looked like a lovely subject in a sixteenth-century Raphael painting.

"How are things in your store?" Theodosia asked. Brooke was a jewelry maker and the proprietor of Heart's Desire, an upscale jewelry shop that also specialized in buying and selling estate jewelry.

Brooke, a pretty, petite fifty-something with a sleek cap of white hair, waggled a hand back and forth. "So so. I think a lot of folks have fled the summer heat, so business is a little slow." Charleston did seem to lose more than a few of its residents to the beach homes on nearby Kiawah and Hilton Head Islands.

Theodosia pushed back her mass of curly hair. "I've heard that same story from a lot of Church Street business owners," she said.

"But I've got some special pieces I've been working on," explained Brooke. "See here." She fingered a silver pendant that hung around her neck.

At first glance the pendant looked like a lopsided orb. But as Theodosia studied it, she realized that Brooke had

created a marvelous silver sculpture of an oyster, complete with a tiny inset cultured pearl. "It's an oyster pendant," said Theodosia, delighted. Oysters were a favorite staple in Charleston cuisine as well as nearby low-country cooking. Oysters from the surrounding marshes were eaten raw, fried with cornmeal batter, and cooked in pies. In fact, when the first settlers sailed into Charleston Harbor, they named it Oyster Point because of the huge heaps of bleached oyster shells that were piled at the tip of the peninsula.

"Some of the models will be wearing these pendants at Fashion Bash next Saturday," Brooke told her. "So you never know. With that kind of notoriety, things at the shop could turn around fast."

"Delaine's got you roped in, too?" asked Drayton as he bustled over to Brooke's table.

"Are you kidding?" laughed Brooke. "Once that lady gets her hooks in you, it's all over."

"Tell me about it," said Drayton.

Two hours later it was all over but the cleanup.

Drayton sat sprawled on a chair. His bow tie drooped, his eyes drooped, even his gray hair looked frazzled. "I'm never pouring another cup of tea in my life," he declared. "My career's over, I'm throwing in the tea towel."

Slowly, almost painfully, Haley untied her apron. What had once been pristine white was now smeared with jam and honey. A splotchy-looking tea stain spread out from the center. "We need a bigger kitchen," she moaned. "I felt like a rat caught in one of those awful lab experiments. Drop a few kernels of corn and see which way Haley spins in her cage."

Standing at the counter with Haley, Theodosia surveyed the damage. Dirty dishes and teapots were stacked everywhere. Tables and chairs were awry. Even their counter displays had been devastated. This afternoon's high tea had proved so pleasurable to many of their customers that they'd clamored to take home little touchstones of the event. Tins of tea, jars of jelly and DuBose Bees Honey, gift baskets filled with tea, tea strainers, and teacups had sold like hot cakes. Even the T-Bath products, Theodosia's innovative new bath soaks and shower gels that contained soothing green tea and bits of lavender, had flown out the door. Theodosia figured she'd have to phone their supplier first thing Monday and order several more cases.

Haley picked up one of the Crown Ducal cups and saucers and frowned. "I thought we had two of these," she said.

"We did," said Theodosia. "We must have sold one."

"I didn't sell one," said Haley. "Did you, Drayton?"

Drayton sat with his head thrown back, staring at the ceiling. "No idea."

"Hmm," said Haley, scanning the half-empty shelves, ever the compulsive organizer and neat-nick.

"Don't fret about it," said Theodosia. "Just revel in the success." She slid open the drawer of the old brass cash register and extracted two crisp hundred-dollar bills.

"Success? Are you kidding? It was awful," moaned Drayton theatrically.

Theodosia folded the bills in half, handed one to Haley, slipped another one to Drayton.

Drayton immediately straightened up. "What's this?" he asked, fingering the bill.

"A little extra," said Theodosia. "You two worked so hard today and our customers were so complimentary about your efforts."

"And we're still getting our regular salary?" asked Haley.

"Of course," said Theodosia.

"Much obliged," said Drayton, pocketing his bill.

"Cool," announced Haley. She jumped up, threw her arms around Theodosia, and gave her a big squeeze. "Thanks, boss."

"You're very welcome, Haley," said Theodosia, "but please don't call me boss. It makes me feel old."

"You're not old," said Drayton, "*I'm* old. Because right now I'm positively dreading the cleanup."

"Then don't worry about it," said Theodosia. "Just go home and take it easy."

"We're not going to clean up?" said Haley.

"*We're* not going to, *I'm* going to," said Theodosia.

"It'll take hours," warned Drayton. "You don't know what you're letting yourself in for."

"Not a problem," Theodosia assured them. "Besides, haven't you always told me my official title was CEO, marketing maven, and chief bottle washer?"

Drayton was delighted, but not wholly convinced. "You're positive?" he asked. "You really want us to go home?"

"Really," said Theodosia, shooing them both out the door.

It took Theodosia exactly three hours. But she wasn't alone in her endeavor. After bidding so-long to Drayton and Haley, she went upstairs and roused Earl Grey. Stretched out in her kitchen, waiting patiently for his beloved mistress, the dog was delighted at the prospect of going for a quick walk. Of bounding down the block, blowing off steam, and stretching his legs.

But the very best part was yet to come. Because after their walk, Theodosia gave Earl Grey permission to do what he loved best. She allowed him to come back to the tea shop with her.

With the radio playing and Theodosia shuttling dirty dishes, Earl Grey was in doggy heaven. He followed her from table to table, tea room to kitchen, happily matching strides with her and dogging her every step.

At one point Theodosia leaned down and gazed into Earl Grey's soft brown eyes. "You like this, don't you? Spending a little quality time together in the tea room?"

Earl Grey touched his nose to her hand, gave a gentle lick. *Yes.*

"You know," she told him, "we haven't been to the O'Doud Senior Home for a while. What do you think, big guy? Are you up for it?"

A couple years ago, Earl Grey had passed his TDI test and earned his therapy dog certification. That accomplishment had won him admission to freely enter the O'Doud Senior Home with Theodosia. Donning his official blue nylon vest with his Therapy Dog International patch on it, Earl Grey was always a big hit with the residents. One woman, Flossie, a longtime resident who'd suffered a debilitating stroke, was fearful of using her left arm again. Yet she made amazing progress when Theodosia and one of the physical therapists positioned Earl Grey to the left of Flossie's wheel-chair. Yearning to pet "the darling pup," as she called him, Flossie struggled mightily to stretch her long-unused muscles in an attempt to cup her wrinkled hand atop Earl Grey's soft head. It took Flossie five tries, but the sixth time, she was successful. And Theodosia, thinking later about how the old woman had persisted in her attempt to pet Earl Grey, had shed tears of joy.

Watching her bustle about the kitchen from his alert "sit"

position, Earl Grey's long tail beat a rhythm on the wooden floor.

"Good boy," Theodosia told him. "Time to go visit our old friends. Let me make a couple calls."

When Theodosia and Earl Grey climbed the back stairs to their apartment, it was exactly 8:00 P.M. Too early to go to bed, too late to really do anything. So Theodosia decided to flake out for the rest of the evening. Maybe pour herself a glass of wine, play a relaxing CD, and for sure put her feet up. And of course, have a little nosh.

Haley had been considerate enough to leave behind a "care package" for Theodosia. Leftovers from the day's two tea parties, but still very tasty. A dab of fruit salad, three small tea sandwiches, and a slice of quiche. So, as she pulled the cork from a chilled bottle of Pouilly Fousse, Theodosia also popped the quiche into the microwave and heated it up.

Woof.

Theodosia turned on her heels to find the inquisitive eyes of Earl Grey focused intently upon her.

"I suppose you're pretty hungry, too," she said to him. Scooping a cup of kibbles from the Scooby Doo cookie jar that held Earl Grey's food, she dropped the dry morsels into his dish.

But the dog just sat and stared at her, daring her to do better.

"I take it my culinary creation isn't quite up to snuff?" she asked him.

Come on, his shiny brown eyes pleaded.

Theodosia dug in her refrigerator for a carton of plain yogurt, then scooped a giant dollop onto the dry kibbles. "There you go, buddy. *Topping.*"

Topping was one of the magic words in Earl Grey's lexicon. For the dog suddenly dove at his silver dog dish with all the enthusiasm of a major league ball player who'd just whacked out a strong line drive and was headed for first base.

Theodosia slid her warmed-up quiche onto a pretty Limoges plate, added the tiny sandwiches and daub of fruit salad, then grabbed her glass of white wine and headed for the couch.

Life was pretty perfect, she decided as she munched her food and sipped her wine. The Indigo Tea Shop had netted a very tidy profit today—more than sixteen hundred dollars when you totaled up receipts for all the lunches and the add-on purchases that included tins of tea, teapots, and some of the T-Bath products. Pretty terrific results for a single day's work.

Gazing about her apartment as she enjoyed her dinner-time leftovers, Theodosia was pleased at how well her renovations were going. A couple years ago, she'd been a shabby chic kind of girl, enamored with all the delights of flaking white paint, antique wicker, and Country French decor.

But over the last year or so her tastes had begun to change. While she still adored the subtleties of the French palette—the ivories, pale pinks, and pastel blues—the colors and decor in her apartment had now taken on more of an old world patina.

Pale peach walls had been replaced with a rich Chinese red done in a marbleized technique. Chairs and a sofa that had once been upholstered in chintz and prints were recovered in elegant mauve damask. Accent pillows were velvet and fringed. The tone, the entire *attitude,* of her apartment was so much richer now.

Two seascape paintings that had always looked a little too moody for her living room suddenly looked right at home with this new subdued, elegant interior. Two more Aubusson rugs were acquired at auction, and Drayton had located an antique mirror with an over-the-top wildly rococo frame. Now it hung over the fireplace, a perfect accent piece.

Dabbling a toe in the realm of decorating, Theodosia found that she absolutely *adored* this look that was so distinctly Old Charleston.

Would you believe it? Now she was seriously considering eggplant walls and a Chinese screen for her dining room!

Wow, she thought, *pretty soon my little apartment is going to take on the patina of one of Timothy Neville's fancy drawing rooms.* Timothy Neville, the curmudgeon president of the Heritage Society, was famous for his tortoiseshell-look high-gloss walls, Louis XVI furniture, and over-the-top finery.

Well, Theodosia decided as the telephone shrilled at her elbow, *I could find myself in worse company.*

"Hello?" she answered.

"Theodosia!" came a warm greeting. It was Jory Davis, the young attorney who was, as Charlestonian ladies of a certain age would say, currently *squiring* her about town.

"How did your teas go?" he asked.

"Fabulous," she told him. "We even had to turn people away."

Jory let out a low whistle. "I'm impressed. I know that tea is wildly popular, but I had no idea ladies were so infatuated with attending *formal* teas."

"Listen, my friend," she told him, "sometimes attending a tea is the *only* shred of sanity left in a woman's life. Between kids and jobs and husbands and boyfriends, or ex-husbands or—"

"I get the idea," Jory laughed. "It's the perfect opportunity for women to really talk, isn't it?"

Recalling some of the snatches of conversation she'd heard earlier today, Theodosia had to agree. Whispered secrets about boyfriends and husbands, quirky bosses, strange friends, and problem children had flown fast and furious today. However, she wasn't about to spill any of those confidences. At the Indigo Tea Shop, teatime was also sacred time.

"I was wondering if you'd like to go for a sail tomorrow?" said Jory. "I figured you could use a little R and R after the last couple days."

Jory was well aware of her grizzly discovery in the water last night and had been more than sympathetic.

"Perfect," said Theodosia. She made a quick mental inventory of what Haley had stashed in the refrigerator downstairs, figured she could rustle up a fairly decent picnic lunch. "Want me to bring along some food?"

"I was hoping you'd volunteer," said Jory.

"Okay then," said Theodosia. "I should meet you . . . when?"

"How about the Charleston Yacht Club at around ten o'clock. I'll get there early and rig the sails. Then all m'lady has to do is step aboard. How does that sound?"

"Works for me," said Theodosia. "See you then."

"Pleasant dreams, kiddo," said Jory Davis.

As Theodosia hung up the phone, her eyes fell on the stack of grant applications that sat on the coffee table in front of her sofa. Naomi Morison, a friend of hers at the Charleston Arts & Science Foundation, had asked if she would read a dozen or so of the grant requests that had been submitted to the CASF and make a preliminary recommendation.

The CASF was a philanthropic foundation that awarded grant money to worthy arts and science projects. From the cover sheet that Naomi had sent along with her packet, Theodosia knew that the CASF had funded such diverse projects as the Charleston Children's Puppeteer Club, an archaeological dig at the old Haislet plantation out near Mount Pleasant, and the restoration and preservation of a turn-of-the-century blacksmith shop. In past years, the CASF has also given funding to the Charleston Sea Turtle Protection League as well as the Heritage Society.

Theodosia sighed. She was not unused to this kind of work. She sat on the board of directors of Big Paw, Charleston's service dog organization, and had also done a good deal of pro bono publicity work for Spoleto, Charleston's major arts festival. Of course, this was the first time she'd actually been asked to read grant requests and make specific dollar amount recommendations. It seemed like a fairly daunting task. There were so many worthwhile projects and organizations and just a finite amount of funding available. Oh well . . . perhaps one of the grant requests would pop out at her . . . stand head and shoulders above the rest.

Yawning, she cast a sleepy eye toward the stack. At least she *hoped* one would.

CHAPTER 5

SOMETHING WAS INTERRUPTING Theodosia's dream of a
perfect journey through Tuscany. Rolling yellow hills
and purple fields were fading fast as a piercing sound in-
vaded what had been a lovely, contemplative landscape,
slightly along the lines of an Impressionist painting. The
piercing sound of . . . what?

Telephone! Wake up, lazy. It's morning.

"Hello?" Theodosia fumbled for the old-fashioned
French-style telephone that sat on her night table.

"Theodosia? Sorry to wake you, but it's very—"

"Drayton?" she said.

"Yes, it's me. Sorry to be in such a tizzy, but they found
the boat."

*Boat? What boat? Was Drayton talking about Jory's
boat? No, he couldn't be.*

She yawned. "Slow down, Drayton. Tell me what's going
on."

"It was just on the early-morning news. A small boat

washed up near the old lighthouse on Sullivan's Island."
Drayton paused. "They think it might be Harper Fisk's
boat."

"Who thinks that?" asked Theodosia. She sat up, swung
both feet out of bed, slid them across the small rug by her
bed. When they touched the cool floorboards of her bedroom, it seemed to have a stabilizing effect on her.

"Believe me, I never would have jumped to that conclusion myself," said Drayton. "But it's what the Channel
Sixteen reporter said. One of those eager beaver direct-
from-the-scene fellows, you know the type."

So Harper Fisk fell out of a boat after all, thought
Theodosia.

"Listen," said Drayton, obviously very worked up about
this new development. "We've got to get over there! Maybe
try to get a look inside that boat." He paused. "Theo?"

"I'm thinking, Drayton."

What can I do? She peered at the numerals on her antique
clock. It read seven-thirty.

"Theodosia?" said Drayton. Now he seemed on the verge
of hysteria.

"Tell you what," she said to Drayton. "I'll pick you up in
fifteen minutes, okay? Be on the curb outside your house."

*Fastest, most direct way to Sullivan's Island is straight
across the harbor. Take off from the Yacht Club, cut around
Patriots Point, head toward that lighthouse.*

Relief was apparent in Drayton's voice. "Thank you,
Theo. I *knew* I could count on you. You know this means a
lot to me."

"I know that, Drayton."

"Theo," he said, urgency coloring his voice. "You can get
a boat?"

"Yes, Drayton, I can get a boat."

* * *

"Jory," began Theodosia as he picked up his phone. "Slight change of plans. Can you borrow a speedboat?"

Jory Davis was still a little sleepy. "Uh . . . yeah. Sure." In the background was the whoosh of running water and the clatter of a pan. *He must be must be stumbling around his bachelor's kitchen, making coffee.* The image may have caused her to smile, but she didn't let up on her sense of urgency.

"Right away? Now?" asked Theodosia.

There was a slight hesitation then Jory said, "Shouldn't be a problem. I've got a set of keys for Paulie Foster's boat. It's a big Sea Ray Amberjack. Say, you want to tell me what this is all about?" Jory was starting to wake up fast.

Theodosia paused.

"Holy smokes," said Jory, suddenly catching on. "This is about the other night, isn't it? The Harper Fisk thing?"

"Absolutely it is," said Theodosia.

"Okaaay," said Jory. "So we'll still meet at the Yacht Club . . ."

"But we'll have to condense our timetable considerably," said Theodosia. "See you on the dock in fifteen minutes?"

"Fifteen . . . ?" came Jory's surprised voice. But he was talking to dead air.

Slap, slap, slap.

The twenty-seven-foot Sea Ray Amberjack carrying Theodosia, Jory, and Drayton barreled across Charleston Harbor, its 240-horsepower Mercury outboard emitting a powerful whine and arcing out a giant spray of foam. Buzzing along at a brisk sixteen knots, they could see Shutes Folly Island just off to their left. Beyond that was the much

larger Garden Island, where the World War II aircraft carrier
Yorktown was permanently moored at Patriots Point.

Though morning haze still hung over the harbor, it would
burn off by ten o'clock, and Sunday in greater Charleston
would prove hot and steamy. A typical July day conducive
to lazing in a hammock, sipping iced tea in the back garden,
or heading for the low-country to seek out a fish fry or shop
at one of the farmers' markets, abundant with fresh produce.

But on Sullivan's Island, one of Mount Pleasant's three
barrier islands, and the course that Jory Davis had set for
their speeding boat, the ever-present sea breezes would provide cooling relief.

Not that thousands of Charleston area natives wouldn't
take to the waters anyway, since Charleston was the unofficial boating capital of the South. Fishing boats, sailboats,
charter boats, tour boats, and personal watercraft plied the
harbors, the Cooper and Ashley Rivers, the Intercoastal Waterway, and the little rivers and inlets that led to the low-
country. South Carolina was a state that ranked third in the
United States for number of registered watercraft per capita.

"Where do you think that boat washed up again?" Jory
asked Drayton as they began to close in on Sullivan's Island.

"Just down from the lighthouse," responded Drayton.
Obviously not thrilled to be a passenger in the speeding Sea
Ray, Drayton had white-knuckled the trip all the way across.

Theodosia squinted into the distant haze. She could
barely make out the old lighthouse on the far end of the island, but Jory, old salt that he was, had immediately spotted
it and set a direct course toward it.

Five minutes later, they were closing in. Jory cut the en-
gines and the Sea Ray puttered slowly toward shore.

Theodosia peered at the expanse of white sand beach.

There sat an abandoned boat all right. A Boston Whaler with a V-hull that had obviously washed in, then been hauled up a few feet onto the narrow strip of beach. Just beyond, parked on the access road, Theodosia could see two panel trucks with TV microwave equipment on top. Three cars were parked in a blacktop parking lot that fronted the beach. A squad car with lazily flashing red and blue lights, a white Toyota truck, and a burgundy Crown Victoria.

That Crown Vic belongs to Tidwell, thought Theodosia. For the old boy to be up and out so early on a Sunday, *something* must be going on.

Jory cut the engine completely and let the Sea Ray drift its way in to shore. A uniformed police officer walked down toward them and stopped just shy of the lapping waves. Holding one hand up, palm facing them in a gesture of authority, he barked: "That's close enough. Please restart your engine and back off."

Theodosia lifted an arm and waved to a blob down the beach that she figured had to be Burt Tidwell. Since she hadn't put her contact lenses in yet, she really couldn't be sure.

"Detective Tidwell, hello!" she called.

The blob raised an arm in return.

Bingo, thought Theodosia.

The uniformed officer, on seeing that their group seemed to be fairly well acquainted with Detective Tidwell, suddenly lost interest and decided to focus his efforts some twenty yards down the beach where an inquisitive posse of preteen boys on banana bikes continued to edge forward.

Drayton was the first to jump from the Sea Ray and slog through the breaking surf to the shore. It was the first time Theodosia had ever seen him totally unconcerned about getting his linen slacks damp or ruining his leather loafers.

"Is this the boat?" he called to Tidwell. "Did this belong to Harper Fisk?"

A man wearing mirrored sunglasses, a yellow polo shirt, and khaki slacks walked across the sand from the parking lot to confront him. The man put hands on hips, obviously not pleased. "Who the heck are you?" he asked Drayton as Theodosia watched from the Sea Ray.

Drayton extended a hand, which the man in mirrored sunglasses was slow in shaking. "Drayton Conneley. My friend, Theodosia Browning, and I found Mr. Fisk's body two nights ago down on Halliehurst Beach. We heard that his boat might have washed up here." Drayton's gaze shifted to the small boat some twenty yards down from them.

"Guess you heard right." The man in the mirrored sunglasses stared at Drayton. Drayton stared back, keeping his cool.

A *standoff*, thought Theodosia, immediately deciding she'd put her money on the indomitable Drayton.

Luckily, Detective Tidwell came sauntering over. Dressed in a flapping black shirt that looked more like the spinnaker for a sailboat and nondescript gray slacks, he clutched a red-and-white-striped paper bag in his hands. Every few minutes Tidwell would dip a chubby paw into the bag and pop something into his mouth. Theodosia couldn't tell if Burt Tidwell was chowing down on fried clams or popcorn shrimp. Whatever salty, fried treat it was, it suddenly appealed to her. With a light supper last night and no breakfast this morning, she was starving.

"Ah, Mr. Conneley," said Tidwell in a maddeningly bright voice, "I see you've met our Detective Hudson."

"Yes, hello there," said Drayton, favoring Hudson with a perfunctory smile.

Detective Hudson ignored Drayton and turned to address

Tidwell. "Tell your friends to back off. This is my case, my investigation."

Theodosia watched in amusement as Burt Tidwell rocked back on his heels and flipped a fried clam or popcorn shrimp or whatever it was into his mouth. Catching it expertly, like a trained seal, he seemed to take great relish in savoring the tasty morsel.

"Five minutes, Hudson," Tidwell told the other detective. "Five minutes."

Without waiting for an answer, Detective Tidwell turned and ambled down the beach toward the washed-up boat. Deciding she'd better make hay while the sun was still shining, Theodosia jumped from the speedboat and splashed through the water to intercept Tidwell.

"Shrimp?" he asked her as her bare feet dug into the sand and she climbed up the sand dune to meet him. He held out his striped paper bag enticingly.

"Thanks." Theodosia dug in, found a tiny, still-warm fried glob, and popped it in her mouth. Crunchy batter, still steamy inside, yielded a fried shrimp seasoned with cayenne pepper and lemon salt.

"Do you think it's Harper Fisk's boat?" Theodosia asked Tidwell.

The detective merely shrugged. "Let's have a look."

Theodosia and Drayton followed Tidwell some twenty feet down to where the Boston Whaler was pulled up some six feet above the surf line. The faded registration numbers read 273809 and the name, *Mary Lynn*, was stenciled to the side of its bow.

"Must have washed up during the night," Tidwell told them. "Some kids found it this morning when they came out scouting for hermit crabs and sand dollars. They called it in. Kojak here was on duty, but he doesn't know what to make of it." Tidwell jerked his head toward Hudson, the man in the mirrored sunglasses and yellow shirt who was jabbering on his cell phone in a self-important manner.

The three of them peered into the boat. It was a curious-looking boat, fairly small in size, but sporting that deep V-hull that definitely marked it as an oceangoing craft. A fifty-five-horsepower Evinrude motor hung off the back.

"There's a plastic map case sitting on the seat there," noted Theodosia. stretching up on her tiptoes.

"But no map," said Tidwell. "Of course, that's certainly no indication of foul play. The map could have fallen in with Harper Fisk and simply floated away. Or disintegrated once it hit the water."

Drayton peered over the gunnels of the boat, his eyes nervous and searching.

"See anything out of the ordinary?" Theodosia asked him.

He stared into the boat awhile longer, then shook his head miserably. "No, not really."

"You folks about ready to leave?" Detective Hudson had come up behind them and stood staring at them. His barrel chest stuck out, his hands were set firmly on his hips. Everything about Hudson's pose was confrontational.

"They're just about ready to take off," replied Tidwell.

But Theodosia had other things in mind. "Boost me up, Drayton," she muttered under her breath.

"What? Oh." Drayton leaned forward and knitted his fingers together. Theodosia stepped lightly into Drayton's waiting hands and, in a matter of seconds, bounded up and over the side of the listing boat.

The features on Detective Hudson's disapproving face suddenly morphed into a thundercloud. "Awright, I've had just about enough of you people!" he barked. Positioning himself directly in Tidwell's face, he lambasted his fellow detective: "If you want to twiddle away your entire Sunday snooping around one of my cases, that's fine with me—just as long as you stay the hell out of my way! But I heartily suggest you lose the civilians if you know what's good for you!"

Theodosia stared down at Detective Hudson. He really was throwing quite a hissy fit, she decided.

What happened to cooperation among brothers in blue? And why on earth is Tidwell "unofficially" investigating?

She stared at the two men, wondering what was going on.

Suddenly, something sparked in Theodosia's brain.

Is the Charleston PD trying to force Tidwell into retirement? Is Tidwell just a supernumerary these days? He's certainly getting up there in age. Is there a mandatory retirement age or does the PD do what a lot of other companies do—just let their people languish until they leave out of sheer boredom? Hmm, that is a possibility.

"Miss Browning," called Detective Tidwell, "that's quite enough. Now give me your hand." Rather than sounding miffed, Tidwell sounded slightly amused. He seemed to enjoy antagonizing Detective Hudson.

But Theodosia was still poking around. "There's some other stuff in here," she said. She kicked at a faded orange life preserver that sat in two inches of dirty water under one of the seats. "There's a thermos bottle here, too. And two plastic cups."

Both Drayton and Tidwell peered over the side.

"I said *now*!" Detective Hudson almost choked on his own words.

Clambering out of the boat, Theodosia jumped down and landed lightly on her feet in the sand.

Detective Hudson was speaking on his cell phone again,

striding back and forth, trying to look official, or menacing, or whatever he decided should be his mood *du jour.*

"That's right," he barked into the phone. "I'll be at Chalmer's Yachts, then I'm heading in." He stabbed murderously at the END button, then hooked the phone back onto his belt.

"Why Chalmer's?" Theodosia asked him.

Detective Hudson flashed her a look of utter disdain. "Didn't you catch the sticker, lady?"

"Gotcha," she replied, thinking to herself, *Sure thing, genius.*

"Good," replied Hudson. "Now get lost."

"You look like the cat who just swallowed the canary," Drayton told Theodosia, once they'd bid good-bye to Tidwell and were back standing in front of the Sea Ray. "What gives?" he asked.

She glanced around, making sure they were clearly out of earshot of Detective Hudson. "Do you see that little decal on the boat? The one that says CY-22?"

Drayton shaded his eyes from the sun, peered back down the shoreline at the beached Boston Whaler. "Yes. At least I *think* I do. What's it mean?"

"Detective Hudson thinks it came from Chalmer's Yachts," said Theodosia.

"Did it?" asked Drayton.

She nodded toward the Sea Ray that bobbed directly in front of them. "What do you think?"

Drayton studied the Sea Ray. "It's got the same sticker! Harper's boat must have come from the same place we picked up this tub," said Drayton as they splashed back through the surf and clambered aboard Jory's borrowed boat.

"You got that right," said Theodosia.

"Excellent," said Drayton. It was the first time Theodosia had seen him smile in two days.

"Stand by to fasten the bowline," yelled Jory as he maneuvered the Sea Ray into its mooring at the Yacht Club.

Leaping from the Sea Ray onto the pier, Theodosia wrapped a line snugly about one of the wood pilings. She waited as Jory tossed her the stern line, then she looped that line around a second piling and slowly pulled the Sea Ray in, snugging it up against the rubber buoys that hung from the pier and kept the hull from scraping.

"Careful, Drayton," Theodosia cautioned as Drayton stepped down off the boat still wearing his wet shoes. "This part's a little tricky."

"I'm fine, I'm fine," he assured Theodosia and Jory. "In fact, you've both been wonderfully indulgent with me."

"Hey, not a problem," said Jory as he jumped onto the pier. With his long legs, it wasn't much of a leap. "If one of my friends drowned at sea, I'd want to try and figure out what happened to him, too."

"Was it his boat?" came a whispery, parchment voice. "Was it the *Mary Lynn*?"

Startled, the three of them whirled around to find a tall, white-haired man staring intently at them. His white cotton shirt sported red and blue epaulets on the collar.

Military, was Theodosia's first impression. But when she looked again more carefully, she realized the sport shirt was just cleverly designed to *look* like military insignia. This old fellow was clearly a civilian.

"Buddy," said Drayton, a note of surprise in his voice. "What are you doing here?"

"Why did you ask about the *Mary Lynn*?" asked Theodosia, her radar perking up. *Who was this older gentleman who seemed to have a sense of what they'd just been up to?*

The old man's face shed its mask of sadness and he responded with a quick smile. "Forgive me, permit me to introduce myself. I'm Lieutenant Benjamin Clark, *Buddy* Clark. Drayton and I are old acquaintances."

"Lieutenant," repeated Theodosia.

"U.S. Navy," said Benjamin Clark. "Retired, of course."

"Buddy's one of the fellows in the English Breakfast Club," said Drayton. "Friends of Harper Fisk. Remember? I told you about them."

"Yes, of course," said Theodosia, extending her hand. "Fellow tea drinkers. So nice to meet you, I'm Theodosia Browning. I own the Indigo Tea Shop."

Benjamin Clark accepted her hand gingerly. "Ah . . . Drayton's mentioned you a number of times."

"And this is Jory Davis," said Theodosia. "He ran us over to Sullivan's Island where, I'm afraid to report, we did indeed find the *Mary Lynn* washed up."

Benjamin Clark nodded sadly. "I caught something about it on the TV news earlier and I was afraid it might be poor Harper's boat." A look of abject sadness washed across Buddy Clark's face. "Poor Harper . . . to end up like that."

"Buddy, did you know Harper was going out in his boat?" asked Drayton.

"And do you know if he took off on Thursday or Friday?" added Theodosia.

Benjamin Clark suddenly looked overwhelmed. "No, not really. I hadn't talked to him for a few days. But Harper was forever making forays out into the harbor or puttering up and down various rivers around here. Charting shipwrecks and such was kind of his hobby."

"You must be pretty familiar with some of the Charleston

Harbor shipwrecks yourself," said Theodosia. "Seeing as how you're a former Navy man. Were you stationed here at Charleston Naval Base?" The Navy yard in North Charleston had been a major naval station up until 1993, when it was finally decommissioned.

"No, I'm afraid not. Most of my career was spent at Fort Worden near Seattle. Now, sadly, that's been decommissioned as well." Buddy Clark swiped at his face with the back of his hand. "There'll be hell to pay if this country ever has to fight a real war again."

"I thought our new supercarriers couldn't even clear some of those older harbors," said Theodosia. "And our submarines rarely have to come in to port."

Benjamin Clark's eyes met hers in a searching, probing manner, then they flicked over toward Drayton. "You were right to go work with this one," he said with what seemed like false heartiness. "She's a very clever girl."

CHAPTER 6

❦

"*IT SOUNDS LIKE* you-all had a very weird weekend," said Miss Dimple, dumping four lumps of sugar into her Dragon Pearl Jasmine and stirring it thoughtfully. She had knocked on the front door of the Indigo Tea Shop early this Monday morning, bearing her ledgers and figures and tabulations for the past week. But very little real business had taken place yet. Theodosia, Drayton, and Haley had been busily regaling her about the sad recovery of Harper Fisk's body and the discovery of his boat yesterday.

"Frankly," said Miss Dimple, reaching for a second miniature almond cake and fixing her gaze on Theodosia, "I would have jumped out of my skin if I'd been swimming in the ocean and encountered a dead body!"

"I almost did," said Theodosia. No sense pretending to have been brave, the whole encounter *had* been terribly unsettling.

"Poor Drayton." Miss Dimple reached a chubby hand across the table and patted his hand. "Lost a good friend."

Her gold bangles jangled gently. "That's what happens when you start getting up there in years. Death isn't just an abstraction anymore, it becomes all too real."

"Theodosia doesn't think Harper Fisk's death had anything to do with his age," said Haley.

Miss Dimple leaned forward, interested. Her penciled brows shot up in surprise. "You suspect foul play?" She searched their faces for any additional hints.

Drayton screwed his face into a look of abject misery, but remained mum on the subject.

"Maybe," said Theodosia cautiously. "But let's just keep that between the four of us for now, okay?"

Miss Dimple pantomimed a zipping motion across her lips. "You don't have to worry about me, honey, my lips are sealed."

"Drayton and I want to check a few things out first," Theodosia added.

Miss Dimple nodded. She had the utmost trust and confidence in Theodosia. Why, it had been Theodosia, after all, who'd helped coax her out of retirement by lining up a few freelance bookkeeping jobs with the merchants up and down Church Street. When her old employer, Mr. Dauphine, had died, Miss Dimple's paycheck had also dried up. And Theodosia had rescued her and helped preserve her dignity. As such, it wasn't likely Miss Dimple would betray any confidences!

"Miss Dimple," piped up Haley, "you haven't asked us about the special-event teas we had on Saturday."

Miss Dimple focused her gaze on Haley. Of all the tea shop employees, Haley was her favorite. She was so young and full of enthusiasm and so often over the top. "I was about to, dear," said Miss Dimple. "But I'm assuming the teas were an enormous hit. As is everything you dear folks set your minds to."

"The place was packed," said Haley, still flushed with their success.

"I knew it," said Miss Dimple. "I just knew you'd get a full house. Very impressive and good for the bottom line, too."

Drayton, who'd been scratching notes in his black leather journal for the past fifteen minutes, now lay his Mont Blanc pen down and stared into the distance.

"You look perplexed," said Haley. "What's the matter?"

"We need reorders on almost everything," he said. "Those ladies really cleaned us out on Saturday. I was in such an all-fired rush to get home and put my feet up, I didn't realize how many tins of tea, jars of honey, and gift baskets we'd actually sold. It's really quite remarkable."

"Plus I sold at least a half-dozen antique teacups and saucers," said Theodosia. Her collection of antique cups and saucers had reached such critical mass that she could no longer display them all upstairs or even down here in the tea room. And since she hadn't as yet amassed *quite* enough money to purchase one of the elegant old mansions in the historic district, the only logical conclusion was to sell off some of the teacups. It broke her heart, but it was better than letting them languish in storage somewhere. At least *someone* would be enjoying the lovely Maling teapots and the teacups by the likes of Crown Ducal, Aynsley, and Royal Winton.

"You know," piped up Haley, "we should consider doing a candlelight tea sometime."

Drayton peered at her over his glasses, looking like an owl all done up in a bow tie. "We did one last fall," he said. "It was billed as a mystery tea."

"Well, this would be the same thing," said Haley, "but without all the spooky stuff." She turned to Theodosia. "*You* like the idea, don't you?"

"Haley, I have the utmost confidence in you," said Theodosia. "If you say we should have a candlelight tea, then I'm all for it."

"Strikes me as more of an autumnal event," said Drayton. "I'm envisioning cool breezes, flickering candles, and tables draped with rich tapestries. As far as choice of teas go"—he steepled his fingers together and looked thoughtful—"it would have to be steaming pots of Lapsang Souchong and Oolong tea. Lapsang is *so* deliciously rich and smoky. And if we also served a Formosan Oolong, we'd pick up that extraordinary peach and chestnut bouquet."

"I've got a recipe for baked salmon wrapped in prosciutto," said Haley.

"Excellent entree," agreed Drayton. "But could we add a green tea marinade?"

"I don't see why not," said Haley. "And maybe a crusty piece of *fougasse* with olives?" She smiled at Miss Dimple. "That's really just flatbread with olives."

Miss Dimple rolled her eyes in great appreciation. "Do these two *ever* take a break?" she asked Theodosia. "It strikes me they're constantly tossing out *zillions* of utterly brilliant ideas!"

"They don't seem to have an off switch," agreed Theodosia. "In fact, they've been known to phone me in the wee hours of the morning with recipes, promotion concepts, or new ideas for tea blends."

Theodosia's voice carried not one whit of criticism. This was, after all, what set her heart to glowing. A small creative group that wasn't afraid to bounce ideas off one another. Not everything they came up with was superstellar, of course, but *most* things worked quite well. In fact, this creative daring and camaraderie was what made coming to work every day so exciting. You never knew *what* recipes or schemes might be hatched!

Glancing at his watch, Drayton slid back his chair and leapt to his feet. "Time to brew some tea," he announced. "We open in less than five minutes!"

"What are you going to tantalize us with today, Drayton?" asked Theodosia. He was puttering about behind the counter, getting ready to brew up three different pots of tea.

"I thought I'd do a pot of that Chinese Hyson," he told her. "It should be oddly complementary with Haley's miniature almond cakes." Hyson was a Chinese green tea that was fragrant, light, and mellow.

Theodosia nodded. "Perfect. What else?"

"Keemun," said Drayton. "There's nothing like a smooth black tea with a superlative bouquet."

The Chinese Keemun or the Taiwanese?"

"We'll go with the Chinese today," Drayton told her. "The Keemun Hao Ya. I'm awfully partial to that slightly roasted taste."

"And then the African tea we talked about?" asked Theodosia.

Drayton nodded. "Yes, the Rooibos." Rooibos, or Redbush, was a tea that grew just north of Capetown, South Africa. It had been getting a lot of buzz in the media lately and Theodosia was anxious to see how her customers would take to it.

Drayton masterfully juggled tea tins, teapots, and tea kettles as he assembled his morning tea offerings.

"Can't I help?" asked Theodosia.

"I'm fine here," he told her, "but I could certainly use your help on another matter."

"What's that?" asked Theodosia.

"I spoke with Timothy Neville last night. He mentioned that there was a master list of gifts on Harper Fisk's computer."

"Okay," said Theodosia. She had a pretty good idea what Drayton was suggesting.

Drayton cocked one eyebrow at her. "You *know* I'm an absolute computerphobe."

That much was true, thought Theodosia. But she also knew that Drayton didn't just abhor computers, he abhorred anything that smacked of being technological. No VCR, DVD, or Palm Pilot for Drayton Conneley. Oh, no. Vinyl records were fine with him, as well as movies viewed in theaters, and old-fashioned paper and pens. Drayton's technophobia bordered on that of a confirmed Luddite.

"Tell you what," said Theodosia. "If we're not too busy later on, why don't we stop by Harper Fisk's store. It's only a few blocks away." She saw the look of gratitude that flooded his face, and was flustered for a moment. "His computer *is* at his store, isn't it?" she added. "I mean, I just assumed it was."

Drayton struggled to keep his composure. The sight of Harper Fisk lying dead on the beach was still fresh in his mind. "Your guess is as good as mine," he said, his voice thick with emotion.

"Well," said Theodosia, "let's just ease into this then. Maybe drop by with some tea and scones, deliver our condolences to his business partner, see how everything plays out."

"Thank you, Theo," said Drayton. "You're an absolute lifesaver."

*　　*　　*

The next hour was fairly busy for a Monday. Regulars dropped by for cups of tea to go, as well as Haley's fresh-baked pastries and scones. And since they were smack dab in the middle of a Charleston summer, Drayton had also added iced tea to their menu. Today the Indigo Tea Shop was offering lemon mint tea with real lemon verbena, as well as a tea sangria made from English Breakfast tea, white grape juice, and fresh fruit. As usual, all the to-go's were poured into distinctive indigo blue cups with white snap-on lids, the bakery goods packaged neatly in indigo blue bags.

When Delaine stopped by around 10:00 A.M., accompanied by her sister, Nadine, Theodosia took a few moments to wander over to their table and greet them.

Delaine was still in a twitter over Saturday's upcoming fashion show.

"You know I *still* have to talk to you about Fashion Bash," said Delaine, ducking her head coquettishly and throwing Theodosia a sly look. "I really need to pick your clever little brain about a couple things."

Uh-oh.

"Sure thing," Theodosia told her. "But, Delaine, you know I'm not the fashion guru *you* are. Every time you've selected clothes for a fashion show then matched them to your models, the results have been fairly spectacular." Indeed, Delaine *had* pulled off a wonderful fashion show for the Ladies Garden Club some four months earlier.

"Flattery will get you everywhere," quipped Nadine from her now-familiar position at Delaine's elbow.

"Theodosia's right," said Miss Dimple, wandering over to Delaine's table and jumping head-first into the conversation. She had finished her bookkeeping chores and was ready to leave, her ledgers tucked under one plump arm.

"We all have complete faith in Delaine because she runs the most elegant boutique in Charleston. In fact, I don't think there's anything comparable unless you travel south to Palm Beach or north to New York."

"You know, sweetie," said Delaine, clasping one of Miss Dimple's hands with both of hers. "I just received the most *marvelous* shipment of silk scarves. Jewel tones. Deep claret, royal purple, emerald green. *Très elegant.*"

"Jewel tones are *so* flattering to older complexions," Nadine added helpfully.

I'm outa here, thought Theodosia as she hustled back to the kitchen to pick up another tray of scones. *And pardon me, is it just my perception or does that sister of Delaine's have an awfully sharp tongue?*

CHAPTER 7

⁂

*T*HE *LEGACY GALLERY*, Harper Fisk's antique store, was located in a redbrick building fronted with ornate white columns and topped with a red slate roof and a sharply peaked cupola. Bushy palm trees swayed in the warm breeze and flanked the front window where *Legacy Gallery* had been hand-painted in gold scrolling letters.

Theodosia and Drayton had strolled the few blocks from Church Street to King Street, the heart of Charleston's antique district, then hung a right at Fulton. The Legacy Gallery was about half a block in, adjacent to a fascinating-looking store by the name of Worldly Possessions that featured French and English porcelains.

"This was a good idea," said Drayton as they paused outside the Legacy Gallery. He shifted the box of scones he was carrying from one arm to the other.

"You think the shop's open?" asked Theodosia.

Drayton squinted as he pushed the shop door open. "I believe so. The lights are on, anyway."

The first thing that caught Theodosia's eye was an English-style highboy with a spectacular burled walnut veneer. Then her eyes flickered to an elegant scallop-edged tea table with tripod base. Finally, she spotted the small group of people perched on a selection of Queen Ann and Chippendale-style chairs.

"My goodness," announced Drayton, sounding startled, "it's the English Breakfast Club."

"Drayton!" A pretty brunette who looked barely thirty years old suddenly launched herself from her chair and ran to him. Throwing her arms about him, she buried her face in his jacket lapels. "What a sad time this is for all of us," she said tearfully. Balancing his box of scones, Drayton patted her shoulder in a commiserating gesture.

This has to be, thought Theodosia, *the young partner, Summer Sullivan.*

A quick glance told Theodosia that the three older gentlemen who were now struggling to their feet were, indeed, what was left of the English Breakfast Club. They had obviously been sitting here with Summer Sullivan, sharing a cup of tea and mourning the loss of Harper Fisk.

The pretty brunette released Drayton from her embrace and turned toward Theodosia with a sad smile on her face. "Hi, I'm Summer Sullivan," she said, offering her right hand. "I was Harper's partner."

Theodosia's first impression of Summer Sullivan was that she was a quiet beauty. Her skin glowed, seemingly without benefit of makeup, lush dark hair fell to her shoulders, and her dark brown eyes looked luminous if not a trifle brooding. Then again, Summer Sullivan had just lost her partner and mentor. It was entirely appropriate for her to be a bit subdued.

Glancing about, Theodosia recognized Benjamin "Buddy"

Clark, the retired naval officer they'd run into yesterday at the Yacht Club. And there were two men she didn't know.

Summer Sullivan rushed to introduce everyone.

"Theodosia . . . you *are* Theodosia, aren't you?" said Summer Sullivan. "Drayton's mentioned you many times."

"Yes, I am and it's lovely to meet you," said Theodosia. "Although I certainly wish it were under happier circumstances."

Summer Sullivan favored her with a shy smile. "Theodosia, this is Professor Archibald Gibbon." She indicated the older gentleman with a beefy red face who stood next to her. "He's a professor of nautical archaeology at Charleston University."

"Hello," said Theodosia, shaking hands with Professor Gibbon.

"And this," said Summer, "is Lawrence March. Larry owns March Forth, the antique shop just around the corner."

"Great name," said Theodosia as she shook his hand.

Lawrence March favored her with a shy smile. "People are always telling me that. Once you hear the name, you never forget it."

"You're right," agreed Theodosia as she studied this small man with wire-rimmed glasses and a heroic mane of white hair. "And that, of course, is the hallmark of any good brand name."

"Theodosia used to be in marketing," Drayton quickly explained.

Buddy Clark nodded politely at Theodosia. "Nice to see you again," he told her. "We met yesterday," he told the others.

"Good to see you again," murmured Theodosia.

Two more chairs were immediately pulled into the circle for Theodosia and Drayton, and Summer Sullivan found

cups and saucers for them as well. As Drayton quickly volunteered to pour tea, Summer arranged their offering of
scones on a lovely Chinese blue and white plate. The plate
was carefully passed around the circle and everyone politely
helped themselves.

"You must think it's positively awful of me to open
the store today," Summer began, gazing at Theodosia and
Drayton.

"Not at all," said Drayton.

"The truth of the matter is," said Summer, "I didn't know
what else to do. And when I thought about it, really analyzed
things, I knew Harper would have wanted it this way."

"I think you're right," said Drayton. He cleared his throat
self-consciously. "I *know* you're right."

"Has Drayton told you about us?" Professor Gibbon
asked Theodosia. "The English Breakfast Club?" He chortled halfheartedly. "Bunch of old fogies sitting around sipping tea, that's us."

"He told me that Harper Fisk had a group of very dear
friends," said Theodosia. "And that he generally regarded
them as family."

Professor Gibbon looked pleased. "Family, eh? Well, I
guess we sort of are."

"What exactly *is* nautical archaeology?" Theodosia asked
Professor Gibbon, trying to get his mind off the recent
tragedy. "The whole thing sounds fascinating but, I must
confess, I'm not entirely sure what's involved."

Professor Gibbon cleared his throat as though he were
about to begin a classroom lecture. "Nautical archaeology is
simply the study of underwater archaeology sites," he told
her. "Shipwrecks, reefs, geological anomalies, that sort of
thing. In the case of shipwrecks, we employ magnetometers
and global positioning devices that work off of satellites to tri-

angulate and hopefully pinpoint key sites. Then we document via underwater sketching and photography to determine if further research is warranted."

"Did Harper Fisk ever work with you on this?" Theodosia asked, recalling that Drayton had mentioned Harper Fisk's passion for trying to pinpoint underwater shipwrecks.

"Goodness no!" exclaimed Professor Gibbon. "Harper was really an amateur treasure hunter. While we may have shared an interest in what had been lost to the sea, you wouldn't say we ever *worked* together."

Professor Gibbon studied his empty plate, and the silence in the room seemed to stretch out endlessly.

Theodosia turned to face Summer Sullivan. "This must have been a terrible shock for you." She reached over and patted the young woman's hand. "If there's anything Drayton or I can do to help . . ."

Summer returned Theodosia's smile somewhat wistfully. "That's so kind of you. I don't know if you realize this, but Drayton here was the one who called me Friday night and broke the news about Harper." She nodded toward him. "He didn't want me to hear about his death from the police."

"Or, heaven forbid, television news," said Drayton.

Theodosia nodded. She wasn't a bit surprised by Drayton's actions. That was the kind of person he was. Always concerned with the feelings of others.

"Drayton tells me you'll probably continue to operate the shop," said Theodosia. She glanced around at the eclectic jumble of furniture, antique silver, architectural antiques, and a corner display that was all red and orange Chinoiserie. "It's a marvelous shop," she added. "Had you and Harper been working together for a long time?"

"Just two years," said Summer. "I used to be one of those amateur dealers who hauled their junk around in an old station wagon, traveling from flea market to tag sale." She laughed. "In fact, that's how I met Harper. He bought almost half my load one day at a crazy days celebration over in Orangeburg. After he hammered me down on price, he told me I had a good eye."

From the looks of the objects in the store and the care that had gone into arranging the displays, it was obvious both partners had a real sense for what today's customer was searching for.

"Anyway," continued Summer, "Harper and I got to talking and one thing led to another. I'd always planned to move to Charleston and hopefully open my own shop someday. That was my dream . . ." Summer hesitated a moment, her throat constricting and her voice suddenly growing hoarse. "Harper gave me that chance, my big break. He welcomed me into his shop and had been easing me in as his junior partner via a 'sweat equity' plan we worked out. I took a lower salary in exchange for a percentage of the business." Summer's eyes glistened and tears suddenly spilled down her cheeks. "Now, of course, the shop is mine. Sadly, I've inherited it." Summer rubbed at her reddening nose with the back of her hand. "Of course, I'd give the whole lot to have him back."

"Of course you would," said Lawrence March. "We all would." His gnarled hands grasped the frayed armrests on both sides of his chair and he heaved himself up. "This old street isn't going to be the same without Harper Fisk. Besides serving as chairman of the Antique Merchants Association, the man was always there for you. Someone from another shop couldn't identify a silversmith's mark or was unsure about the provenance of a painting, they'd come see Harper. He knew. He always knew."

Professor Gibbon pulled out a hanky and blew his nose

loudly. "Harper Fisk was one heck of a guy," he said. "We *were* like family."

"Still are," said Lawrence March. He reached down, put a hand on Professor Gibbon's shoulder, and patted it. "We're *still* the English Breakfast Club."

Professor Gibbon glanced up at the group with watery blue eyes. "What's left of us," he said.

CHAPTER 8

"SOMETHING SMELLS HEAVENLY," said Drayton as he and Theodosia came through the back door of the Indigo Tea Shop.

Haley met them in Theodosia's office with hands planted firmly on her slim hips. "Where have you two *been*?" she demanded. "I've been going absolutely *batty*. It's a good thing Miss Dimple was still hanging around. I had to put her to work!"

"You put a seventy-two-year-old woman to work?" asked Drayton. "Are you insane?"

Now Haley advanced on Drayton, brandishing a wooden spoon. "Hey, buster, what was I supposed to do? You left me here all by my lonesome."

"Haley's right," said Theodosia as she dropped her purse and straw hat on top of her cluttered desk and headed for the tea room floor. "Shame on us for leaving Haley all alone. Things got busy and she still had lunch to prepare. It wasn't fair."

"Plus you guys set up all those extra outdoor tables," grumped Haley. "It's a good thing they didn't fill up, too. *Then* where would we have been?"

"Oh, Miss Dimple," said Theodosia as she breezed into the tea room. "Let me do that. I'm *sooo* sorry we had to put you to work."

Miss Dimple, who was busy ladling spoonfuls of Munnar tea into a Brown Betty teapot, threw Theodosia a mischievous grin. "Well, I'm not a bit sorry," she said, with what seemed like genuine gusto. "I've been having the time of my life! Course, I don't know where a darn thing is and I can barely tell an Earl Grey from a China Black, but working here is definitely a *kick!*"

"Really?" asked Theodosia. The older lady's enthusiasm stopped her dead in her tracks.

"Yes, really," Miss Dimple assured her as she added hot water to the Munnar. Within seconds a bright, coppery liquor steamed in the teapot, a rich, aromatic tea from the southern tip of India. "Truth be known, dear, I'm glad Haley was in a bit of a tizzy. It's fun coming to someone's rescue. Especially at my age."

"Why, Miss Dimple," said Theodosia, quickly appropriating the teapot. "You're barely middle aged."

"Only if I plan to live to be a hundred and forty," she quipped back.

"Miss Dimple," said Drayton, bustling out through the curtains. "You poor dear. I'm so sorry you got roped in. It's my fault completely. I coerced Theodosia into going over to Harper Fisk's antique shop and then time just *unraveled* on us."

Miss Dimple waved a plump hand. "Forget about it, Drayton, Theodosia's already done the apology bit. I told her it wasn't a problem, I've been having *fun*."

"Well, at least let us *pay* you," said Theodosia, sliding open the drawer of the old brass cash register. "After all, you came here to do our bookkeeping and instead ended up serving tea."

"Just give me a little lunch," said Miss Dimple. "I've been scurrying about out here, pouring tea, and the smells issuing from Haley's kitchen are absolutely heavenly."

"What *is* Haley making for lunch?" Theodosia asked Drayton. Now that Miss Dimple had broached the subject, something *did* smell wonderful.

"I believe it's grilled shrimp with tropical fruit salsa," said Drayton.

"Wow," said Miss Dimple, clearly impressed with Haley's cooking prowess. "Tropical fruit salsa. What's tropical fruit salsa?"

"Haley's version appears to be a marinade of chopped mango, tomato, and cilantro seasoned with fresh ginger and lime," said Drayton.

"That *does* sound divine," said Miss Dimple. Her eyes had grown increasingly larger at the mention of every savory ingredient.

Theodosia glanced out across the tea room. Only two tables were occupied and those were by people who'd dropped by earlier for tea and scones. They'd no doubt be leaving any minute. But the lunch crowd would definitely be piling in soon, she decided. Probably in a matter of minutes.

"Say," said Drayton to Theodosia. "Sorry about this morning."

"What's to be sorry about?" she asked, reaching up to straighten the display of teacups.

"You know, the computer thing. We never got around to it."

Theodosia shook her head sadly, recalling all the tears and sad faces. "It just wasn't the right time, Drayton."

He nodded sagely. "Better to wait a few days."

"This is for Miss Dimple," said Haley as she emerged from the kitchen bearing a luncheon plate. Plump pink shrimp had been grilled to perfection and drizzled with a colorful melange of salsa blend.

Drayton gazed at the luncheon dish hungrily. "You're serving it on a bed of . . . what?"

"Asian cole slaw," said Haley, with just a slight hint of attitude.

"You have a lot more of this, yes?" asked Drayton.

Haley put the plate in Miss Dimple's eager, outstretched hands. "We'll see," she said. "First Miss Dimple eats and then we have to accommodate our *paying* customers."

"I assure you, Haley, I have been thoroughly chastised," said Drayton. "So there's no need to continue taunting me with the remote possibility of getting a taste of this fine dish." Drayton was a shrimp lover of the first magnitude and had been known to make emergency excursions to the little fishing village of Shem Creek to visit their various "raw bars."

The ring of the telephone punctuated his sentence. Haley grabbed the phone with one playful swipe, still not meeting Drayton's pleading gaze. "Indigo Tea Shop," she said. Haley listened for a brief second, then held the receiver out for Theodosia. "It's for you," she said in a stage whisper. "That pushy producer from Channel Eight who stopped by a few weeks ago."

Theodosia nodded as she accepted the phone. A couple weeks ago, she'd been asked to do a segment on tea for the midmorning *Windows on Charleston* show on Channel Eight. She'd decided it was one of those offers that sounded good at the time but probably wouldn't come to fruition anywhere in the near future.

"Theodosia," barked the strident voice of Constance Brucato, the executive producer of *Windows on Charleston*. "We need to set up a taping time. Pronto."

Oops. It suddenly looked like a TV segment might be looming on the horizon far sooner than Theodosia had thought possible.

"Constance," said Theodosia. "I didn't expect to hear from you this soon." Constance Brucato was a tiny dark-haired woman with the metabolism of a gerbil. She was in a constant state of excitation, trying to do twenty things at once. Theodosia decided the woman had been well named.

"I'll cut right to the chase," said Constance. "I ran my concept of doing a couple tea segments by the big boys here at the station and they *loved* the idea. *Jumped* at it, as a matter of fact. Tea's a hot commodity right now, as you well know. Iced tea, bottled tea, chai lattes, tea parties, tea shops . . . the darned stuff is everywhere!" Constance rattled on. "Women in particular are embracing tea, and women are the target audience for *Windows on Charleston!*"

"When were you thinking of taping the segments, Constance?" asked Theodosia. "And how many segments would you want?" Theodosia was praying that Constance would tell her they'd want to do the production this fall. Things were busy enough right now.

"We need to tape this week," announced Constance.

Frowning, Theodosia hesitated. "I wish I'd had a little more warning on this," she said. "I'm not sure we can accommodate you."

"Listen, Theodosia," said Constance, launching into an impassioned plea. "This is big time. We're talking four tea segments to start. Maybe one on tea in general. You know . . .

different varieties, different flavors. Then segments on how to stage a fancy tea party, which foods to serve with tea, and maybe another on the Japanese tea ceremony or something exotic like that. I haven't worked out the exact details yet, I'm more of a concept person. *You're* the tea expert, you tell me."

"We can't possibly do all that in one week," protested Theodosia. When she'd taped thirty-second TV commercials in the past, she'd always had at least six weeks lead time for preproduction. After all, you had to deal with sets, props, lighting, crew, talent, scripts . . . the works. TV always *looked* easy, but the prep time was a killer.

"Not to worry," Constance assured her. "This week all I want to do is bring my crew by the Indigo Tea Shop and soak up some atmosphere. You know, tape some footage that can be cut into quick little promo spots. Then, in another few weeks, you and I will get together and hash out the actual segments."

"But you definitely need to tape this week?" asked Theodosia.

"Theo, what can I tell you," chirped Constance. "My production assistant, Amy, leaves for a two-week trip to New Zealand next week and my editor is pregnant. The doctor says she could deliver any minute!"

"And you're sure you want me," said Theodosia, stalling. With her advertising and marketing background, she was used to being the one *behind* the camera.

"Yes, you," said Constance. "Of course, you. I want to capitalize on this big resurgence in tea drinking, really ride the crest of the wave. And it certainly doesn't hurt that you're an entrepreneur, a *female* entrepreneur. In case you haven't noticed, Theodosia, Charleston doesn't exactly have a wealth of high-profile businesswomen running around."

Constance paused, ever the hard-headed TV producer. "Plus, you basically hit all our demographics dead on."

"Which are?" said Theodosia.

"Twenty-eight to fifty-five, female, fairly well educated. Plus you launched that line of T-Bath products. They're still selling well, right?"

Theodosia thought back to her last P & L statement on the T-Bath products. "In six months we sold maybe eight hundred units out of the tea shop and another fifteen hundred via our website," she told Constance.

"See!" Constance chortled gleefully. "That's *beaucoup* newsworthy! In fact, the Charleston Chamber of Commerce ought to name you businesswoman of the year!"

"I don't know about that," protested Theodosia. *Good-ness,* she thought. *I can think of a dozen women who are doing the same thing I am. Running a small business, turn-ing a small profit. And all the while dealing with diverse is-sues such as sales and marketing, inventory, taxes, leases, and occasionally, problematic customers.*

Why, Delaine does it with her Cotton Duck clothing store, Brooke Carter Crocket at her jewelry store, Heart's Desire, and Nell Chappel over at the Chowder Hound Restaurant.

"Anyway," said Constance, interrupting Theodosia's thoughts, "we still need to tape right away."

"What's right away?" asked Theodosia.

"Let's see here . . ." There was a rustle of paper and Theodosia guessed Constance was paging through her scheduling book. "Yeah, how about Thursday?" Constance asked.

"Thursday's an awfully busy day for us," said Theodosia. "Drayton's got a tea tasting in the morning and we've got a group from the Lady Goodwood Inn scheduled for the afternoon." She was nervous as to how her customers would react to a TV crew moving in lock, stock, and barrel. It was bound to be terribly disruptive what with cameras and lights and electrical cables snaking underfoot.

How would I react, she asked herself, *if I was trying to enjoy a nice blackberry scone and cup of Darjeeling and somebody stuck a camera or microphone in my face? It would go against everything the Indigo Tea Shop was supposed to represent—a cozy, quiet respite from the hubbub of the outside world!*

"How about taping in the evening," Theodosia suggested carefully. "I could invite a few friends in and we'd—"

"Theo, I'm afraid we're locked in on this." Frustration edging toward disapproval was evident in Constance's voice. "My crew is doing a piece on the Bach Society this Wednesday, then the big cat show starts Friday. All of next week is reserved for summer gardens. It's now or never."

The silence on the phone stretched out.

"Okay," Theodosia agreed, "Thursday it is." She knew this kind of publicity was hard to come by. It didn't usually get dropped in your lap quite so easily. For her to write and produce a TV spot and then buy airtime would cost thousands of dollars. This was, literally, a gift from the gods, she told herself. Better accept it graciously.

"A TV spot," exclaimed Haley, "that's fantabulous!"

"Not a TV spot per se," Theodosia told her. "Channel Eight just wants to capture some of our atmosphere so they can cut together two or three promo spots. Constance says we'll hash out the actual segments later."

"Can I be on TV?" Haley asked excitedly. "I'd *love* to be on TV." She posed dramatically, presenting her profile, all long hair and button nose. "I'm ready for my close-up, Mr. DeMille."

"Well, I'm not," sniffed Drayton. "I think the whole idea is a little crass, if you want to know the truth. I realize, Theodosia, that the publicity aspect of this is tremendous, but you'll understand if I don't choose to participate."

"Drayton, you'd be fabulous on camera," gushed Haley. "You're a natural-born actor. Don't you think he is, Theo?"

"You'll get no argument from me," said Theodosia as she took a nibble of salad. The three of them were sitting at the table nearest the kitchen, enjoying a late lunch. Only three tables of customers lingered and they were almost finished. Drayton had given them final refills on cups of Assam tea and then unobtrusively presented them with their luncheon checks. It was only a matter of time before they'd wander up to the counter to pay.

"But, Drayton," said Haley, "what if *Windows on Charleston* wants to do a segment on tea *blending*? You're our big honcho in charge of that. In fact, you've made the Indigo Tea Shop *famous* with your seasonal blends. At Christmas people come from miles around to buy tins of your Applejack Spice Tea and your Cooper River Cranberry. In hot weather, we can barely keep the Audubon Herbal in stock."

"It's flying off the shelves now," noted Theodosia. She picked at her salad as she made notes on her Dayrunner calendar. Unfortunately, all the slots seemed to be filling up at an alarming rate.

"I suppose you're right," said Drayton unhappily. "So I'll probably have to appear on-camera, too."

Theodosia patted Drayton's arm. "There, there, we'll deal with that if and when we get to it." She studied her calendar again. "I wish I could find a little breathing room this week," she mused.

"A social life. The woman actually enjoys a social life,"

said Haley. "Must be nice. Pray tell, what is it that's crowding your schedule and rendering it so totally impossible?"

"Well," said Theodosia, ticking off her obligations on her fingers, "I'm supposed to take Earl Grey to the O'Doud Senior Citizen Home tonight, attend a gallery opening with Delaine tomorrow night, and Wednesday is the big anniversary party at The Featherbed House, which, of course, we're all invited to. And now we're taping all day Thursday, and Saturday is Delaine's big Fashion Bash at the Garden Gate Restaurant. Trust me, I *know* Delaine's going to try to rope me in on something."

"You forgot one thing," said Haley, squinting at her.

"What's that?" asked Theodosia.

"You have to figure out who killed Harper Fisk."

"What!" Drayton's reaction was so strong, he tipped over his teacup, splashing the last of his Oolong all over the linen tablecloth. "What are you talking about?" he asked as he blotted furiously.

Haley cupped her chin in her hands and propped her elbows on the table, studying him. "That certainly got you going," she told Drayton.

Drayton focused a murderous glare at Haley, which she promptly ignored. "If you ask me," said Haley, rattling on with the supreme confidence born of a twenty-two-year-old, "that young woman who was Harper Fisk's partner seems awfully suspicious."

"What she really seems is awfully nice," said Theodosia. She knew Haley was prone to jumping to conclusions due to sheer youthfulness and exuberance. On the other hand, Haley had remarkably good instincts about people. "What do you know about Summer Sullivan, Haley?" asked Theodosia.

Haley shrugged. "Not much. Drayton was telling me

about Summer while you were yacking on the phone with that producer. It seems fishy that she inherited his shop just like that."

"I thought I'd stressed that they'd been working together for two years," cut in Drayton. "They were *colleagues*." Drayton furrowed his brow and gazed at Haley. "You make it sound as though Summer came scratching at his door like a stray cat looking for a handout."

"From what I understand, Summer helped him significantly expand the business," said Theodosia.

Drayton reached for the teapot and carefully poured himself a fresh cup. "Oh, absolutely," he said. "Summer Sullivan has an amazing eye for architectural relics. She sleuths out buildings that are being torn down or renovated, then negotiates with the owners or, in some cases, the wrecking crews, to salvage various parts that would otherwise be discarded and tossed into dumpsters."

"What kind of parts?" asked Haley, screwing up her face in a gesture of sudden interest.

"Oh . . . cupolas, cornices, balustrades, old doors, stained glass windows, various odds and ends. You name it," said Drayton. "Anything that could fall victim to a wrecking ball or jack hammer."

"That kind of stuff is *still* getting knocked down?" said Haley. "How sad. Haven't people learned any lessons at all?"

Drayton shook his grizzled head. "Sadly, architectural preservation is *not* top of mind for most people." He cleared this throat. Clearly this was a subject that tore at his heart. "Anyway," he continued, "Summer Sullivan is an apparent whiz at what is now being termed architectural salvage. She added a whole new dimension to Harper Fisk's business. In recent months, they've been getting calls from people in

Atlanta, Savannah . . . you name it. Builders, contractors, preservationists, and just plain folks who are working diligently to restore old buildings."

"Summer Sullivan sounds like an awfully sharp girl," said Theodosia. Maybe she should mention Summer Sullivan's name to Constance Brucato, she thought to herself. The young woman's penchant for architectural preservation would surely make for a fascinating segment on *Windows on Charleston*. "Anyway," said Theodosia as an aside to Haley, "when we visited with Summer earlier today, she seemed completely bereft."

"That's right," said Drayton. "And as far as what happened to poor Harper Fisk, we're just going to have to wait for the coroner's report."

"Coroner's report!" barked Haley. She eyed Theodosia and Drayton with suspicion. "Don't tell me you're working with that nasty fellow Tidwell again."

"I wish you wouldn't talk like that," said Drayton. "He's been awfully helpful thus far."

Somewhat chastised, Haley stood up and began to pile dirty dishes onto a tray. "I thought he was on his way out," she murmured quietly.

Theodosia caught Haley's remark. "Where did you hear that?" she asked. *So there is something in the air about Tidwell's possible retirement.*

Haley shrugged. "Oh, you know my friend, Jimmy Cardavan, who writes for the *Charleston Post and Courier*? He got promoted from copy intern to junior reporter on police beat. He told me his boss was thinking about doing a story on the Charleston Police Department clearing out all their dead wood. Tidwell's name came up. I guess because he hasn't been around for a while."

"Really," said Theodosia. This was startling news. "Are they working on this story now?"

"I don't think so," said Haley. She shifted from one foot to the other. "You want me to call Jimmy and ask him?"

Theodosia considered this. "Let's hold off for the time being, okay?"

"Sure," said Haley, surprised by the look of consternation that flickered across Theodosia's face. "Whatever you say."

CHAPTER 9

~~~~~

LIMPID, BROWN EYES stared at Theodosia from under a mop of curly honey-colored hair. Then the little spaniel suddenly cocked his head as if to say *I know you,* and greeted Theodosia and Earl Grey with a gregarious *woof.*

"You finally got him!" exclaimed Theodosia as she knelt down on the green-tiled floor of Florida Singleton's room. Theodosia and Earl Grey had arrived at the O'Doud Senior Home about an hour ago and, so far, had spent all their time going from room to room, visiting with various residents.

Florida Singleton's old eyes sparkled as she reached out a gnarled hand and placed it gently on the head of her little Brittany spaniel. "Say hello to Sam Henry, the newest member of my family," she told them proudly.

Florida was a tiny woman, nut brown with a frizzle of gray hair. A year ago she'd suffered a bad case of viral encephalitis, which had turned into epilepsy. Now Florida had been diagnosed with complex partial and absence seizures.

Unable and afraid to live by herself in her apartment, Florida had been confined to the O'Doud Senior Home for the past eleven months. Now, it would appear Florida had finally received her walking papers in the form of a small, shaggy dog. Because this wasn't just any dog, this was a seizure alert dog.

Theodosia had met Florida some six months ago and wondered then if a seizure alert dog could help restore some of Florida's independence. She'd brought up the idea at a meeting of Big Paw, the Charleston service dog organization, of which she was an active member. Intrigued with the idea of expanding their assistance dog repertoire, the group had put the word out to various breeders in the area. A seizure alert dog, it seemed, wasn't so much *trained* for the task as he was *born* to it. Certain dogs simply experienced an intense feeling or intuition when a person they were close to was about to suffer a seizure. Scientists had even speculated that certain canines were more *attuned* to electrical activity in the body, while other dogs were utterly clueless. The trick, of course, was to find one of those rare animals who possessed that canine sixth sense.

Sam Henry had been in the assistance dog program for four months, living in a foster home, when Theodosia and Jackie Bachman, the training director, had taken him over to meet Florida one day. Florida and the dog had bonded instantly. But the question remained. Did Sam Henry have the gift?

That issue was resolved some twenty minutes into their visit when Sam Henry suddenly started whimpering and throwing pleading looks at Florida. Then, Florida's eyes began to glaze over and her facial muscles grew tense. As Theodosia fled to alert a nurse, Sam Henry leapt into Florida's lap and began licking her face. That small, almost insignificant act *interrupted* the seizure. And Florida came out of it, dazed, shaken, and utterly amazed at the miracle the little dog had wrought.

"We go home next week," Florida told Theodosia proudly. "Sam Henry's been living here with me for the past two weeks, and so far he's stopped three seizures and remained with me through one. Florida gazed with adoration at her little dog and Sam Henry reciprocated by wagging his tail and giving her his "good dog" look.

"Best of all," Florida continued, "Sam Henry seems to know exactly when I begin to show *signs* of an impending seizure. The little guy whimpers and puts a paw on me, telling me I need to get to a safe place. You know, go sit in a chair or lay down on my bed so I don't have to worry about falling and breaking bones."

"It's a miracle," said Theodosia as she sat cross-legged on the floor, one arm slung around Earl Grey's neck, the other scratching Sam Henry under the chin. She never failed to marvel at how assistance dogs brought such real and immediate joy to people—whether they were trained as therapy dogs like Earl Grey or as seizure alert dogs, Seeing Eye dogs, or hearing dogs. In Theodosia's mind, dogs were precious creatures who were capable of bestowing great love and kindness.

"You'll still come visit us, won't you?" asked Florida, clearly torn between leaving old friends and regaining her independence.

"Count on it," said Theodosia as her cell phone shrilled inside her purse.

Stepping out into the hallway with Earl Grey, Theodosia punched the receive button. "Hello?" she said.

"Theodosia, hi." It was Jory Davis.

"Hey, I'm surprised to even hear from you," she said. "I

figured you were still over in Columbia." Jory had told her earlier that he'd be over at the state capital all day, taking depositions on a real estate case and probably filing an appeal.

"We're just on our way back now," Jory told her. "Passing through the city of . . . uh, I think it's Swansea." Jory paused. "Listen, Theo, I just heard a very strange bulletin. There's been a shooting over at Buddy Clark's house. You know, Benjamin Clark, the retired Naval officer?"

Jory's news caught Theodosia by surprise. Buddy Clark was one of the members of the English Breakfast Club, after all.

"What happened?" she stammered. "How did you hear this?" She knew Jory Davis had driven to Columbia with another lawyer from his firm. *Did they hear this on their car radio? Or had they heard a rumbling just as they departed the court house?*

"Billy's got a police scanner in his Beamer," chuckled Jory. "Just what every good old boy Southern lawyer needs, right?"

But Theodosia was focused only on the shocker news Jory had just delivered. "Tell me what happened," she said.

"As you might imagine, information was sketchy," said Jory. "But it sounds as though Buddy was out in his backyard and somebody took a pot shot at him."

"With a gun? A rifle?"

"Don't know," replied Jory. There was a patch of loud static then Jory said, "Sorry, we just drove through an underpass."

"And this shooting just happened?" she asked.

"Yeah," said Jory. "Minutes ago. Pretty wild, huh?"

But Theodosia was already thinking about how she could get in touch with Burt Tidwell. *Or better yet, could I just drop by the crime scene? Where the heck does Buddy Clark live anyway? Over here near the university? Maybe in the historic district?*

"Jory? Thanks for calling. Thanks so much," said Theodosia. "I'll catch you later, okay?"

There were two Benjamin Clarks listed when Theodosia called directory assistance. One on Chapel Street and one on Bull Street, close to the City Marina.

Bull Street, has to be it, Theodosia decided as she loaded Earl Grey into the back of her Jeep and roared off into the night.

Her hunch proved correct. Lieutenant Benjamin "Buddy" Clark lived over on Bull Street in what had once been an elegant three-story Charleston single home. Although there were many variations of single homes, Clark's was a turn-of-the-century Victorian with all the requisite cupolas, balustrades, and wooden lace. It had also seen better days.

Because Charleston single homes were so old, many had interiors that boasted ornate plaster work, cypress paneling, and marble fireplaces. But the Charleston weather, with its full complement of heat, humidity, hurricanes, and dampness, wreaked terrible havoc on the exteriors. If you didn't constantly maintain them, you could lose them. And Buddy Clark's house looked like it might be a lost cause. The two-story piazza on this formerly grand home sagged badly, paint flaked from the exterior, a front window was pitted and cracked, the shrubbery next to the house completely overgrown.

Since this was a typical Charleston single house, snugged smack dab up to the sidewalk, with no front yard, all activity seemed to be taking place in the street directly in front of Buddy Clark's house. Blue and red police lights pulsed, uniformed police officers clutched clipboards with great authority, and a gaggle of onlookers milled about on the side lines.

Theodosia cruised by, hung a right at the corner, and came around to the back of the house. There was activity here, too, but not as much. She threw her Jeep into park and snapped a leash on Earl Grey. *A woman walking a dog down an alley at night will probably be construed as a friendly neighbor, right? Easier to get close to the action this way.*

Buddy Clark's backyard exhibited as much disrepair as his house. Like many Charleston homes, it had a fairly elaborate garden tucked behind it. But this garden obviously hadn't been maintained for years. Once verdant, it was now overgrown, a virtual jungle. Mimosa trees clumped together with dense stands of oleander and loquat, choking out the center fountain that had probably run dry years ago. This was no longer an elegant oasis of calm, it looked more like the tangle of kudzu-choked brush like you'd see in the low-country.

Edging up to a crumbling brick wall, Theodosia surveyed the scene. Buddy Clark's backyard was lit by a single bright light that hung above a side door. Just to the left of that door, at about eye level, two police officers wearing black shirts that said CRIME SCENE on the back seemed to be digging something out of the wall.

Digging out a slug? Yeah, probably.

Some six feet away Buddy Clark stood talking with Detective Orrin Hudson.

Recognizing him immediately, Theodosia curled her mouth in distaste. Fresh in her mind was her encounter with the acrimonious Detective Hudson last Sunday. He had been sharp-tempered and rude, just this side of disdainful when she'd spoken with him. She doubted he'd undergone any sort of transformation in manners since then.

As if he'd read her mind, Detective Orrin Hudson suddenly swiveled his head and focused in her direction. His eyes landed on Earl Grey, then her.

"Hey," he called. "Get out of here! Sensky, Emmett, can't you two do nothin' right?" he called to two nearby officers.

"Hello, Detective Hudson," Theodosia called to him, "nice to see you again." *When in doubt, use politeness as your weapon. It's worked before, let's see if it works here.*

"It's Theodosia Browning," she added in what Drayton often called her innocent yoo-hoo voice. "We met last Sunday over on Sullivan's Island? Remember?" said Theodosia with forced cheeriness.

Hudson continued to stare at her. Buddy Clark simply gazed at the side of his house where the bullet or slug or whatever it was had ostensibly struck. He made no attempt to meet Theodosia's gaze. Probably didn't even realize she was there.

"At the boat?" Theodosia added, giving a friendly little wave to Hudson.

Hudson turned his back to her and gestured for Officer Sensky to take Buddy Clark inside. "Get his statement and be sure to write it out legibly," he barked to the officer.

Theodosia took a bold step forward, crunching weeds underfoot. "Is Mr. Clark all right?" she asked.

Hudson sighed and shook his head. With exaggerated gestures, he pointed at the retreating Buddy Clark accompanied by Officer Sensky. "See for yourself," he said.

Once the camel gets his nose in the tent, it's all over, Theodosia thought to herself. *And here we go.*

"I heard someone took a shot at him," Theodosia ventured.

"Looks that way," said Hudson. The expression in his eyes was flat and bored. No mirrored sunglasses today, Theodosia noted. None needed. Hudson had his intimidation tactics down perfectly.

"What do you think happened?" she asked.

Orrin Hudson stuck his tongue in his cheek and glanced sideways.

"Probably was a shot fired from a passing car or pickup truck. A couple peckerwoods out for a few beers and a joyride. Showing off, trying to act smart."

Someone just happened to fire a shot at him, Theodosia thought to herself. *In what appears to be a very quiet neighborhood that's off the beaten path from more-traveled thoroughfares. No rowdy bars or blues clubs around either. Hmm.*

"And Buddy's for sure okay?" Theodosia asked.

"Who?" Hudson's eyes flicked back at her. He was fast losing interest in this little game.

"Lieutenant Clark," said Theodosia.

"He's fine. As you saw, I sent him in to give a statement. The man's a little shaken up but—"

"Are you going to check his hands for powder residue?"

The question just popped out, surprising Theodosia as much as it did Detective Hudson.

"What?" Hudson stammered. The outrage and anger in his voice were obvious. He practically put his head back and howled at her. "Lady, just who do you think you are? This ain't Forensics 101, and none of us are looking to audition for a starring role in a crime scene TV show. This happens to be the *real world* by way of Charleston." Hudson put his face close to hers and she could feel tiny droplets of spit bounce against her cheeks. "Buddy Clark didn't *do* nothin', get it? Somebody *else* was responsible."

Hudson grabbed at his belt with both hands and did a quick hitch of his pants.

A very male gesture, Theodosia decided. *Territorial.*

But Hudson wasn't finished chewing her out yet. "Accidents happen, okay? Rednecks get plastered and climb into big honkin' pickup trucks and sometimes get a notion to shoot up the town. It ain't no big deal unless somebody gets hurt. And nobody got hurt tonight." He pulled a piece of Juicy Fruit from his pocket, tossed the wrapper into the weeds, and crumpled the gum into his mouth. "Now, stop making mountains out of mole hills. And if you know what's good for you, you'll get out of here and let me do my job!"

There was a low growl from Earl Grey, and Theodosia gave a sharp tug on his leash. The dog didn't much like it when his mistress was threatened.

"Emmett." Hudson gave a sharp nod to a uniformed officer, who promptly got to work stretching a roll of black and yellow crime scene tape across the driveway. "String up that tape and don't let nobody near here. That's an *order.*"

Emmett nodded, all ears and shaved neck on a gawky six-foot-six frame.

"Then get me one of those twenty-three slash seventeen forms to fill out," barked Hudson. "And a ball point pen that *works!*"

Theodosia stepped back into the alley with Earl Grey, relegated now to the subset of gawkers and onlookers. It was clear something had happened here tonight. Buddy had looked shaken and emotions seemed to be riding high.

But the whole episode didn't feel right.

Theodosia dug in her purse for her cell phone, then punched in the numbers for Jory's cell phone.

"Hello, Theodosia," he answered.

"How did you know it was me?"

"Lucky guess." Jory Davis laughed a rich, melodic laugh. "What did you find out?"

"The police say a couple rednecks were cruising the neighborhood and accidentally fired a shot."

"You *went* to the crime scene? My gosh." He was nonplused that she'd acted so quickly. "Well, that *sounds* like a plausible story," said Jory.

Theodosia hesitated. She'd heard all sorts of stories about how calls on cell phones could be easily intercepted and overheard. But at the same time, she *needed* to talk this over with Jory while it was still fresh in her mind.

"Here's my take on it," began Theodosia. "I can see *one* accident happening within a small group of friends . . ."

"Friends being the English Breakfast Club," said Jory.

"Yup," said Theodosia. "But *two* accidents in the course of what . . . three or four days? One fatal accident and one near-miss? That type of coincidence seems to stretch the bounds of logic."

"Now that you mention it . . . I'd probably have to agree with you," said Jory.

Staticky silence hung between them.

"Maybe someone's out to get rid of the English Breakfast Club?" ventured Theodosia. The words tasted harsh in her throat.

"Whew," said Jory. "Big leap."

"Big guess," said Theodosia. "What do *you* think?"

"Hey," said Jory Davis. "I'm one of the legal eagles who help put the bad guys on trial. Of course, I don't actually go out and *track* them down." He paused. "More and more, that seems to be your territory," he said, trying to make light of what seemed to be shaping up as a very serious matter.

Remembering Harper Fisk's cold, lifeless body bumping against her like a cold plastic buoy in the Atlantic Ocean just three nights ago, Theodosia took Jory's words to heart. "I suppose you're right," she told him. "If it's anyone's territory, it's mine."

CHAPTER 10

❧❧❧

SUNLIGHT STREAMED THROUGH the heavy-leaded windows of the Indigo Tea Shop, bouncing a kaleidoscopic burst of sunbeams off the brick walls, pegged wooden floors, and floor-to-ceiling warren of cubbyholes that held shiny tins and jars filled with piquant and delicate loose leaf teas.

In Haley's kitchen, orange juice, blackberries, sugar, cinnamon, nutmeg, and cloves bubbled together in a heavy sauce pan, just one step in the making of her famous blackberry cobbler. In time, fresh sweet cream would be whipped into heroic, fluffy mounds to top that summertime treat.

Out in the tea room, Drayton bustled about, dressed in a linen blazer, starched white shirt, and spiffy polka dot bow tie. Because Haley's bakery selections today included sweet potato muffins, ginger-pear scones, and blackberry cobbler, all offerings that were summery and sweet, he had carefully selected several teas he thought would pair nicely with them.

Dragon's Well, a green tea from Central China, was a

pale golden tea with a refreshing, slightly sweet flavor. Taken hot, without benefit of milk, cream, or sugar, it was both refreshing and oddly cooling.

Then there was Drayton's old favorite, Shou Mee. This was a white tea from the Fujian Province in China. Again, it was drunk straight and offered a sweet, flowery taste that should be highly complementary to today's baked offerings.

Drayton's fingertips danced across a row of tea tins that sat high up on a shelf. *Now where is that other one?* he mused. It was a special blend he'd created but didn't serve all that often.

Haley emerged from the kitchen to stare at him. "Well," she said, wiping her hands on her apron, "have you made up your mind yet?"

Drayton grasped one of the tins, pulled it down from the shelf. "Do you recall that lovely Java Ginseng blend I created? I was thinking of brewing a pot or two today."

"I *love* that blend," Haley told him. "Indonesian black tea with just a hint of ginseng and cardamom. Very mellow." She reached up and poked a hank of hair behind her right ear. In her pale pink T-shirt and long gauzy floral skirt, she looked pretty and perky and about sixteen years old. "What about offering iced lemon verbena again? We sold a *ton* of that the other day."

"Your wish is my command," responded Drayton.

"Well, you're *easy,*" laughed Haley as she pulled the brown paper wrapping off a bundle of linen napkins that had just been delivered by the laundry, and set off to distribute them among the various tables. Haley, always the compulsive neat-nik, loved getting everything all set up and ready for their first early-morning customers.

In fact, everything at the Indigo Tea Shop was extremely calm and copasetic until Theodosia came galloping in to tell them the news about poor Buddy Clark getting shot at last night.

"Oh my goodness," said Drayton. Pouring a cup of Dragon's Well tea for himself, he stopped midway and set the teapot down unsteadily. "It's happened again."

"What's happened again?" asked Haley.

"I believe Drayton was referring to the English Breakfast Club," said Theodosia. "Last night's little shooting melee was the second accident to befall one of its members."

"Whoa," said Haley. "I'd call Harper Fisk's drowning more than an *accident*. And now you say this fellow Benjamin Clark was shot at?"

Drayton stumbled to the closest chair, put a hand to his heart, and sat down heavily.

"Drayton, are you okay?" asked Theodosia. The poor man had turned absolutely white.

"I think so," ventured Drayton. "But I must say I'm stunned, truly stunned."

Haley finished pouring Drayton's cup of tea and brought it over to him. "Drink this," she said gently. "It'll make you feel better."

Drayton obediently took a sip. "It *doesn't* make me feel better," he told Haley, "but at least it's a civilized response to some rather uncivilized news. You're quite sure Buddy's all right?"

"Yes, he seemed fine," said Theodosia. She paused, thought about what she was about to say, then plunged ahead. "Drayton, does the notion of Buddy Clark getting shot at seem a little far-fetched to you?"

Drayton took another sip of tea and shook his head slowly. "Yes, it does." He peered up at Theodosia, searched her face. "You want to tell us where you're going with this?"

Theodosia looked oddly uncomfortable. "What if it just

looked like something happened to Buddy Clark . . ." she began. "Do you see what I mean?" There was a pleading note to her voice.

"You think this Buddy Clark guy might have *staged* last night's incident?" piped up Haley. "Or had something to do with Harper Fisk's death?"

Theodosia stared at Haley, considering both questions. "I don't know," she said finally. "Buddy Clark certainly *acted* strangely this past Sunday when we ran into him on the dock at the yacht club. I don't know. I probably have this all wrong."

"I sincerely hope you do," said Drayton. "It gives me the shivers to think that someone within the group might wish ill of the others. Or that someone outside the group was attempting to pick them off."

Haley's eyes were big as saucers. "Why would someone want to do that?"

Drayton gazed into his teacup as though the answer might be contained therein. Finally, he just shook his head again. "I have no idea," he said. "No idea whatsoever."

Even though Drayton was in a thoughtful mood for the rest of the morning, his teas were a major hit. It seemed that *everyone* wanted a cup of the Dragon's Well tea to go along with one of Haley's sweet potato muffins or ginger-pear scones. The blackberry cobbler wasn't even offered, it was being held in reserve for the afternoon tea crowd.

Lunch would be simple today and in keeping with the hot weather. Chilled peach soup and chutney chicken salad sandwiches served open-face on thin slices of nut bread.

Around eleven o'clock Delaine Dish came sashaying in. Wearing a navy sheath dress that skimmed her slim figure, her wrists jangling with eighteen-karat gold bangles, and her long dark hair woven up in a psyche knot, Delaine was the picture of elegance and refinement.

"Drayton," she cooed as she ran brightly polished nails across the lapels of his wheat-colored linen jacket. "You're always so beautifully turned out. I simply *adore* a man who takes pride in his appearance."

Drayton smiled tolerantly. He had just talked to Buddy Clark via phone, and Buddy had assured him he was just fine. "Where's your lovely sister?" he asked Delaine.

Delaine waved a hand airily. "Gadding about. Out shopping, I suppose." She narrowed her green eyes as Theodosia came bustling out from behind the velvet curtains, carrying an armload of T-Bath products that had just been delivered to her back door via UPS.

"Theodosia!" called Delaine. "*Pardon.* Do you have *un momento*?"

Of course she didn't have a moment to spare, but Delaine was bearing down on her with that I'm-helpless-as-a-newborn-lamb look.

"What's up, Delaine?" asked Theodosia as she briskly stacked boxes and bottles of T-Bath products on the shelves of the old wooden secretary. Set next to the stone fireplace, it served as the perfect display case.

"Honey, you've just *got* to help me," Delaine implored. "I'm up to my *eyeballs* with things to do for Saturday's big Fashion Bash. And I frankly need someone with more than a modicum of *taste* to accompany me to Garden Gate Restaurant to help finalize the arrangements."

"And I'm your pigeon?" Theodosia leveled her gaze at Delaine. *It would have to be now.*

"You're not my pigeon, Theo, you're my friend," said Delaine. She waggled a finger at Theodosia. "Remember, you *did* promise to help . . . and it *is* a fund-raiser for the

Heritage Society. There've been so many people who swore they'd volunteer their time, then simply dropped by the wayside. *Fini.* For heaven's sake, Theodosia, *you* wouldn't do that to me, too, would you?" Delaine's voice rose to a sharp squawk, causing people at several tables to turn around and stare.

"No, of course I wouldn't," said Theodosia. She *had* promised to help Delaine. She just wished Delaine hadn't requested a command performance right this minute!

Garden Gate on Cumberland Street was a power lunch restaurant. Its dimly lit interior sported black leather bumper car booths, tiny glowing lamps atop each table, and lots of gleaming wood and shiny brass appointments. Rich oil paintings graced the walls.

The owner, Gordon Sargent, had kindly offered to cater Delaine's Fashion Bash luncheon at cost. Which meant that, after charging all her luncheon attendees a hefty sixty dollars a ticket, Delaine would clear a cool three thousand dollars to plunk in the Heritage Society's coffers.

Theodosia and Delaine pushed their way toward the deserted hostess stand. They'd arrived slightly before the lunch crowd was poised to hit, before the bankers and lawyers and ad guys sat down to snarf their radicchio salads and grilled snapper.

"Were you planning to have the tea in Garden Gate's party room?" Theodosia asked. Off to their left was the large dining room, to their right a clubby-looking bar. Theodosia knew Garden Gate had another large party room *somewhere*. She remembered being in it when she'd attended a Christmas party here last year.

"No, no, no," said Delaine as she herded Theodosia on

through the restaurant toward the back door. "Our group will be *outside*." There's a reason they call this *Garden* Gate."

Emerging on the outdoor patio was a pleasant and amazing contrast after the dark atmosphere of the restaurant. A fountain spattered merrily in the center of a small, circular pool. Wooden lattice walls covered with a tangle of vines surrounded the large, sunny patio. Against these rough-hewn walls, stands of dogwood, mock orange, and camellias formed a delightful faux forest. Scattered about were a dozen or so wrought iron tables and chairs accented with colorful umbrellas emblazoned with the usual Cinzano and Perrier logos.

"You like?" asked Delaine.

"It's great," enthused Theodosia. "What a terrific place to hold a tea and fashion show." Open to the sky, yet still sheltered from the hot Charleston sun by the riot of trees, large potted plants, and table umbrellas, the patio was pretty, inviting, and tranquil.

"My dear Miss Dish, is that you?"

Theodosia turned to see a good-looking man in a beautifully tailored summer suit come rushing across the patio, smiling brightly at them.

"Say now," the man exclaimed. "I didn't mean to interrupt your inspection tour, but my office is right over there." He turned slightly and gestured toward the far wall of the courtyard. A riot of greenery cascaded across more latticework, hiding what appeared to be a small window framed by wooden shutters. "You see?" he said. "I even used to have a teeny, tiny window. Then we added staff and had to move a few inside walls."

"Theodosia Browning, meet Gordon Sargent," gushed Delaine. "Gordon is our genial host and *impresario* of the Garden Gate Restaurant."

Gordon Sargent grasped Theodosia's hand warmly. Dark-haired and olive-skinned, he smiled widely, revealing dazzling white teeth. "And you're the lady with the tea shop!" he exclaimed. "Delaine's told me all about you. Welcome."

Theodosia found herself warming up to Gordon Sargent almost immediately. He had the forthright, friendly manner of a skilled restaurateur. And in the two years that Garden Gate had been open, he had certainly garnered more than his share of favorable write-ups and reviews in the local press. His inventive menu, what Gordon Sargent liked to call "nouvelle coastal cuisine," included such delicacies as pecan-crusted grouper in champagne sauce and smoked Carolina shrimp with citrus marinade. Pushing the limits of Carolina cooking, his offerings were a far cry from the region's traditional fare of crab cakes and oyster stew.

The three of them wandered about the patio, Delaine chattering blissfully away about Saturday's upcoming event.

"That's an interesting piece," Theodosia remarked as she stopped to admire a stone statue of a cherub carrying an urn on one shoulder. Somewhat pebbled and distressed in appearance, the statuary was tucked into a copse of rhododendrons and azaleas, looking all the world like something from a Roman ruin.

"Like it?" Gordon asked her.

"Very much," said Theodosia.

"It came from an old church that was demolished over near Monk's Corner," Sargent told her. "Sad to think something that pretty was almost cast away."

Theodosia stared at Gordon Sargent intently. "How exactly did you come by this piece?" she asked.

Gordon stuck both hands in his pants pockets and rocked back on his heels. "Oh, I'm a fairly lucky guy. The lady I'm dating is an antique maven. She's got a real knack for ferreting out this kind of thing."

"Summer Sullivan?" exclaimed Theodosia. *Wasn't this a coincidence?*

Gordon's face brightened even more. "Good gosh, you two know each other? Hey, that's great. Small world, isn't it."

"Actually," said Theodosia, "I just met Summer for the first time yesterday morning. Her partner, Harper Fisk, was a good friend of Drayton Conneley, my assistant."

Gordon stared at her intently then snapped his fingers as though he'd just put two and two together. "Oh, my gosh! You were the lady at Halliehurst Beach!" His mood shifted suddenly from that of genial host to one of somber reflection. "That must have been *awful* for you. Swimming out and finding poor Harper Fisk's body like that."

"Awful for Harper Fisk, too," murmured Delaine. "But we don't want to get sidetracked by something so *dreary* when we have big plans to discuss."

But Gordon Sargent wasn't nearly ready to drop the subject.

He shook his head sadly. "I've been going out with Summer for about six months now. She's a pretty happy-go-lucky girl. But the last three days have been pure hell for her. She's completely broken up over Harper's death. As you can imagine, they were very close."

Theodosia's heart went out to the girl. She couldn't imagine how *she'd* feel if she ever lost Drayton. Just like the relationship that must have existed between Harper Fisk and Summer Sullivan, Drayton was far more than an employee to her. He was a critical part of her business team and one of her best friends. Yes, she'd be absolutely devastated. As devastated as Summer Sullivan probably was right now.

"Yes, poor Summer," said Delaine, not seeming to muster up more than a modicum of empathy. "You know," she said brightly, gazing about the patio garden and smiling contentedly to herself, "our Fashion Bash was originally advertised as simply a luncheon tea. But seeing all this *marvelous* flora and fauna has inspired me to give it a little *added* emphasis."

"What do you have in mind, Delaine?" asked Theodosia. *Trust Delaine to change things at the last minute. And what exactly does she need me for? She seems to have everything already decided on.*

Delaine spun on her high-heeled sandals to face them. Her green eyes glinted, impending drama was written on her face.

"Just look around," she extolled them. "We are in an incredible *English* Garden. Mr. Gordon Sargent's fantasy garden!"

Gordon gave a dazed, somewhat bewildered smile. It was obvious he wasn't used to someone like Delaine coming in and doing a number on him either.

"Now picture, if you will," continued Delaine, "the utterly *exquisite* fashions we'll be showcasing." She paused dramatically. "Lots of summer lace. Very soft, almost *handkerchief* thin, white cotton skirts and cropped pants. And camisole-style tops with lace, tiny eyelets, and gauzy ribbons. Then there's an exquisite *ivory* collection for evening wear," she continued. "Dresses and pant suits, still summery light, but far more formal. I mean, I've already sold two of these pieces as *wedding* gowns. Of course, these were not first-time brides, but *mature* women, one on her second marriage, another on her third."

Gordon stared at Delaine, enraptured. Obviously he'd also never had experience with a woman like Delaine in the throes of a *big idea*. Theodosia, on the other hand, had witnessed Delaine's revelations on an almost weekly basis for several years running. She knew that Delaine *did* have good ideas, it was the theatrics that took their toll.

"Delaine," said Theodosia, a faint smile playing at her lips. "Let's cut to the chase. What exactly are you suggesting?"

Delaine whirled on her. "Thank you, Theodosia. You're always so good at centering me, at grounding me."

"So this new theme would be . . ." began Gordon, trying his best to keep pace with the conversation.

"Lavender and Lace," purred Delaine. She held up a finger to Gordon. "Don't try to talk me out of it . . ."

"I wasn't," he stammered.

"Yes," Delaine tilted her face upward and smiled a distant, dreamy smile. "I see bouquets of fresh lavender overflowing at each table." She was on the move now, her concept really sweeping her away. Gordon followed at her heels. From somewhere he produced a tiny leather notebook and began frantically jotting down notes. Theodosia tried to keep from giggling. When Delaine got wound up, she was a sight to behold.

"For our beverage we should serve lavender iced tea," proclaimed Delaine. "And we must place tiny lavender soaps and lavender sachets at each place setting as favors. And tie lavender ribbons and little pieces of lace to all the chairs."

"Pretty," murmured Theodosia. *So this is why Delaine strong-armed me into coming along. She wanted an audience.*

"You mentioned lavender tea," interjected Gordon Sargent. "Which brings to mind an idea. If you'll excuse me for one moment . . ." And off he dashed toward the kitchen.

"Oh, Theodosia," exclaimed Delaine, clutching Theodosia's arm, "we *do* work well together, don't we?"

"We're a regular Jekyll and Hyde," responded Theodosia.

"And isn't Gordon Sargent an absolute *dreamboat*?" asked Delaine, dropping her voice to a low growl. "So elegant, so European."

"He's definitely deserving of all the rave reviews," answered Theodosia, noncommittally. In the last month or so, Delaine had broken off from dating Cooper Hobcow, a somewhat infamous criminal attorney. She hoped Delaine wasn't setting her cap for Gordon Sargent. After all, the man was already romantically involved with Summer Sullivan.

"You know," said Delaine, "Gordon Sargent is actually related to the *real* Sargent, the American painter!"

"To John *Singer* Sargent? Where on earth did you hear that?" asked Theodosia. That would be quite a surprise, since before Gordon Sargent hit it big with Garden Gate Restaurant, he was supposed to have run a modest little seafood restaurant called the Harbor Grill over in Myrtle Beach.

"And the rumor is," whispered Delaine, not the least bit deterred by Theodosia's skepticism, "that he has a *real* Sargent hanging right here in the bar. The painting of the two very romantic-looking dancers with the musicians in the background. I hear it's worth an absolute fortune."

"Do you think he inherited it?" asked Theodosia. She knew there was no arguing with Delaine regarding *provenance* or authenticity.

"Oh, honey," purred Delaine, "I wouldn't be surprised. With a family heritage like that . . ."

As if on cue, Gordon Sargent came bustling out of his kitchen bearing a marvelous old silver samovar.

"When you mentioned the lavender iced tea, this samovar came to mind as the ideal serving piece." Gordon set the samovar down on a wrought iron table and the three of them gathered around it.

An elaborate tea heating and brewing apparatus, the samovar was invented in Russia during the eighteenth century and soon became the symbol of a family's prosperity and cordiality. The samovar was generally placed in the center of the table and family and guests would gather round it to be served hot tea with sugar. The gleaming silver samovar that Gordon Sargent had just presented was obviously a fine Russian antique. Shaped like a decorative vase, it featured an elaborate spigot.

"It really does exude personality, doesn't it?" said Gordon, pleased with his find.

Theodosia considered the idea. The samovar hinted at exotic lands where tea was a way of life, a deeply ingrained part of the culture. Plus, the samovar was a drop-dead gorgeous serving piece. It would lend an exotic feel to the whole event.

"It's perfect," Theodosia told Gordon Sargent. "Do you want me to make the lavender tea or should I have—"

Gordon Sargent held up a hand. "Just send a couple tins of your lavender tea over and we'll do the rest. Garden Gate will take care of everything. Don't worry about a thing." He grinned widely. "Never mind that I put in fourteen-hour workdays."

"Remember now, you must use *fresh* lavender as garnish," said Delaine, batting her eyelashes at Gordon.

But Gordon had turned his attention to Theodosia.

"Will you be attending the service tomorrow?" he asked her.

She shook her head. The idea hadn't really crossed her

mind. In fact, she wasn't sure she'd even *known* there was a service tomorrow for Harper Fisk.

"Apparently his body was released yesterday by the police," said Gordon. "He's being cremated this afternoon and Summer is planning to bury his urn in the family plot. You should come," invited Gordon. "It's just going to be a small graveside service at Magnolia Cemetery."

"Sounds so sad," said Delaine.

"It *is* sad," said Gordon. "Harper was the last of the Fisks."

"So I'd heard," said Theodosia.

So Harper Fisk's body has been released from the county morgue. Obviously the police have decided to treat it as an accidental death. Which means there'll be no further investigation. No official investigation, anyway.

"I'll try to make it," Theodosia told Gordon Sargent as they turned to leave. "I really will."

Back in the darkness and cool of the restaurant, Delaine was suddenly craning her neck every which way, doing some serious table spotting.

"Will you look at that!" she exclaimed. "Grace Broadmoor is having lunch with Sarah Jane Hastings. And I thought they weren't even on *speaking* terms! Theo, dear, if you don't mind, I'm just going to make a teeny, weeny little detour. I'll see you tonight. At the gallery opening. Okay?"

Without waiting for an answer, Delaine barreled into the main dining room to exchange air kisses with her lunching friends.

On her way toward the door, Theodosia glanced into the bar and wondered about the oil painting in question. The so-called John Singer Sargent.

Got to check this out, she told herself.

Walking into the bar, her sandals whispering softly on the

plush carpeting, she went directly to the far wall where the painting was hung.

It was a rich and handsome piece. Two Spanish dancers romantically entwined, a small group of musicians playing in the background.

The painting was beautifully placed, too, and served as the main focal point within the bar. Centered on the cranberry red wall, a low mahogany side table had been placed directly beneath it. On the table was an ornate chimney-style brass and black enamel lamp.

Theodosia bent close and peered at the painting. *Was it real?* she wondered.

She studied the painting carefully, noting the way the light shone against the beaded surface. Then, because no one was around and the bartender seemed fairly well occupied with whipping up a couple Cosmopolitans, she picked up the brass lamp and held it near the painting. The light played across the canvas, revealing a pebbly, uninterrupted surface. Very convincing, to be sure, but not quite the look of old oil paint on hand-gessoed canvas. No, the painting was cleverly done, but it was definitely a reproduction.

Theodosia moved the lamp back into place. *Very clever,* she thought again, knowing that every restaurant needs some sort of gimmick these days, and every restaurateur a marketable story or unique persona. Thanks to her past life in marketing, promotion was one thing she understood exceedingly well.

CHAPTER II

"*THANK GOODNESS, YOU'RE* back," Haley hissed from the kitchen as Theodosia let herself in the back door and hurried through her small office. With its antique wooden desk, tuffet-style chair, and celadon green walls that showcased a montage of posters and photographs, it was ordinarily a very attractive office. But today everything looked a mess. Empty shipping cartons were stacked everywhere, packing material littered the floor and obscured the Aubusson rug, her desk was piled high with tea catalogs.

"What's wrong?" asked Theodosia. Usually when she stepped out for a few hours, things didn't go crazy on her. This was the second day in a row that they had. *Not good,* she told herself. *Not good. Running a small business is a contact sport. Better stay in contact.*

"Drayton's in an absolute tizzy," warned Haley. "Summer Sullivan called a while ago and he was on the phone with her for almost twenty minutes. She's completely panicked . . . everything's been erased from Harper Fisk's computer!"

Theodosia frowned, feeling the slightest prickle of unease. *The odds against another bad break happening to someone in the English Breakfast Club had to be about a million to one. Yipes.*

On the other hand, maybe it was just a simple computer glitch—not as bad as Drayton made it sound. Drayton didn't know beans about computers and Summer Sullivan could have just overreacted. Maybe Summer didn't realize that Harper probably had some sort of backup system, a zip drive or some such thing. Or if he hadn't been that fastidious, he might have backed his work up on disk.

"I'll talk to Drayton," said Theodosia. "See if I can help."

Drayton was pouring tea when he saw Theodosia emerge from the back. He hustled over to her, slopping tea as he went.

Very uncharacteristic of him, Theodosia noted. He *must* be upset.

"Did Haley tell you?" Drayton whispered frantically. "Everything's been erased! Harper's business information, his personal files, all his notations on gifts to the Heritage Society! Everything!"

"You're sure it was erased from the hard drive?" asked Theodosia.

Drayton fixed her with a blank stare. "I don't know," he sputtered. "It's been erased from the *computer*. The thing that looks vaguely like a TV set and sits in the office at the Legacy Gallery. I don't know how the darn thing *works*, I just know the information is *gone*!"

"Was there a power glitch?" Theodosia wondered out loud as Haley emerged from the kitchen with an extra plate of ginger-pear scones.

"I don't *know*!" snapped Drayton. "I just know the whole thing *sounds* fishy."

"I told you I didn't trust Summer Sullivan," piped up Haley. "I think there's more to her than meets the eye."

"Tell you what," said Theodosia, glancing around the tea room quickly. "Soon as we finish with this luncheon crowd, we'll run over there. Okay?"

Poor girl has enough on her plate, thought Theodosia. *And now Haley wants to accuse her of wrongdoing. No, it didn't feel right.*

Drayton bobbed his head tightly. "Okay."

Summer Sullivan seemed flummoxed beyond belief. "I was just on this computer yesterday afternoon," she wailed, "and it was working fine. I know I'm no techno guru, but I've got a fairly decent working knowledge of computers."

"And this computer's definitely not working, right?" said Drayton. "Everything's erased?"

"Erased, crashed . . . whatever," said Summer Sullivan. "If there are still readable bits and bytes within this machine, they're locked up tight."

Summer Sullivan gazed helplessly at Theodosia. "I didn't know who to call," she said. "Drayton told me if I needed *anything* to just call the tea shop. Then when I did, he assured me you were a whiz with computers." She stopped, tried to pull herself together. "I'm sorry to impose on you and pull you away from your business. I'm sure you're frightfully busy."

"Don't worry about it," said Theodosia. "We're happy to help. Let me take a look." Slipping into the chair that faced the computer, Theodosia began tapping computer keys. Although she worked on an iMac at home and this was a PC, she knew that computers were all basically the same. The

OS or operating system might carry a different name, but they still responded to pretty much the same commands.

Except for this one. It powered up just fine, the application icons popped up nicely on the screen, but that was it. Once it reached that point, the computer just seemed to stall out. To freeze.

Was the motherboard fried? No, then she wouldn't have gotten as far as she did.

Had there been a power glitch? Could be. But it still wouldn't account for the computer simply freezing at a certain point.

Worse yet, had someone gotten inside and erased or stolen all the information? Then planted a bug? Eeeuyh . . . that was the unthinkable.

If the information was just erased, even accidentally, there was a good chance it could be retrieved from the hard drive. It might be a little gibberishy, but the basic information would still be there. On the other hand, if the contents had been stolen, if Harper's computer had actually been *hacked,* then the contents might be gone for good. And of course, computer hackers and crackers were notorious at planting little bugs and bombs within a computer's code.

"You have an Internet connection, correct?" asked Theodosia.

Summer Sullivan nodded.

"Got a high-speed DSL line? Receive lots of e-mails?" asked Theodosia.

"Tons," said Summer. "From all over the country."

Theodosia made a face. "Tell me what was on this computer."

Summer Sullivan gave a helpless shrug. "Pretty much everything. Our customer mailing list, billing information, shop inventory, tax records, Harper's personal correspondence, his maps . . ."

"His maps?" said Theodosia.

Yes." Summer seemed to be biting her lower lip to keep from crying. "As you probably know by now, searching for old shipwrecks was Harper's absolute passion. He was forever reading historical accounts in old books, journals, newspapers, and such. Then he'd piece together the information and see if he could figure out where a certain ship had gone down."

"He'd plot it on a map," said Theodosia slowly.

"Precisely," said Summer. "He always called it his *watery grave* project." She gave a little shiver. "Harper had a rather morbid sense of humor, just ask anyone who knew him." Summer glanced up at Drayton. "Right, Drayton?"

Drayton gave a theatrical roll of his eyes. "Harper was a real character, there's no denying it."

"Anyway," Summer continued, "once Harper attempted the actual location plotting, he used some kind of CAD-CAM program. He was actually quite skilled at it. A couple times the National Park Service even borrowed his maps when they were researching sunken ships of an historical nature."

"Did Professor Gibbon ever borrow these maps?" Theodosia asked, recalling Professor Gibbon's association with the University of Charleston's Underwater Archaeology Program.

"I don't know," said Summer. "Scouting out sunken wrecks was Harper's thing, I was only concerned with the shop." She paused. "And I do have a personal life."

Theodosia smiled kindly at Summer, thinking back to her meeting with the good-looking Gordon Sargent a few hours ago.

"Summer," said Theodosia. "Do you think Harper might have stumbled upon something that was really important?"

"I don't know," she said softly. "I do know that he told me there was treasure to be found. But realize, that *wasn't* what motivated him. Harper was far more interested in the historical aspect of the shipwreck and the thrill of possibly determining an exact location. He didn't dive for it or anything. Probably couldn't have, he suffered from asthma."

"Do you dive?" asked Theodosia.

Summer shook her head. "Nope. I'm no adrenaline junkie. And diving always seemed a little too dangerous for me."

"If Harper Fisk stumbled onto something important," said Theodosia, "that may have been the reason he was out in his boat." She softened her voice. "It could also have been the motive behind his murder."

"Murder!" cried Summer, her face contorting into a look of both surprise and pain. "What are you *talking* about? The police ruled Harper's death an accident! They said there *wasn't* any foul play!"

"Did you know that someone took a shot at Buddy Clark last night?" Theodosia asked her.

Summer's eyes grew big. "What! Are you serious? Is Buddy all right?" Summer took a step backward and crossed her thin arms over her chest. "Good lord, what's going *on*?"

"I'm not sure," said Theodosia. "But this computer thing is awfully suspicious. It's entirely possible someone jacked in with intent to steal information, then sabotaged the system."

"But what were they *looking* for?" said Summer. She paused, swallowed hard, gazed at Theodosia and Drayton with a look of fear and disbelief. "And what if they didn't find it? What if there's something *here* in the shop that they're looking for?"

"Oh dear," said Drayton, glancing about quickly. "Summer's right. If someone thinks Harper discovered gold bullion or some other treasure of great value at the bottom of Charleston Harbor, and they didn't find the map, they're going to come looking! Here!"

"I'm going to lock up the store," declared Summer. "Put a sign on the door that says we're closed until further notice. I don't *need* this kind of stress." She put her head in her hands and rubbed at her eyes. "What a crappy week this has been."

Theodosia put her arms around the girl as Drayton whipped out his handkerchief and offered it to her.

"Lock up and go home," Theodosia advised her. "And please don't worry. I promise you, Drayton and I will look into this. We're going to talk with . . ." She paused. "Well, let's just say we've got *contacts* within the Charleston Police Department. We'll touch base there. And then I'm going to take your computer to a real expert who can give us a definite read on what kind of problem we're looking at." Theodosia knelt down and began disconnecting cords. "Maybe it's nothing, maybe we've alarmed you for no reason at all."

"Theodosia's right," said Drayton, patting Summer on the shoulder. "Try not to worry. *Please.*"

"Are you the only one who has keys to this shop?" asked Theodosia.

"Yes," sniffed Summer, "I'm the only one."

"Well, *that's* good," said Drayton. He grunted as Theodosia plunked the computer into his arms. "Don't we need that?" he asked, glancing at the monitor.

Theodosia shook her head. "Nope."

"Will you be attending the service tomorrow?" Summer asked in a small voice. "At Magnolia Cemetery?"

"Of course," Drayton assured her.

"We'll both be there," said Theodosia, gathering up the last of the cords.

"Thank you," sobbed Summer. "You're both so very kind."

CHAPTER 12

*T*HE *PAINTINGS WEREN'T* exactly masterpieces. In fact, Theodosia decided, the Touchstone Gallery, usually purveyors of fairly tasty paintings, sculptures, and photography, had rather scratched the bottom of the barrel with this show.

There were twenty-five paintings hung in the spacious five-room gallery. All set off against the Touchstone's whitewashed walls and enhanced by the drama of high ceilings and creaking wood floors. Once an old textile mill, the Gautreaux Building on Elliott Street that housed the Touchstone Gallery had been rehabed into what so many old inner-city brick buildings had now become. A warren of shops, galleries, offices, and restaurants.

Theodosia cocked her head, studying an oversized canvas that exploded with a riot of intensely bright pinks, blues, yellows, and greens. The subject was a Caribbean villa, replete with a verandah strewn with tables, chaise lounges, and potted plants, the hint of a jungle hillside, and an ocean vista. The painting was flashy, but not terribly dramatic. Eye candy to hang above a floral sofa. Or to add splash to a commercial office space.

Although the painting was priced at well over two thousand dollars, it looked for all the world, Theodosia decided, like a painting you could pick up for twenty-nine dollars at a starving artist sale. One of those paintings that had been air-brushed assembly-line-style by young art students, some of whom probably *were* close to starving, then schlepped cross-country for two-day blowout sales in hotel ballrooms.

"Spectacular, isn't it?" breathed Delaine. "If I only had a free wall in my shop, that painting would be perfect."

"Absolutely perfect," parroted her sister Nadine, who had tagged along with them.

"Who's the artist again?" asked Theodosia. She'd glanced at her program a half-dozen times, but for some reason, the name of the artist just wouldn't stick. *I wonder why? Maybe it's because Delaine and Nadine keep chattering away? Or because this stuff just isn't my taste?*

Delaine rolled her eyes. "Dulcie Kramer is the artist. "Honestly, Theodosia, you're *so* preoccupied. I don't believe you've heard a word I've said all evening."

"Is the artist from here?" asked Theodosia, trying to be polite.

"Nooo, I don't think so," said Delaine, surreptitiously pulling out a pair of reading glasses and scanning her program. "Though I believe she did study here." Delaine's finger tapped at the artist's bio in the program. "Yes, right here at the Charleston School of Arts. About ten years ago."

"Now she lives in Key West," Nadine added, trying desperately to be part of the conversation.

"That explains it," said Theodosia.

"Explains what?" asked Nadine suspiciously.

"Her use of colors," said Theodosia. "Charleston colors are hazy and ethereal. Always slightly muted. I think it has something to do with our air quality."

The two sisters stared at Theodosia as though she'd suddenly started spouting Greek.

"Think about the colors you see in the historic district," Theodosia enthused. "Salmon pink, oyster white, pale blue. A French palette. Very subtle and refined. Compared to Charleston, Key West colors are a lot more vibrant and tutti-frutti."

"Tutti-frutti," repeated Delaine. "That doesn't sound like a particularly *technical* analysis to me."

"Believe me, it's not," Theodosia assured her.

"Well," said Nadine, a little huffily. "I think the woman is a *marvelous* painter. Obviously the gallery thinks so, too. After all, she's only thirty-four and they're already having a retrospective."

"It is amazing," agreed Theodosia.

Delaine sipped from a glass of white wine she'd picked up at the buffet table earlier. "Don't you want a glass of wine, Theodosia?"

But Theodosia wasn't paying particular attention. As she wandered about the gallery, she was thinking back to the hurried conversation she'd had with Detective Burt Tidwell. After she and Drayton had dropped off Summer's computer at a trustworthy computer repair shop and returned to the Indigo Tea Shop, she'd phoned Burt Tidwell. She wanted to get his take on the shooting that took place last night at Buddy Clark's home. Did he know about it? Did he think it was in any way related to Harper Fisk's drowning?

But Tidwell had been surprisingly closed mouthed. Since he wasn't officially assigned to the Harper Fisk case, he told her he couldn't be overtly involved.

So what's the opposite of overtly? That's an easy one. Covertly. Echoes of the CIA. Hah, that should appeal greatly to Burt Tidwell's sense of gamesmanship.

Tidwell had promised to keep an ear open and get in touch with her and Drayton sometime tomorrow. Frustrated that she hadn't learned more, and that Tidwell hadn't been more forthcoming, Theodosia had called Jory Davis at his office to bring him up to speed on the situation. But since he was hip deep in engineering a real estate foreclosure, he hadn't been able to spare more than a few minutes.

Bored, growing more and more concerned with what might befall the *next* member of the English Breakfast Club, Theodosia gazed at another of Ms. Dulcie Kramer's tropical paintings. This one, of a courtyard garden with pillars that seemed to sprout from nowhere, was even more garish. Bright colors of coral, orange, red, and purple were splashed freely across the canvas. Good colors, to be sure, but a trifle hot for a garden. Gardens were supposed to be cool and lush and verdant, weren't they? Of course they were, she decided, thinking back to Gordon Sargent's lovely patio garden from earlier today.

Theodosia, Delaine, and Nadine wandered into the last of the gallery rooms, one that also had a doorway that led back out to the main corridor. Theodosia knew there were several other shops and galleries located down this hallway. In fact, a low conversational buzz told her there was a good chance a second gallery opening was being held tonight.

Theodosia peered around the doorway into the corridor. Yes, she'd guessed correctly.

Down to her left was a gaggle of people, all clutching glasses filled with the same de rigueur white wine. *Your typical gallery opening white wine,* she thought to herself. *The caterers must bring it in using tankers.*

Theodosia turned back and plucked at Delaine's sleeve. "Come on," she urged her friend. "Let's have a little fun." Then she disappeared around the corner.

"Theodosia!" said Delaine. "Just where do you think you're . . ."

Delaine stepped out into the corridor, where a waiter from the *other* gallery opening promptly refilled her wineglass. ". . . going." She finished her sentence and blinked at the waiter. "Thank you."

Catching up with Theodosia some thirty seconds later, her sister in tow, Delaine hissed her displeasure into Theodosia's ear. "We can't just *crash* this party!"

"We're not crashing," Theodosia told her smoothly. "This is a public art opening." She looked around at the gaggle of interesting-looking people. "As a matter of fact, it might just be a *better* art opening."

Actually, Theodosia noted, it wasn't art per se at this gallery, but a showing of black-and-white photography. Dramatic, oversized prints that captured some of the marvelous landmarks that dotted Charleston. The Powder Magazine, the Old Exchange & Provost Dungeon, and the ruins of Fort Sumter, out on Sumter Island.

"Now this I like," said Theodosia, enthused. They were standing before a photo of the Thomas Elfe House. Built in 1760 by Thomas Elfe himself, one of the most acclaimed cabinetmakers of the Colonial era, the tiny single house was an architectural gem.

"These photos are awfully . . . um . . . stark," said Delaine, gazing around. She was obviously unhappy with the subject matter as well as the gallery attendees. The crowd at the Touchstone Gallery had been a fun, *fashionista*-type crowd. She and Nadine had been enjoying themselves immensely as they chatted up the various guests. But *these* people were a different crowd entirely. In fact, many of the people who seemed to be carefully studying the black-and-white photographs were dressed in bohemian black and sported spiky hair and multiple earrings. They ranged from looking downright scruffy to a trifle academic.

"I think these photos are amazingly rich," said Theodosia. "Notice the description? The photographer shot color film but printed his negatives in black and white. A tricky way to achieve great depth of tone."

"I didn't know you could even do such a thing," said Nadine, glancing at Delaine and letting loose a long sigh.

"One of my art directors used that technique once in an annual report for a high-tech company," said Theodosia. "The effect was very dramatic and understated. Just like these photos."

"Theo," purred Delaine, "we're going to go back to the other gallery. Will you be joining us?"

"In a little while," said Theodosia, suddenly spotting a familiar face. She made her way through the bustling main gallery to a side gallery that was hung with smaller photos highlighted by pinpoint spotlights.

"Professor Gibbon?" said Theodosia.

The tall, balding man with the perpetually red face turned toward Theodosia and blinked. "Yes?" He didn't seem to recognize her.

"It's Theodosia Browning," she said, introducing herself. "We met yesterday at Harper Fisk's shop?"

Recognition suddenly dawned in Professor Gibbon's eyes. "Oh my goodness, of course!" he exclaimed. "You're Drayton's friend. *Please* forgive me, I don't mean to be antisocial. I've just been so enthralled by these photos that I seem to have zoned out."

"They really are wonderful," agreed Theodosia.

"Top notch," said Professor Gibbon, suddenly showing a lot more enthusiasm. "You know, the photographer, Arthur Fielding, is on our faculty at Charleston University. That's why I'm here. Had to drop by and show my support." Professor Gibbon gestured to two young men who hovered nearby. "These are a couple of my grad students. Delmar Cooper and Stanley Young. Dragged 'em along for company."

"Cooper and Young," said Theodosia. "Sounds like an accounting firm."

There was good-natured laughter and some more hand-shaking and then Professor Gibbon excused himself. "Got to go give my congratulations to Arty."

Theodosia faced the two students. "You're both studying nautical archaeology with Professor Gibbon?" she asked.

Cooper and Young both gave polite nods.

"Sounds fascinating," she said.

"It is," said Cooper, the taller of the two. "We just started preliminary work on the Capers Point wreck."

"What kind of wreck is it?"

"Actually," said Young, "it could be the second oldest wreck site in the United States. If our data proves correct, the wreck would date back to the fifteen seventy-two expedition of Don Renaldo de Prado."

"We're trying to obtain funding right now," added Cooper, "so we can dive down and take a look-see using underwater robotics. But the money's not exactly forthcoming."

Theodosia nodded. She'd written a few grant proposals herself, requesting funding for Big Paw, and it had been tough going, even with a social services grant request.

"First Professor Gibbon took a run at the NSF," said Young. "You know, the National Science Foundation."

"I imagine applying for NSF money is highly competitive," said Theodosia.

"You don't know the half of it," said Cooper. "There are about fifty grants awarded every year but five *thousand* applications."

"Did Professor Gibbon get his grant?" asked Theodosia.

Both young men looked glum. "No dice," said Cooper. "But he recently submitted to a different funder where he thinks he'll have a better chance. Too bad the whole process is so darned cutthroat."

Young shook his head philosophically. "It's a shame. Makes really good professors resort to tactics they normally wouldn't want to."

"Like what?" asked Theodosia, intrigued by this comment and suddenly remembering the stack of grant requests at home on her cocktail table that *she* was supposed to review.

"Oh, you know, rush the research, hype a few facts, stuff like that," said Young. "Not illegal stuff, just a few . . ." He looked around, suddenly worried Professor Gibbon might overhear him. "You know . . . gray areas."

Theodosia nodded, wondering exactly what it was Professor Gibbon had done that pushed him into the gray area.

And then, because the two young men were still staring politely at her, she said: "I take it you're both photography buffs?"

Cooper shrugged and gave a sheepish grin. "Nah, not really. Professor Gibbon just needed a ride over here. I think he took his car in to be detailed or something. Anyway, we were the ones still working in the lab." He nudged Young with his shoulder, as if to say, *We were the unlucky stiffs who got corralled.*

Young picked up on his friend's wry humor. "Yeah," laughed Young. "We were handy."

CHAPTER 13

❧❧❧

BLUSH NOISETTE ROSES trembled with droplets of dew. Azaleas, camellias, tea olive shrubs, and loquat entwined to create living walls of plant life. Sweet jasmine wrapped its delicate tendrils around ancient, tilting wrought iron fences that bounded Civil War graves of hand-hewn marble.

Wednesday dawned hot and humid in Charleston. And in Magnolia Cemetery, the flowers, shrubs, and magnificent live oaks draped in delicate mourning veils of Spanish moss seemed to be the only living things that were truly appreciative of the sultry summer weather.

Sitting on a flimsy black metal folding chair, Theodosia fanned herself with a program and prayed for a hint of breeze. Any breeze.

Located at the north end of the peninsula just off East Bay Street, Magnolia Cemetery was a charming, highly atmospheric, profoundly historic cemetery. Often called a "political graveyard" because so many South Carolina politicians were buried there, Magnolia Cemetery was also the final resting place for over two thousand Civil War veterans, including five Confederate brigadier generals.

Originally part of the grounds of the old Magnolia Umbria Plantation, Magnolia Cemetery was still a "working" cemetery. Many prominent Charlestonians had family plots there. Drayton's family still had a plot; so did Timothy Neville, patriarch of the Heritage Society.

Slipping out of her shoes, Theodosia wiggled her bare toes and gave a silent sigh of relief as she gazed at the backs of the mourners who occupied chairs in the two rows ahead of her. She recognized several antique dealers from the King Street area as well as a number of people from the Heritage Society.

And then there was the English Breakfast Club.

Strange thing about that. All the members of the English Breakfast Club had shown up this morning save one. Lawrence March was a no-show.

"How terribly odd," Drayton had remarked in a low whisper. "Summer Sullivan, Buddy Clark, and Professor Gibbon are all here. But no Larry March."

"Maybe he couldn't find anyone to mind his store?" Theodosia offered by way of explanation as she continued to fan herself.

Drayton raised one quivering eyebrow. "It's *possible*," he replied. But from the disapproving tone of his voice, Drayton wasn't allowing much leeway. In Drayton's mind, Lawrence March's absence from Harper Fisk's funeral was clearly a major social faux pas.

Strangely enough, Lawrence March's absence had shot holes in Theodosia's still-shaky theory. Still going on the supposition that Harper Fisk's death had been no accident, she had turned her scrutiny to the three remaining members of the English Breakfast Club who were present.

First and foremost in her mind was Lieutenant Benjamin "Buddy" Clark. He had popped up at the marina last Sunday right after Harper Fisk's boat, the *Mary Lynn*, had been found. He had asked a few questions, acting despondent yet nervous. Then, surprise, surprise, someone had fired a shot at Clark the following night. Could Buddy Clark have *staged* the shooting incident to deflect suspicion from himself and throw it on someone else? Maybe. Did Buddy Clark even own a gun? That remained to be seen.

Then there was Professor Archibald Gibbon. He was a strange duck. Professor of nautical archaeology. *That* was certainly a strong tie-in with Harper Fisk. And from last night's conversation with the two grad students, Cooper and Young, it sounded like Professor Gibbon was feeling a trifle desperate in his attempts to obtain funding. In fact, Theodosia knew that professors were *expected* to bring in money for their colleges and universities. Their tenure and salaries were often tied to their grant-getting track record.

No dough, no show.

If Harper Fisk *had* stumbled upon some critical information concerning an underwater shipwreck, it was possible Professor Gibbon had tried to wrest it from him. If Harper Fisk hadn't been forthcoming, Professor Gibbon could have crossed the boundaries. After all, desperate men often committed desperate acts.

And then there was Summer Sullivan. She was a bit of a wild card. Summer had been Harper Fisk's business partner for the past two years. Their working relationship *sounded* like it was on the up-and-up. But then again, you never know. The amazing disappearing computer hard drive could be a convenient ruse to deflect suspicion. Or cover up valuable information.

As for Lawrence March, proprietor of March Forth, Theodosia had no idea. She didn't really know enough about the man to venture a guess. Now, the fact that he'd been a no-show today seemed slightly suspicious. Of course, there could be any number of reasons why Lawrence March hadn't come. Illness, family emergency, busy schedule, guilty conscience.

Who knows?

As the officiating minister solemnly uttered his parting words to the mourners who were gathered there, Theodosia glanced down at her program. She'd been so busy fanning herself, she hadn't really read it.

A poem printed on the back of the folded sheet caught her eye. It was a poem titled "Ode At Magnolia Cemetery" which had been written by Henry Timrod.

> *Sleep sweetly in your humbled graves,*
> *Sleep, martyrs of a fallen cause;*
> *Though yet no marble column craves*
> *The pilgrim here to pause.*

These were the first four lines of the poem Timrod had written at the end of the Civil War. Written at the end of Timrod's life, too. Haunting and sad, the sentiment was universal in appeal.

The ashes of poor Harper Fisk would soon be interred in this hallowed soil, thought Theodosia. He was also one of the fallen.

Theodosia nudged Drayton with her elbow. Drayton frowned, tilted his head down to her. He'd been focused intently on the minister's sad eulogy.

"Do we have time to stop at Lawrence March's shop?" she asked.

Drayton's gray eyes gazed out over the small grass plot where a tiny hole, barely ten inches in diameter, had been dug to accommodate Harper Fisk's brass urn. Raw black earth was mounded behind it, bouquets of pink musk roses and white lilies stood on either side. He nodded. "We'll make time," he whispered back.

March Forth was located on King Street, a bustling palm tree–studded street where whitewashed buildings stood shoulder to shoulder with classic redbrick buildings. Theodosia pulled her Jeep into an empty parking spot a few doors down from Lawrence Marsh's shop, then waited while a brightly colored horse-drawn jitney rumbled by, filled with tourists. Pushing open the car door, she thought she finally detected a hint of breeze coming off the distant sea.

Lawrence March was seated at a large wooden European trestle table located in the epicenter of his shop. Around him was a maze of tables, sideboards, and antique secretaries, all crammed with antique leather-bound books, porcelain statues, miniature portraits, sterling silver bowls, children's alphabet plates, dolls in period costumes with painted bisque faces, colorful glassware, and Indian baskets. Antique quilts, Chinese screens, and oil paintings covered the walls. Hung from the ceiling were dozens of antique chandeliers. The ones with dangling antique crystals tinkled faintly as Theodosia and Drayton pushed through the double doors and stirred the air inside the shop.

Lawrence March glanced up casually from polishing a porcelain figure of a noble-looking tan and white spaniel. "Hello, Drayton," he said, his voice registering not a hint of surprise.

Drayton favored March with a curt nod.

"Oh, don't do that," said Lawrence March, annoyed now. "I know why you're here and I don't give a hoot. Fact of the matter is, I simply can't *abide* funerals."

"Your presence was greatly missed," said Drayton.

"My presence wouldn't have amounted to a hill of beans," said Lawrence March somewhat petulantly. He shifted his gaze to Theodosia. "Hello, Miss Browning. Nice to see you again. Have you stopped by in a futile attempt to shame and chastise me as well?"

"Actually," said Theodosia, "I'm pretty crazy about that spaniel you're holding."

Lawrence March glanced down at the ceramic dog cradled in his hands. "English Staffordshire, circa eighteen fifty. Care to make an offer?"

"Care to offer an explanation?" said Drayton, not about to let Marsh's absence go unchallenged.

Lawrence March rose to his feet and walked a few paces to a polished wooden secretary that held an entire collection of porcelain dogs.

"If you favor dogs, Miss Browning, take a gander at this canine collection."

Theodosia moved past Drayton to where Lawrence March stood and let her eyes rove across one of the tastiest collections of ceramic dogs she'd ever seen. Most were tan and white spaniels, but there were also a few whippets, hounds, and Pekinese mixed in.

"Don't they have sweet faces?" asked Lawrence March. He plucked a smaller Staffordshire terrier from the shelf and placed it in Theodosia's eager hands. "Wouldn't you like to give this pooch a home?"

Theodosia turned over the ceramic dog and glanced at the price. It was marked nine hundred dollars.

"I can let you have it for six," Lawrence March told her. He leveled his gaze at Drayton, who was still glowering. "When my dear wife, Lucinda, died of pancreatic cancer ten years ago, I swore I'd never attend another funeral again. And I haven't." Lawrence March's old eyes snapped with defiance.

Drayton relented. "All right, Larry. Point well taken."

Theodosia, meanwhile, was wandering around March Forth, trying to get a feel for its owner. Lawrence March seemed like a straight-ahead type of fellow, she decided. She couldn't imagine that he'd had a bone to pick with Harper Fisk. According to Drayton, Lawrence March had been a regular at Harper Fisk's store for a number of years. And she'd heard no rumors of a rivalry or even a falling-out between the two men.

On the other hand, familiarity *can* breed contempt, Theodosia decided as her eyes scanned a lovely Sheraton table that displayed at least two-dozen teacups and matching saucers atop its glowing surface.

"Miss Browning," said Lawrence March, smiling at her. "I just realized I'm hosting the absolute plu-perfect seminar for someone like you."

Theodosia looked over at him. "Pardon?"

"You like old fabrics?" Lawrence March asked her, a twinkle dancing in his eyes.

"Love them," she said. In fact, she had amassed quite a collection of tea towels, linen tablecloths, and paisley shawls.

"And it stands to reason you love tea," continued Lawrence March.

Theodosia peered at him with curiosity. *Where is this leading?*

"It so happens I'm sponsoring a tea-dyeing class this

Friday," said Lawrence March. "My friend, Hillary Retton, from Popple Hill Interior Design, is coming in as instructor. It's what we call a fabric and finish class." He smiled shyly at her. "Would you care to attend?"

Tea dyeing? With old fabrics?

"Are you kidding?" Theodosia enthused. "I'd love to come."

And why not? she decided. *It sounds marvelous. Plus, it'll give me a chance to take a closer look at Lawrence March and maybe even get him to open up about Harper Fisk. See if he knew about any problems Harper might have had with the other members of the English Breakfast Club.*

"I see I have to twist *her* arm," Lawrence March said to Drayton, who was still looking somewhat puckery. "Oh buck up, Drayton," March continued. "You look like you swallowed a lemon."

CHAPTER 14

✦

TEA KETTLES WHISTLED and chirped, customers had been dropping in every few minutes for takeout or a sit-down cuppa, but Haley had held down the fort with very little effort.

"How was the memorial service?" she asked Theodosia and Drayton as she sped by them carrying an ornate silver tray bearing small plates of shortbread squares topped with homemade lemon curd.

"Awfully sad," said Drayton. "Although I must say, Magnolia Cemetery was as beautiful and soothing as ever."

Haley was back in a wink to grab a newly filled teapot of Gielle Garden Darjeeling.

"That Darjeeling's *second* flush, you know," Drayton was quick to point out. He'd already removed his jacket, rolled up his sleeves, and donned a long white apron.

"I know, I know," said Haley.

"Means your water temperature better be a trifle hotter and your steeping time a minute or two longer."

"I've got it," said Haley. "But thanks anyway, Drayton." She never failed to marvel at how Drayton so deftly kept track of the various steeping times and water temperatures for all the different teas. Then again, brewing and blending was what he did. Tea was Drayton's passion.

"Your grilled sirloin smells heavenly," said Theodosia as she emerged from the back. "What magic have you been working with spices?"

"Not all that much," Haley replied. "Just slathered the meat with my special tea-bone sauce. Once the steak chills, I'll slice it extra thin and serve it on tiny baguettes with a garnish of watercress. For a side salad I'm doing bibb lettuce with fresh tomatoes and buttermilk dressing. Simple but tasty."

"Though the dressing's sinfully rich," said Theodosia.

"I should say so," agreed Drayton. He glanced at the sweating, half-filled pitchers of iced tea that sat on the counter. Obviously the Indigo Tea Shop had already done a land office business in take-out iced tea. "Do we need more of this?" he asked, hefting one of the pitchers.

"Yes!" exclaimed Theodosia and Haley in unison.

By the time Burt Tidwell dropped in around one-thirty, lunch was pretty much history. Theodosia, Drayton, and Tidwell took the table nearest the kitchen so they could chat undisturbed, while Haley patrolled the tea room with a pitcher of iced tea in one hand, a pot of hot Assam tea in the other.

"Detective Tidwell," said Drayton. "We have enough sirloin tidbits for the makings of perhaps one more sandwich. Are you interested?"

Tidwell's beady eyes fairly gleamed. "Kind of you, Drayton. It's always difficult to postulate on an empty stomach."

Theodosia didn't imagine that Burt Tidwell ever did much postulating on an empty stomach, but she was willing to indulge him today. Especially if he'd come bearing information.

Theodosia and Drayton sipped their iced tea while Tidwell made short work of his sandwich.

"This is no ordinary sauce," he remarked with great appreciation.

"Haley whips green tea with lemon juice, soy sauce, and honey," said Drayton. "And I think some ginger and chili pepper."

"Tasty," said Tidwell, licking a finger. "It imparts an extra zing."

"Detective Tidwell," said Theodosia. "Could I also offer you a cup of tea?"

Tidwell leaned back in his chair with what appeared to be a good deal of satisfaction. "What was it Dickens said?" Tidwell rolled his eyes skyward as though trying to recall. "Oh yes, it was, 'My dear, if you could give me a cup of tea to clear my muddle of a head, I should better understand your affairs.'"

"Very good," said Drayton, impressed.

Theodosia returned with a small blue and white teapot and poured Tidwell a cup of Chun Mee, a pale yellow tea that yielded a smooth plum-like flavor. Grown in northern China, Chun Mee was also known as "Precious Eyebrows."

"I know what's occupying your mind," said Tidwell, gazing placidly at her as she took her seat at the table.

"What's that?" asked Theodosia as the sides of her mouth twitched faintly. Tidwell certainly had keen powers of observation, she decided.

"You're no doubt wondering if I took a good, hard look at Lieutenant Benjamin Clark." Tidwell paused and took a sip of tea. "Or any of the *other* members of the so-called English Breakfast Club."

"Well," said Drayton, leaning forth anxiously. "Have you?"

"Not really," said Tidwell.

"Well, at least give us your thoughts on Buddy Clark," said Theodosia. "Do you think someone actually took a shot at him?"

Tidwell favored her with a mild gaze. "Probably. The most likely scenario is that it was indeed accidental."

"Is that so?" said Drayton. "I thought perhaps someone fired a shot directly at the poor devil."

Tidwell took another sip of tea. "Doubtful. The slug entered the house some two feet above Clark's head. If someone had been aiming at him, they were a pretty poor shot."

"Could he have staged it himself?" asked Theodosia.

Tidwell shrugged. "Don't know. No one ever checked to see if Lieutenant Clark owned a rifle. Or any other guns, for that matter."

"Why not?" asked Theodosia.

"No reason to," said Tidwell.

Drayton furrowed his eyebrows and the words he delivered were short and clipped. "But you're still of a mind that Harper Fisk might have been the victim of foul play."

"Yes, I am," said Tidwell.

"Yet you suspect no one in the English Breakfast Club," said Theodosia.

"They were his friends," replied Tidwell mildly. "Some of them are *your* friends, are they not?" he asked Drayton.

"Acquaintances," corrected Drayton. Theodosia noted that, more and more, Drayton was distancing himself from the group.

"Detective Tidwell, what if one of the English Breakfast Club members *did* have a motive?" asked Theodosia.

"Motive would be critical," said Tidwell, the irony in his voice apparent.

Gritting her teeth, Theodosia wanted to reach out and shake the man. Tidwell was being purposefully obtuse and stubborn, giving them terse two- and three-word answers. And for what reason? His own amusement? Didn't matter, his method was maddening.

Let me fill you in on a few facts," barked Theodosia. "Four days after Harper Fisk's body was found floating in the ocean, his computer was *tampered* with. All the information he had stored on his hard drive is *missing*. And we're talking business information as well as maps and notations on area shipwrecks that might still possibly contain valuable cargo."

Tidwell nodded. "Strange, I'll give you that."

"Now chew on this," she continued. "Professor Archibald Gibbon, our resident underwater archaeologist, is apparently desperate to obtain funding in order to study an old shipwreck he's pinpointed. It's entirely possible that some of Harper Fisk's detailed maps could provide him with valuable information."

Tidwell absorbed this fact as well. "Go on," he urged. "And since you are both so utterly fixated on the English Breakfast Club, pray tell what's your assessment of Mr. Lawrence March? What's his desperate situation or homicidal motivation?"

Theodosia and Drayton exchanged glances.

"We don't know that he has one," said Drayton.

"Well, that hasn't stopped you thus far," replied Tidwell.

Drayton rose from the table so fast, his teacup almost toppled over. "Detective Tidwell," he said, drawing himself into a ramrod posture, "I've endured just about enough of your flippant remarks. I thought you were our ally in this investigative endeavor. Forgive me, I have obviously completely misjudged." And with that, Drayton stalked off toward the kitchen.

"I hope you're proud of yourself," said Theodosia accusingly.

"What?" said Tidwell, all innocence. *"What?"*

"Drayton is one of the finest and most honorable people I know. His dear friend, Harper Fisk, was buried this morning and you sit there and taunt him, mock him. Shame on you, Detective Tidwell. I, too, thought you were our friend."

Tidwell stared back hard at Theodosia. There was not an ounce of remorse or shame on his face.

"Friendship has nothing to do with it," replied Tidwell. "A homicide investigation is based on facts, not innuendo. When we collect additional facts or discover something truly concrete, we shall proceed posthaste."

Angered, Theodosia turned her gaze away from Tidwell, only to see Delaine push her way through the front door. Delaine hesitated for a moment, scanning the faces in the early-afternoon tea crowd, then brightened when she caught sight of Theodosia. Giving a quick wave, Delaine proceeded to make a beeline for the table where Theodosia and Tidwell were seated.

"Drat!" exclaimed Tidwell. Now it was his turn to jump to his feet and hurriedly toss his napkin onto the table. "I cannot *abide* that woman," he muttered. "She has the brain capacity of a doodle bug." And Tidwell was gone. Scooting across the shop and out the door with all the moves of a world-class sprinter. Theodosia was astounded, she'd never seen a man that large move so fast. It had to be some kind of record.

"I declare," said Delaine, gazing after Tidwell. "He *is* the rudest man I've ever encountered! Not even a howdy-do. See if I slave away in a hot kitchen to bake my famous Huguenot Torte for the policemen's charity gala."

"Don't hold it against him," urged Theodosia. "Tidwell's snit has nothing to do with you, he's just wound up and in an all-fired hurry."

"Zooming off to solve another murder in his oh-so-subtle Crown Victoria?" asked Delaine. She plunked herself down at the table with a very grande dame *to-the-manor-born* attitude and peered closely at Theodosia. "I hope *you're* not tangled up in some nasty investigation again. A tiny wrinkle etched itself above her perfectly waxed brows. "I worry about you, Theo, I really do."

"I'm fine, Delaine."

"I'm your friend, so I can say this, Theo . . ."

"What's that, Delaine?"

"You should pay more attention to Jory Davis," she warned. "Nice young attorney like that is quite a catch."

Theodosia decided to let Delaine's somewhat tacky innuendo roll off her back. Jory was certainly in her mind, but he wasn't what was worrying her right now.

"Would you like some iced tea?" Theodosia asked her. Now that Tidwell had departed, Haley had finally emerged from hiding in the kitchen with a fresh pitcher and a tray of glasses.

"That would be lovely," declared Delaine. She waited primly while Haley poured her a frosty glass, then took a delicate sip. "Mmn, delicious. But, you know, I've gotten totally off track. There *is* a reason I stopped by."

"You wanted to talk about Saturday's Fashion Bash, right, Delaine?" said Theodosia.

"Yes, and you *did* promise to help," Delaine reminded her.

"I will," said Theodosia. "I have."

"Good," said Delaine. "Now that we've got *that* settled, I need you to brainstorm a really special event."

"You've already got the luncheon tea and fashion show all planned," said Theodosia. "They're going to be fantastic . . . what more do you need?"

Delaine dug in her tiny clutch purse for a mirror and lipstick. "But I want Fashion Bash to be *super* special." She uncapped the lipstick, waved it in the air like a magic wand. "Something all our guests will remember with great fondness." She finally focused and deftly reapplied a coat of hot pink lipstick. "Oh, and it would be good if whatever you came up with was also a fund-raiser." Delaine suddenly grimaced. "My costs are running a touch higher than I'd anticipated."

"I thought Gordon Sargent was catering the luncheon at cost," said Theodosia.

"Yes, yes," said Delaine impatiently, "but then we added the lavender bouquets and the trinkets . . ."

"You mean the favors?" said Theodosia.

"Right," said Delaine nervously. "The sachets and the soaps and things are wonderful, of course. But it's all beginning to add up. So think of something to help defray costs, will you? You're so clever and promotion minded."

Theodosia sat back and racked her brain. *There isn't much time and Garden Gate's patio doesn't have a lot of space. What can we do that's simple, yet will help raise a little extra money? A better question might be, why does Delaine constantly expect people to jump through hoops?*

"What about a silent auction?" suggested Theodosia. "You could put together a dozen or so sweetgrass baskets and fill them with fun items. You know, a couple tins of tea, bath salts, a box of chocolates, maybe a scented candle . . ."

Delaine's face brightened immediately. "Honey, I love it. It's *perfect.* You know what else? I'll bet Brooke Carter Crocket would donate a couple of those free-form pendants she crafts out of sterling silver. The ones that look like darling little sculpted oysters. Some of the models will be wearing them anyway."

"Those pendants *are* gorgeous," said Theodosia. "I wouldn't mind having one myself."

"And my dear friend, Celerie Stuart, makes these marvelous beach harvest arrangements. You know, wreaths and door swags made out of items that she collects from South Carolina beaches? She literally combs the beaches picking up driftwood and shells and all sorts of dried reeds and twigs."

"Sounds intriguing," said Drayton as he popped out of the kitchen bearing a fresh pot of tea.

"Drayton!" called Delaine. "You're looking slightly peaked today. Everything all right?"

"Right as rain," said Drayton as he moved on to refill teacups at another table.

"So we'll go with the silent auction idea then?" asked Theodosia, anxious to pin Delaine down.

"I positively *adore* the suggestion," gushed Delaine. "Go ahead and pull together those tea baskets, will you?"

"Me?" Theodosia squeaked in a high-pitched voice.

Delaine cocked her head and gave an expectant stare. "Well, *you're* the big tea honcho around here, aren't you? You certainly don't expect *me* to do it. I mean, I'm not exactly sitting around twiddling my thumbs. For goodness' sakes, I'm the one staging the fashion show! It was my idea to produce this whole Fashion Bash extravaganza and sell tickets in the first place. And believe me, Theodosia, I've still got a jillion things to do!" Delaine began ticking off tasks. "We've *still* got fittings with most of the models. I haven't *nearly* accessorized all the outfits. And I haven't decided what my *grand finale* piece will be! Cotty Walton suggested a wedding dress, but that seems so tediously *conventional*. I'd like to end this event with a colossal bang! Something folks will remember forever!"

"Delaine," said Theodosia tiredly. "Enough. I'm sufficiently convinced." *Browbeaten* is more like it, she wanted to add, but didn't. It wasn't easy trying to win with Delaine. Most of the time it wasn't even worth the effort to try.

"Haley!" cried Delaine, motioning for her to come over to the table.

Haley advanced toward Delaine cautiously.

"Honey, I'm going to *need* you this Saturday," said Delaine in her best pleading tone.

Haley glanced at Theodosia. "What for? To set up?"

Delaine offered a rueful smile and shook her head. "No, honey," she said, "I'm gonna need your beautiful little bod."

"*My* bod?" repeated Haley slowly. "What are you talking about?"

"Isn't it every girl's dream to be a model?" asked Delaine with a coy smile.

"You want me to *model*?" said Haley. Panic was evident in her voice.

Delaine stood up and draped an arm possessively around Haley's shoulders. "Cassie Everson was going to model this adorable white chiffon party dress with a ruffled bodice, but now she's dropped out . . . something about her grandfather being ill." Delaine waved a hand as if to indicate this was a minor inconvenience for everyone.

"Chiffon party dress?" said Haley, her eyes glazing over.

"Ruffled bodice?" This kind of clothing was a little out of Haley's league. She wasn't sure if she should feel pleased or put upon.

"That's right," said Delaine with a winning smile. "You're the only other person I know who can squeeze into a size four."

Drayton chose that moment to drift by again. "Well, don't look at me," he joked, obviously in a better mood again. "*I* certainly can't squeeze into a size four."

But Delaine suddenly turned on Drayton with a hungry, appraising look. "We're going to need *your* help this Saturday as well, Drayton."

"What?" said Drayton, doing a double take. "Oh no," he protested, suddenly catching her drift. "Saturday's my day off. I have very specific plans to attend an estate sale over in Jasper County."

"No," said Delaine, "I'm afraid I'm going to have to buttonhole you to be my master of ceremonies."

"Whaaat!" said Drayton.

"Just listen to that marvelous voice," purred Delaine. "You're a born public speaker. No wonder, year after year, you're reelected parliamentarian of the Heritage Society. With a voice like that, who *wouldn't* come to order?"

Haley was so bent over with laughter she was almost choking.

"Drayton!" said Delaine with a petulant frown. "This is a *fund-raiser* for the Heritage Society. Surely you can see your way clear to assist us in raising much-needed dollars."

Theodosia and Haley watched Drayton squirm as Delaine continued to harangue him. They both knew that Drayton was helpless as a fly once Delaine cast her insidious spider's web. They watched, fascinated, as Drayton's protests grew weaker and weaker, then finally diminished entirely.

Eventually, his shoulders sagged and his gray head began to bob in agreement with Delaine's words.

She's got him, thought Theodosia. *Another one bites the dust.*

"Of course, Delaine," said Drayton in a voice that broadcast utter capitulation. His mouth worked furiously, yet no words seemed to be coming out. Finally he mumbled, "Of course you can count on me to narrate your fashion show."

CHAPTER 15

FIRST CREATED IN the Pacific Northwest by Native Americans, planked fish has been embraced in recent years by adventuresome chefs of the Carolinas. The preferred wood for cooking the local salmon, bluefish, and even striped bass has been a one-inch plank of cedar or alder, soaked in water with a few small holes judiciously drilled into it. The fresh fish is placed atop this plank, rubbed with seasonings, drizzled with olive oil, then set atop a hot grill to cook for a good thirty minutes or so.

The result, if chefs and their dinner guests can hold out that long, is a supremely moist roasted fish that has absorbed the rich scents of both wood and smoke.

Mark Congdon had drilled and soaked his cedar planks earlier today and was now playing head chef at tonight's big bash celebrating the fifth anniversary of the Featherbed House.

One of the premier bed-and-breakfasts on the Battery, the Featherbed House had enjoyed five banner years in Charleston. And Angie and Mark Congdon, the genial proprietors, had invited everyone they knew to join them in their garden tonight for the special celebration.

"Are your cookers supposed to smoke so profusely?" asked Drayton. He had a watchful eye on the two giant barbecue grills that contained the planked salmon.

"Always do," said Mark Congdon.

"And you dare not lift the lid?" said Drayton, fascinated at this new grilling technique.

"You can, but I don't advise it," said Mark.

"Drayton, you're such a control freak," said Haley. She and Theodosia had just arrived, walking the few blocks over to the Featherbed House from Church Street together. Though Haley had made rumblings about finding a bigger apartment, she still resided in the small garden apartment just across the back alley from the Indigo Tea Shop.

"*I'm* the control freak?" came Drayton's outraged voice. One eyebrow quivered then shot up. "You're a fine one to talk. I've seen you positively break out in *hives* if someone dares make a suggestion in your kitchen." Drayton was right, Haley was a little kitchen Nazi.

"That's different," grinned Haley. "When I'm on my turf, I'm boss. Right, Theodosia?"

"I don't know if it's right," drawled Theodosia, "but that's the way it seems to shake out."

"Our Indigo Tea Shop friends!" exclaimed Angie Congdon as she sped across the brick patio to greet them. "Glad you-all could make it tonight."

"Hi, Angie," exclaimed Haley. "Happy anniversary." She handed her a bouquet of flowers tied with silver ribbon. A little ceramic goose dangled from the bow.

Besides being known for their genteel hospitality, the Featherbed House was also famous for their enormous collection of geese. Ceramic geese, brass geese, wooden geese, and stuffed geese were perched in the lobby, the stair landings, and every spare nook and cranny.

"Oh my goodness," said Angie, taking the bouquet from Haley. "Beautiful flowers and another little goose to add to our gaggle. This one's adorable, thank you!"

"Actually," said Haley as she began to wander off toward the cookers, "Hattie Boatwright put it together." Hattie Boatwright owned Floradora, the premier floral shop on Church Street.

"Oh, Hattie does almost all our centerpieces, too," enthused Angie to Theodosia. "She's the best. Oh *hello*, Marianne," she said to a woman who'd also just arrived. "Theodosia, do you know Marianne Petigru? She's one of the decorating geniuses behind Popple Hill Design."

And Marianne Petigru rented her carriage house to Harper Fisk, Theodosia remembered. *Isn't this serendipitous.*

"Excuse me while I put this gorgeous bouquet in water," said Angie, beating a hasty retreat to the kitchen.

"You're Delaine's friend, aren't you?" said Marianne Petigru, smiling at Theodosia, who just this moment realized what a stunning-looking woman Marianne was. Tall, thin, dressed in chic black linen slacks and matching sleeveless vest, Marianne Petigru looked like the young, hip designer she was. Her short, blond hair was slightly spiky and her skin glowed with a golden tan. Theodosia knew Marianne and her partner, Hillary Retton, were the hottest interior designers in town and now she wondered if, besides owning an enormous home in the historic district, Marianne might also have a nice little condo on Hilton Head or Kiawah Beach. She looked *that* rested and sublimely toned from tennis or golf.

"Did Delaine strong-arm you into attending Fashion Bash this Saturday?" asked Theodosia.

Marianne laughed. "She tried to but I'm already committed somewhere else. She did, however, hit us up for a couple gift certificates for her silent auction." Marianne suddenly peered at Theodosia with mock suspicion. "Wait a minute, as I seem to recall, the silent auction was *your* idea! Or at least that's what Delaine's been boasting."

"Guilty as charged," admitted Theodosia. "I hope Delaine didn't apply too much pressure." *Delaine not apply pressure? That was a good one.*

Marianne dismissed the remark with an offhand wave. "Not really. We're always glad to help out. The Heritage Society's a very worthwhile cause."

"You live just down the block, right?" said Theodosia. She thought for a moment. "The Victorian home on Lenwood?" In fact, Marianne Petigru's old Victorian was an absolute showpiece. An 1850s house complete with multi-gabled roof, turrets, domed skylight, and all the requisite gingerbread work.

"That's the one," said Marianne. "It may be on the historic register, but privately my husband and I have dubbed it the albatross. The darn thing *looked* structurally sound when we bought it, but the foundation needed a tremendous amount of work. Still does." She shook her sleek head. "You put money in the ground, you never see it again. People think *decorating* costs money, they have no idea how much construction companies sock you for structural repairs. It's *endless*."

"You were renting your carriage house to Harper Fisk," said Theodosia.

"Still am," said Marianne. "He's paid through next

month. Or I guess now it's technically correct to say his *estate* is paid up." She gave a rueful smile. "Poor man."

"So his home hasn't been cleared out yet?"

"No, nothing's been done. Everything seems to be in limbo . . ." Marianne's eyes suddenly went wide and she covered her mouth with one hand. "Oh, my gosh," she exclaimed. "Theodosia. Now I remember hearing . . . you were the one who discovered Harper's body!" Marianne reached out and grasped Theodosia's arm. "Oh dear, that must have been a *terrible* shock for you." Her sympathy was evident.

"It was a pretty bad moment," admitted Theodosia.

Marianne glanced around quickly, as if she was afraid of being overheard.

"Is it true Harper's computer was emptied out?" she asked.

So that tidy little fact is already in the rumor mill, thought Theodosia. *Ah well, I'm not surprised.*

"Looks that way," replied Theodosia. "His partner, Summer Sullivan, is pretty upset."

"She's not the only one," said Marianne. "I know that some of his things were supposed to go to the Heritage Society, and some were supposed to go to Summer at the shop. But of course I'm absolutely *clueless* as to what's going to happen. He had no family, no nothing . . ."

"You were close to Harper?" asked Theodosia.

Marianne considered this. "Close enough. We'd chitchat every couple days. About gardening and decorating and things."

"Did it seem to you that Harper was disturbed about something?" asked Theodosia. "Did you think something was bothering him?"

Marianne thought for a moment. "No, not really. At least

I can't think of any instance where he seemed worried. Harper was a fairly even-tempered guy. An old sweetie, really. Last time we talked, he asked if I was interested in acquiring some Japanese antiques. He knew I was decorating a home over in Wild Dunes for a couple who's absolutely ga-ga over all things Japanese. You know, antique screens, *Ukiyo-e* prints, old fans, *oribe* ceramics."

"The antiques he offered you were from his shop?"

Marianne shrugged. "I guess so." She thought again. "No, that doesn't sound right. Let me think for a moment. Seems to me the antiques belonged to a friend of his." She nodded once, sure of her recollection. "Yes, now I remember. Harper knew someone who'd acquired the pieces quite some time ago and was now interested in selling them. As I seem to recall, this friend needed money."

"Do you remember who Harper's friend was?" asked Theodosia. "Did he mention a name?"

Marianne narrowed her eyes. "He was like . . . maybe someone who was formerly in the military?"

"Was he in the Navy?" asked Theodosia. "Was it Benjamin Clark?"

Marianne snapped her fingers. "That's him. I remember Harper telling me that this Mr. Clark was experiencing some financial difficulties." She cocked her head to one side, as though all the details were coming back to her now. "Clark apparently had some antiques he'd picked up in Japan a number of years ago. A few Utamaro prints and a ceramic vase by Hamada. He'd asked Harper to try to sell them."

"But you didn't buy them. For your client, I mean," said Theodosia.

"No, they'd already overdosed on Japanese prints and ceramics. Any more and their living room would've looked like a sushi bar."

"Do you know if the objects ever got put into Harper's shop? For sale?"

Marianne tossed her hands in the air. "Who knows?" Then a big smile flashed across her face. "There's the lady who might have your answer, though." She pointed across the back garden toward Summer Sullivan, who'd just walked into the party on the arm of Gordon Sargent.

"Talk about luck," breathed Theodosia.

Summer, who looked absolutely fetching in a long sea green dress, was saying her hellos to Angie Congdon. Gordon Sargent had immediately wandered off to inspect the two cookers, where Drayton seemed to have planted himself permanently next to Angie's husband.

What is it about outdoor barbecues that attracts men like flies? wondered Theodosia. *Your typical male can barely turn on the stove, but put him in somebody's backyard with a lighted grill and he's endlessly fascinated.*

"You know Summer, don't you, Theodosia?" asked Angie Congdon as Theodosia strolled over to talk.

Theodosia and Summer smiled at each other.

"Summer's been very instrumental in finding antiques for us," said Angie, bragging up the young antique maven. "She's got quite a knack for ferreting out unusual pieces." Angie pointed to one corner of her spectacularly landscaped garden. "That Ionic-looking column over there in the corner was one of Summer's finds. And she unearthed the carved goose weather vane that presides over our lobby from a junk store located over in Ninety Six." Ninety Six was the name of a small town in the Piedmont region that took its name from an old British fort that was ninety-six miles from the former capital.

"Do you ever handle any old Japanese ceramics or prints?" Theodosia asked Summer.

"Not too often," said Summer.

"Are you in the market?" asked Angie. "Why, Theodosia," she drawled, a smile lighting her face, "I thought you'd finally settled on an Old South flavor for your apartment. Of course," Angie continued, "just because I've finally settled on my 'country clutter' look doesn't mean I can't keep redecorating. That's the fun of owning a B and B," she confided. "You get to keep redoing the rooms!" In high spirits, Angie wandered off to greet more of her newly arrived guests.

Summer smiled sadly at Theodosia. "I wasn't exactly in the best mood to come here tonight," she explained, "but Gordon thought it might be good for me. He's says I have to keep busy, get out and socialize."

"Gordon's one hundred percent correct," responded Theodosia. "I'm sure this morning's memorial service was terribly difficult for you."

"It was," admitted Summer. "I feel like I've lost a family member. My dad died when I was little, so I guess in my eyes, Harper kind of took his place."

"You didn't close the shop after all," said Theodosia, recalling Summer's dilemma on Tuesday morning, after she'd discovered that the hard drive on Harper's computer was somehow locked.

"No," said Summer slowly. "I reopened the next day. I thought about it long and hard, and came to the conclusion that Harper was really a keep-going kind of guy. I figured he'd want me to soldier on. Harper wasn't the maudlin type either. I know he wouldn't have wanted me to sit around and mope about his passing."

"About the Japanese antiques . . ." Theodosia prompted.

"Oh, right," said Summer. She frowned. "To answer your question . . . no. I don't recall having anything like that in the shop. Not in the two years since I've been there anyway. Are you in the market for something specific? I can surely keep an eye out if you are."

"No," said Theodosia, "it was just a crazy idea. Something for a friend." For some reason she didn't feel like telling Summer about Buddy Clark's wish to sell off his pieces.

"Have you heard anything from your computer expert yet?" asked Summer.

"Not yet," said Theodosia. "I'll give him a call tomorrow, see if he's figured anything out."

"Gosh, you're a friend," said Summer. She gazed earnestly at Theodosia. "I know we don't know each other all that well, but I feel like I've known you for more than just a few days. I suppose because Drayton's talked about you so much."

"Don't believe everything you hear," laughed Theodosia.

"Listen," said Summer. "I'm going to have to go it on my own now. It would be a big help if I knew I could touch base with you once in a while. You know, small business owner to small business owner." Summer coughed slightly, obviously embarrassed. "I hate to use the mentor word, but I supposed that's what I'm really talking about."

"I'd be happy to lend any help I could," said Theodosia. She thought about all the good advice Brooke Carter Crocket at Heart's Desire had given her when she'd first opened the Indigo Tea Shop. It was payback time, and if Summer needed help, she'd for sure get it.

"Thanks," said Summer, obviously grateful. "Hey, look!" said Summer. "Mark's about to serve the fish."

Steam billowed from the uncovered cookers, as Mark Congdon began lifting out his planked fish. He'd had the planks stacked two across and two high in each cooker, so now the makeshift buffet table, really a large board on top of two sawhorses, was rapidly becoming laden with grilled fish. The smell was heavenly, very spicy and aromatic, and the guests were beginning to mill about excitedly.

"Looks like we got here just in time," said Summer.

"Ditto that," rumbled a rich, male voice behind Theodosia.

Theodosia whirled around. "Jory!" she exclaimed. "You made it after all."

He put an arm around her shoulders and pulled her close, touched his lips to the top of her head. "Wouldn't miss it." He grabbed her hand and they wandered off toward a white wooden gazebo laced with vines, while everyone else rushed to queue up in the buffet line.

They kissed gently.

"Aren't you hungry?" Jory asked her.

She smiled at him and they kissed again, this time with a little more intensity. "I'm starving," Theodosia replied as she gazed into his warm brown eyes. "But your diversionary tactics are so much more appealing."

Jory's mouth twitched in a slight grin. "Why, at such a romantic moment," he asked, "do you suddenly sound like Detective Tidwell?"

His remark caught Theodosia off guard. "Oh no, say it ain't so!" she replied with mock horror.

"Well, not really," Jory assured her. "Actually you sound exactly like *you*. Charleston's own amateur sleuth. Which leads me to inquire, have you found out anything more concerning the Harper Fisk mystery?"

"A few things," Theodosia told him as they moved, hand in hand, toward the buffet line. "Buddy Clark . . . you remember Buddy Clark?"

Jory nodded. "Sad old geezer on the yacht club dock, same guy who had the pot shot taken at him the other night."

"That's the one," said Theodosia. "Marianne Petigru told me he was trying to sell off some of his Japanese antiques. Apparently he needs money rather badly."

"Do you think he was desperate enough to steal Harper Fisk's so-called treasure maps?" asked Jory. "Or harm Harper Fisk in the process?"

"I don't know," said Theodosia. "His financial woes are evidence of a sort, but they're not concrete evidence."

"Circumstantial," said Jory, ever the lawyer.

"That's it exactly," nodded Theodosia as the two of them slipped into line.

The buffet Angie and Mark Congdon had prepared was to die for. The planked fish, fillets of both salmon and bluefish it turned out, was smoky and tender, cooked to perfection. Their zealous hosts had also prepared pickled shrimp, pole beans, and sweet corn relish. All this was augmented by enormous platters of fried green tomatoes, fried squash blossoms, and steaming hot corn biscuits.

"This is a cross between low-country cooking and a shore dinner," declared Jory. "I love it." He was piling food on his plate like he hadn't eaten in days.

"You must have skipped lunch again," said Theodosia.

"No," smiled Jory. "I'm just hungry. And all this reminds me of my grandmother's cooking."

How can I resist a man who's still enamored of his grandmother's cooking? Theodosia wondered. *And what does a girl do for an encore? Learn to cook like Grandma? Yikes.*

Theodosia slid a piece of grilled salmon onto her plate and helped herself to a spoonful of sweet corn relish. *Should*

I take a dollop of that caper butter sauce for the fish? Oh, why not.

"Is it possible to run a check on Buddy Clark?" she asked Jory in a low voice.

"What kind of check?" he asked. "Arrest record, outstanding warrants, property tax statements . . ."

"Yes, please," she told him. "All of the above. Plus anything else you can think of and whatever you can find out."

"If you ask me," said a voice behind them, "you ought to check out all three of those old duffers."

Theodosia turned quickly to find Gordon Sargent staring intently at her.

"Every one of those guys seems a little shady to me," said Gordon as he helped himself to a generous scoop of pole beans. "And frankly, I'm worried about Summer. They're forever hanging out at her shop, giving her advice on what to do." He paused. "And she's a very trusting girl. Maybe *too* trusting."

CHAPTER 16

"*CAN YOU BELIEVE* we're all going to be immortalized on TV today!" exclaimed Haley enthusiastically as she filled tiny cut-glass bowls with strawberry preserves.

"Remember," said Drayton as he laid out a roster of tiny silver spoons, "it's merely *videotape*. They're not shooting live."

"Listen to Martin Scorsese over there," giggled Haley. "Hey, so what if it's tape, our TV debut is still going to be a blast."

Drayton edged over toward Theodosia, who was standing at the counter, arranging little tins filled with tea rubs. "You seem awfully subdued on what's supposed to be your big media day," he said. "Did you stay up late partying last night?"

"I wish I had," said Theodosia. "Then I probably wouldn't have checked my phone messages when I came in."

"Uh-oh, bad news?" said Drayton.

Theodosia glanced about the tea shop. So far there was just a trickle of customers. Two tables were filled and a few regulars were coming in for takeout. "Remember I told you I ran into Professor Gibbon Tuesday night? At that gallery opening?"

He nodded. "Hmn, I do recall your mentioning it."

"And I also chatted with those two grad students who gave him a ride over because his car was being detailed?"

Drayton narrowed his eyes slightly. "Pray tell, what is detailing? And what could it possibly have to do with your story?"

Theodosia, who'd once dated a dentist cum motorhead, hastily explained the procedure. "Detailing is when you have your engine steam-cleaned and the so-called car technicians use Q-Tips to swipe and polish every little nook, cranny, and button on your dashboard."

"And this automotive information is pertinent to your phone message last night?" Drayton asked, growing impatient.

"I'm getting to that," said Theodosia. The phone next to them suddenly gave a shrill ring, then just as quickly stopped. Theodosia decided that Haley must have picked it up in the kitchen.

"Anyway," continued Theodosia. "Naomi Morison left a message on my answering machine asking if I'd had a chance to read those grant requests I told you about."

"The ones for the Charleston Foundation you so kindly volunteered to read," said Drayton.

"Well, someone else actually volunteered me, but yes," answered Theodosia. "Naomi was wondering if I'd had a chance to make any final recommendations yet."

"And have you?" asked Drayton.

Theodosia shook her head slowly. "I'd really only read

through four or five of the grant requests, about half the stack. So last night, I thumbed through the rest of them, just to get a feel for what they were about."

"And . . ." prompted Drayton.

"At the bottom of my stack was a grant request from Professor Gibbon," said Theodosia unhappily.

"You're not serious," said Drayton. "Gibbon is looking to the Charleston Foundation to fund his underwater research?"

"Looks that way," said Theodosia. She knew it wasn't all that unusual for arts, scientific, and social service requests to come in to the foundation. They were known for funding a diverse array of projects.

"Tricky," said Drayton, ruminating over her words. "What are you planning to do?"

"Remain impartial?" Theodosia turned her unhappy gaze on him.

Drayton raised an eyebrow. "Is that a statement or a question?" he asked.

"I'm not sure," said Theodosia. "But it's sure one heck of a dilemma."

"On that I wholeheartedly agree," replied Drayton. He blinked, swiveled his head to the right as Haley suddenly came flying out of the kitchen.

"Wowee!" she exclaimed. "You're not gonna believe this!"

"A little civility, please," said Drayton. "This is a tea shop, not open microphone at a Myrtle Beach comedy club."

But nothing could deter Haley from sharing her big news. "I just spoke to Miss Dimple," said Haley in an excited whisper. "She's working over at Pinckney's Gift Shop this morning."

"And what did the old girl say that's got you so a-twitter?" asked Drayton blandly.

"Delaine's sister was arrested for shoplifting yesterday!" blurted out Haley.

"What!" gasped Theodosia and Drayton in unison. This *was* news! Big news.

"At Luna Gold and Gems," said Haley. "Apparently she stuck a gold coin bracelet in her purse and then just waltzed out the door. The owner saw her make the snatch on a security monitor and immediately called the police. I guess he was incredibly outraged."

"I don't blame him," said Drayton.

"You're sure there wasn't some mistake?" asked Theodosia. *Delaine's sister seems a trifle odd, but is she a thief? That seems awfully far-fetched.*

"I don't think so," said Haley. "Miss Dimple says Nadine vehemently denied everything until the police pried her purse out of her hands. And there it was stashed inside, a big bold glittering eighteen-karat coin bracelet. The price tag was still on it, no receipt."

"Oh, poor Delaine," said Theodosia. "She must be mortified."

"Poor Nadine," said Haley. "The cops hauled her down to the station and booked her. Probably fingerprinted her and took some very unflattering black-and-white photos as well."

"Absolutely humiliating," breathed Drayton. "Still, if the woman was caught red-handed . . ."

"She was, believe me," said Haley. "And you know what the amazing thing is? This wasn't the first time! Nadine's done it before! In fact, she's got a record! Apparently, she was attending counseling sessions and everything."

"You're quite positive of that?" asked Drayton.

"Hey, buddy," snapped Haley, "remember last Saturday when I asked if either of you guys sold that Crown Ducal teacup? I had a funny feeling that teacup didn't just waltz out the door on its own."

"Oh dear," said Drayton. "Then the poor woman really *does* have a serious problem."

"So do half the merchants up and down Church Street," pronounced Haley. "Nadine's been shopping and chatting and gadding about all week long. Probably ripping off everybody in sight. And I'm sure all the merchants trusted her because they knew she was Delaine's sister."

"Let's not get too carried away with this, Haley," said Theodosia. "There's only the one instance you know of personally, correct?"

"I guess," said Haley reluctantly.

"Then let's give Nadine the benefit of the doubt."

Haley considered this for a long moment. "I suppose."

"Goodness, this is just going to *kill* Delaine," fretted Drayton. "And wouldn't you know it, her Fashion Bash event is in two days."

"Do you think she'll try to cancel?" asked Haley.

"Highly doubtful," replied Theodosia. "Knowing Delaine's indomitable spirit, she'll try to ignore what's happened and simply rally on." She hesitated as the shop door suddenly opened. All three of them glanced over casually, then suddenly fell dead silent as Delaine walked through the door.

"Delaine!" Drayton uttered a garbled squawk as he struggled to regain his composure.

Dressed impeccably in a summer sundress of pale pink organza, Delaine flounced across the floor and regarded them all with a haughty look worthy of a Romanoff duchess. "Well, I can tell by the looks on your faces that you've al-

ready heard those *ridiculous* rumors." She tossed a matching silk bag on the table. "Isn't that just *peachy*," she spat
out.

"I'm sure there's been a misunderstanding . . ." began
Drayton, ever the diplomat.

Haley stared at Drayton. Hadn't he just said something
about Nadine getting caught red-handed?

"Take it from me, there's been a colossal *misunderstanding*," snapped Delaine with as much force as she could
muster. "I don't know *who* started these hideous rumors, but
there isn't an *ounce* of truth to them."

Theodosia exhaled with a giant gush. "Thank goodness,"
she murmured as the tension slipped from her. *There, that's
it direct from Delaine's mouth. The rumors are totally unfounded. Thank goodness.* "How *do* those things get started
anyway?" she asked shakily.

Delaine shook her head. "Search me. But I can assure
you, I shall be straightening out this hideous mess with the
police later on today."

Confused now, Drayton stared at Delaine. "I thought you
said it didn't happen."

"*Nothing* happened," hissed Delaine. "Except harass-
ment from a local merchant against my poor sister."

"So, just for the record, Nadine *did* get hauled down to
the poky?" asked Haley.

"Again, a *colossal* mistake and a *total* miscarriage of justice," fumed Delaine. "Which shall be straightened out
forthrightly by the top-notch attorney I have just retained."
Delaine gazed at them fiercely, a barracuda smile plastered
across her face. "Now, I'd appreciate it if you would all
kindly *drop* the subject! It's become terribly tedious."

*   *   *

From that moment on, Theodosia, Drayton, and Haley all felt like they were walking on eggshells. For rather than getting a cup of tea to take back to her shop, which was her usual habit, Delaine remained at the Indigo Tea Shop, ensconced at the table next to the fireplace. She had brought along a black leather notebook and her cell phone and proceeded to make several calls, all the while jotting notes.

"I think she's embarrassed to go back to Cotton Duck," whispered Haley to Theodosia.

"Can you blame her?" said Theodosia, gazing at Delaine. "Poor dear."

But Delaine was no longer a "poor dear" one hour later when she was *still* there. Because instead of sipping her cup of Keeman black tea and nibbling contentedly at her cream scone, Delaine had begun prowling about the tea shop, getting everyone in a tizzy. Haley had already forbade Delaine from wandering into the kitchen and Drayton was practically twitching from the stress.

"Now there's someone at the back door," Drayton screeched to Theodosia, who, with a large silver tray balanced precariously on one hip, was busy serving tea.

"I'll get it," yelled Haley. "It's probably UPS with the rest of the T-Bath products."

Theodosia scurried to the counter and set her tray down. "Shouldn't you be getting back to your store?" she asked Delaine somewhat pointedly.

Delaine may be a friend, but enough is enough. Right?

"Not really," said Delaine as she fidgeted with the little tins Theodosia had stacked on the counter earlier. "Janine is taking care of things. I just spoke to her a few minutes ago." She shrugged. "Business is a little slow."

Great, thought Theodosia, *and business here is going crazy. Plus I've got a TV crew arriving any minute.*

"Honest to goodness," declared Delaine, "these are the cleverest things I've ever seen."

"What's clever?" Drayton asked Delaine as he hurriedly squeezed behind the counter to make another pot of tea.

Delaine balanced one of the colorful little tins in her hand. "These tea marinades or rubs or whatever you call them. What do you call them, Drayton?"

Drayton's shoulders sagged in defeat. Once again, Delaine has caused him to lose count of the number of spoonfuls of Ti Kuan Yin, a sweet, fruity Chinese oolong tea, he was measuring out. "They're *rubs*," he told her.

"And you came up with this idea?" asked Delaine, seemingly fascinated.

"Theodosia and I did, yes," said Drayton, trying to resume his counting.

"When do you have time to brainstorm these new ideas?" she asked. "Between running my clothing store and attending social functions, I barely have time to go *grocery* shopping."

"Last winter," replied Drayton. "Theodosia came up with the concept and designed the packaging. I masterminded the various blends."

"So you've got this Spicy Black Tea Rub as well as a Lemon Jasmine Tea Rub. Tell me how you use them exactly?"

"Rubs are just that," explained Drayton. "They're rubbed into meats, fish, or poultry prior to cooking."

"To add flavor?" said Delaine.

"Yes, that *would* be the general idea," responded Drayton. He'd finally gotten his tea scooped into his blue willow teapot.

"You're adding *boiling* water," remarked Delaine as she watched him closely. "I thought boiling water was too hot."

"No, no," said Drayton. "It's actually fine for most black and oolong teas. It's the more delicate green teas and white teas that fare best with hot water. That is, water that's been removed from the burner just prior to boiling."

"Oh," said Delaine. Turning one of the tins over, she began to amuse herself by reading the list of ingredients out loud. As if they weren't already fairly well known to Theodosia and Drayton. "Lapsang Souchong, cayenne pepper, sea salt, garlic, and dried mustard. Very impressive," said Delaine. "What would I use this one for?" she asked.

"Meat," said Drayton, his jaw tightly clenched.

"Delaine," said Theodosia, knowing she had to stage some type of intervention between Drayton and Delaine, before he attacked her with a sugar tongs. "Be a dear and taste these spiced peaches, will you? Haley's trying out a new recipe and I'd love to see what you think. Too much cinnamon? Not enough ginger? You tell me."

Delaine wandered back to her table with the sample Theodosia had handed her. "Yes, of course," she said. "But just the tiniest *taste*. Don't forget, I'm *modeling* Saturday. Got to look my absolute best."

Two minutes later, Jory Davis called.

"What's up?" asked Theodosia. "Find anything out?"

"There was an application for a zoning change at Buddy Clark's residence. From residential to commercial."

"What does that mean?" asked Theodosia.

"That Buddy's going to run a business out of his home?" said Jory.

"That's strange," said Theodosia. "The man's retired. I wonder what he's planning."

"Maybe he's going to open a tea shop," said Jory.

"Be serious."

"Okay, let me take a look at the rest of this zoning app. Jeez . . . it must be twenty pages long." There was a pause then Jory began reading out loud. "Whereas the parcel heretofore known as platte A . . . mumble mumble . . . has been duly . . ."

"What was that?" asked Theodosia. "What was that mumble mumble part?"

"Nothing. Technical lawyer-talk," said Jory. There was a long pause. "Okay, here's the heart of the matter right here."

"What?" asked Theodosia.

"It looks like Buddy Clark is changing his home from a single-family dwelling to a B and B. Or somebody is."

"You think he's going to open a B and B because he needs money?" said Theodosia. She thought about this for a minute. It certainly wasn't unheard of. In a high-tourist town like Charleston, B and B's were wildly in demand and often highly profitable for their owners.

"Either that," continued Jory, "or he's always nursed a secret desire to be an innkeeper."

"*Please* be serious," said Theodosia.

"Maybe he plans to sell out and thinks he can get a better price if the property is rezoned," proposed Jory.

"Do people do that?" asked Theodosia.

"Sure," said Jory. "All the time."

"What would you call that? Pre-rezoning?"

Jory chuckled. "Very good. See, you can do the technical lawyer-talk thing, too. You probably missed your calling."

Theodosia was about to tell Jory about Buddy Clark's desire to sell off some of his Japanese antiques when, suddenly, a man laden down with a video camera, battery pack, cables, and video monitor pushed his way through her front door. Two other men, a lighting technician and a grip struggling with a number of shiny, silver cases, followed in his wake.

Uh-oh, here's that camera crew.

"Oops, gotta go," she said to Jory. "The TV crew's here."

"Break a leg," he told her.

"What's this?" asked Delaine, her green eyes glittering like a Siamese cat who'd just spotted a tasty morsel of fish.

Theodosia tried to make light of it. "Nothing really. Just a . . . um . . . TV crew."

"A *TV crew*!" exclaimed Delaine. "Good heavens, are you shooting a TV commercial?"

"No no, nothing like that," Theodosia assured her, still trying to downplay the event. "Just a small amount of background footage."

But Delaine was not to be deterred. "Footage for what, Theo?" she asked in her sweetest voice.

Drayton, tiring of the cat-and-mouse game going on between Theodosia and Delaine, decided to step in. "Theodosia's going to tape a couple segments for the *Windows on Charleston* show on Channel Eight," he explained. "All about tea. How to serve tea, tea facts, tea lore, that sort of thing. Today they're going to shoot footage that the station can use for promos and maybe the opening seconds of her segment."

"How very exciting," said Delaine, pulling a mirror from her purse and quickly applying a fresh coat of lip gloss. "You're obviously going to want your good customers to be part of this, are you not? An *empty* tea shop certainly would not be particularly inviting."

Theodosia looked around. The tea shop was absolutely jammed, and most of her customers were sipping tea and gazing at the TV crew with genuine curiosity.

"Then stick around," said Theodosia. *Why not? Delaine is obviously down about her sister, and being part of this could give her a much-needed lift. On the other hand, Delaine is as tenacious as a pit bull. If there's a TV crew within a thirty-block radius, Delaine would figure out a way to insert her face in front of the camera.*

"How long are you going to be here?" asked Delaine, flashing a brilliant smile at the cameraman, who was screwing his video camera onto a tripod and sorting though an armload of cables.

The cameraman, who had the words TV 8 and DUANE embroidered across the front pocket of his navy blue polo shirt, shrugged. "As long as it takes."

Delaine stood up and smoothed her skirt. "Oh, Duane, dear. How do you think this pink will read?" she asked, indicating her dress. "Does pink come across well or are there better colors? Should I change into something a little brighter?"

Duane cocked an appraising eye. "You could read as slightly faded," he said. "Red or yellow is better." Just as quickly, Duane turned his back on Delaine, opened one of the large metal cases, and pulled out a lens.

"Theo," said Delaine, "be a lamb and put a little RE-SERVED sign on my table, will you? I'm going to dash back to my shop and do a quick change." She headed for the door.

"Lord love a *duck*!" exclaimed Drayton, his eyes rolling heavenward. "Now we're going to have Delaine making a scene!"

Theodosia patted him on the arm. "Have faith, Drayton. It will all work out."

Just as the three crew members seemed to have their gear strewn in every square inch of the tea shop, Brooke Carter Crocket wandered in. "My goodness, this looks interesting," she said. "What on earth is going on?"

"Filming," said Drayton. He was so addled he had taken to giving one-word answers.

"Taping," corrected Theodosia. "For a couple segments on *Windows on Charleston.*"

"Fantabulous," declared Brooke. "That should give business a nice boost."

"Stay and be part of it," urged Theodosia. "You never know, maybe we can work in a subtle pitch for Heart's Desire as well."

Brooke slid into a chair. "Honey, you don't have to twist *my* arm." She reached into her handbag, pulled out something wrapped in blue tissue paper. "Theo, this is a little something for you." She handed the tissue-wrapped packet to Theodosia.

"What's this?" exclaimed Theodosia, accepting it hesitantly. "Please don't tell me it's a present for no reason at all."

Brooke waved a hand. "It's nothing really. I've just been trying out a few new designs. Consider it market research. Just tell me what you think."

Unwrapping the tissue, Theodosia gazed at a sterling silver turtle pendant dangling from a thin, sparkling chain. "This isn't exactly nothing, Brooke," she told her friend. "In fact, it's downright gorgeous."

"Holy smokes," said Haley as she hustled over to Brooke's table with a tea tray. "That turtle is totally cool!"

"I'm glad you like it," said Brooke as she pulled a second package out of her purse. "Because I've got one for you, too."

"Wow!" squealed Haley. She set her tray down and eagerly accepted her pendant from Brooke. "And it's a *sea* turtle!" she exclaimed, holding it up. "How absolutely perfect!"

"What did you think I'd design?" laughed Brooke. "An old hump-backed snapper like you'd find in the low-country?"

"I bet the Sea Turtle Rescue League could sell these as a fund-raiser," said Haley, gazing delightedly at her pendant. "Once you see one, you have to have it!"

"If I can ever find a skilled jewelry maker to assist me, I shall produce these turtle pendants *en mass* and let your fine organization have them at a wholesale price," pronounced Brooke. "The operative word being *if*. Until then, consider your sea turtles very limited editions. Endangered species, so to speak."

"How can I thank you?" asked Theodosia, thrilled by the new piece of jewelry that now dangled about her neck.

"Just keep doing what you do," said Brooke. "Be a good volunteer and help those little loggerheads make it safely to the sea." Her eyes met Theodosia's. "Hopefully without too many added complications," she said, an obvious reference to the sad discovery of Harper Fisk's body.

"Hopefully," agreed Theodosia.

"Say, Brooke," said Haley. "Did Delaine talk you into donating some of your oyster pendants to the silent auction this Saturday? For Fashion Bash?"

Brooke rolled her eyes. "Did she ever. I take it you guys got hit up, too?

Theodosia nodded. "And you've got me to thank. I'm the idiot who *suggested* the silent auction."

"What's the Indigo Tea Shop putting in?" asked Brooke.

"Tea baskets," said Haley. "See, I was in the process of making them." She pointed toward the counter, where sweetgrass baskets, stacks of tea towels, tins of tea, and individual sets of cups and saucers were strewn. "Then the TV crew came clattering in and shagged me away. They want me to wait until they're all set up. Then they want to *tape* me putting the baskets together," she said happily.

"Fun," said Brooke. "And yes, I am donating four silver

oyster pendants. I just haven't decided if I'll hang them on silk cords or narrow leather thongs."

"I vote for the silk cords," said Theodosia. "More summery."

"I vote silk, too," said Haley, finally transferring the tea and scones from her tea tray to Brooke's table.

"You two *did* hear about Delaine's sister, didn't you?" said Brooke tentatively.

Theodosia and Haley both nodded.

"I understand Sully Mitchner, the owner of Luna, was pretty shook up," said Brooke. "An incident like this is a retailer's nightmare. But *Nadine* did apparently lift the bracelet."

"It's a sad thing," murmured Theodosia.

"And Delaine's in complete denial," Haley added happily.

Theodosia frowned slightly. "We don't know that for sure, Haley."

"Sure we do," chirped Haley. "Delaine was just in here carrying on about how it was all a terrible *misunderstanding*. I'd say getting hauled away by the cops was more than a misunderstanding. I'd say it was—"

"Haley," said Theodosia, "why don't we set up table six for the film crew. Put out a pitcher of iced tea, a plate of scones, and a few sandwiches. Make it a kind of *grazing* table for them." When she'd shot TV spots in the past, the production companies had always put up grazing tables for the crew.

Theodosia's suggestion brought Haley up short. "Oh. Sure. Good idea. I guess you want me to hop on that right now?"

"Could you?" said Theodosia, eager to move Haley off

the subject of Delaine and her light-fingered sister Nadine.

Brooke grinned widely as Haley scampered off. "She's quite a girl."

"Yes, she is," agreed Theodosia.

CHAPTER 17

✦✦✦

S*TARING STOLIDLY AT* the red eye of the camera, Drayton once again uttered his well-rehearsed lines: "And our Charleston's Passion Tea is a special blend of black tea from the Charleston Tea Plantation along with orange blossoms, red sandalwood, elderberry, and of course, passion fruit." Holding the silver tin with the indigo blue label up to his face, Drayton continued to stare straight ahead at the camera once he'd finished his lines, then he finally rearranged his face into an embarrassed smile. It was his fifth take and Amy Chancellor, the *Windows on Charleston* production assistant who'd finally shown up a full hour late, *still* wasn't buying it.

"Drayton," shrilled Amy, "you don't have to *sell* the product quite so vigorously, just *tell* us about it. Try to be conversational and natural instead of uptight."

"Drayton *is* being natural," quipped Haley from off to the side. "He's naturally uptight."

Drayton pursed his lips and rolled his eyes while the crew

and most of the people in the tea room dissolved into giggles. Taping was proceeding at a snail's pace, but the customers seated at the various tables were having a ball. As Brooke had whispered to Theodosia, this was reality TV in the making! Even better than watching an episode of *Survivor*!

"Theodosia, maybe *you* should have a go at it," huffed Amy Chancellor. She was a short-statured, short-tempered redhead who seemed to be taking everything entirely too seriously.

Theodosia waved her off. "Drayton's our master tea blender. If you want someone to talk about our special house blends, he's your man. In fact, I made it quite clear that you'd be working with amateurs when I spoke with your producer a few days ago. And Constance assured me it wouldn't be a problem. She said she was willing to commit the crew for an entire day." *Enough of this petty bullying,* thought Theodosia. *I can be just as assertive when I want to.*

"But this will take *forever*," whined Amy. Cowed by Theodosia's words, she'd switched to another tack.

Theodosia didn't much care. Neither Duane, the cameraman, nor Raleigh, the lighting technician, seemed a bit fazed or flustered by the multiple takes. If anything, they were low key and encouraging, complete professionals who were working hard to make the best of the situation. And indeed, each of Drayton's readings had shown a marked improvement.

"He'll get it," said Theodosia. "Just stay off his back." She grabbed a pot of Darjeeling and slid between the tables, refilling cups as she went.

Delaine, who'd been waiting patiently for a while now, grabbed Theodosia's wrist as she skimmed by.

"When do you think they'll want to tape customer reactions?" Delaine asked in a loud whisper. She was all gussied up in a tomato red linen suit with her long dark hair freshly swirled atop her head.

Theodosia smiled noncommitally as she refilled Delaine's teacup.

"Probably when they're finished with Drayton," she said. "Then they'll want to interview you, Brooke, and maybe two other customers. Once that's in the can, they'll wrap with Haley and I assembling tea baskets."

"Wow," said Delaine, sounding more than a little envious. "I wish I could get this kind of publicity for *my* shop."

"Call one of the producers," said Theodosia. "Mail her a press release, invite her to a trunk show, send out complimentary tickets to Fashion Bash. It all hinges on how you promote yourself," Theodosia went on. She knew that many business owners were nervous about sending out press releases and invitations, feeling those techniques might be perceived as too heavy-handed. What they didn't realize was that TV stations and newspapers were constantly looking for something, *anything*, that was newsworthy. In fact, you were actually doing the media a *favor* by alerting them to special events. And when you got right down to it, what was the worst that could happen? The media didn't cover your event. Big deal. So you keep sending out more press releases. And sooner or later, you score some coverage. It surely wasn't rocket science. In fact, it was pretty much PR 101.

As the phone shrilled loudly, luckily at the end of Drayton's ninth take, Haley grabbed it off the counter. She listened for a couple seconds, then her eyes scanned the tea room, finally falling on Theodosia.

Me? Theodosia mouthed, tapping her chest.

Haley nodded.

Scooting through the green velvet curtain into her office, Theodosia grabbed for the phone on her desk. "Hello?"

"Miz Browning?"

"Yes?"

"This is Earl Jeffries at Renaissance Computer Repair."

"Earl, how are you?" asked Theodosia.

"Just grand, ma'am, but that computer you brought in here a couple days ago seems pretty well fried."

"That's why I brought it to you, Earl. Think there's anything you can do?"

"Well, I'm workin' on it."

"Okay . . ." said Theodosia.

"But don't expect miracles," said Earl.

"I expect you'll do your best, as always," said Theodosia. Earl was obviously having quite a time with the computer from the Legacy Gallery.

"I can get it to boot up okay, but then everything goes a little hinky." Earl hesitated. "Could someone have planted a bug in it?"

"You mean a virus?" said Theodosia.

"Yup. There are lots of nasty ones out there."

Nasty people, too, thought Theodosia. "It's possible," she told Earl as Haley slipped into her office and made a series of hand gestures at her. "Better take precautions, Earl," she told him.

"Don't worry, I always do," Earl assured her.

"What's up?" Theodosia asked as she hung up the phone then spun in her chair to face Haley.

"Summer Sullivan wants to see you."

"She's here now?" asked Theodosia, surprised.

Haley made a face. "Oh yeah, she's here."

"What's wrong, Haley?" asked Theodosia. Haley's normally placid face was arranged in a frown.

She put a hand on one hip and stared at Theodosia. "I gotta tell you, I just don't trust that girl."

"You can't believe she had something to do with Harper Fisk's death," said Theodosia in a low voice.

Haley shrugged. "I don't know what to believe. But I get a . . . what would you call it . . . a weird vibe."

"Well, please try and keep those weird vibes under wraps while she's here, will you?"

"Uh . . . okay." Haley obviously wanted to say more but didn't. "So you want me to send Summer back here?"

"Please," said Theodosia.

Honestly, thought Theodosia. *Haley and her vibes. She could start her own psychic friends network based on the number of vibes she gets. On the other hand, Haley does possess fairly good instincts about people. So maybe I should proceed with a tad more caution.*

"Theodosia!" exclaimed Summer Sullivan as she slipped into the back office. "You've got a regular media circus going on out front!"

"Isn't it fun?" said Theodosia. "Drayton was so adamant about not being taped and now he's out there acting like Mr. Saturday Night. I think it's a kick." She smiled at Summer, waved for her to sit down in the cushy green velvet chair across from her. Scooping up a stack of tea magazines, Theodosia made a halfhearted pass at trying to make her desk presentable. "Sorry it's such a mess back here," she apologized. "I guess we've just been filling too many orders to be orderly."

"Have you heard anything about the computer yet?" asked Summer.

"I just talked with the repair shop," said Theodosia. "They're still working on it." *Tell her, not tell her about a possible bug? No, let's just let this play out. See what happens.*

"Hey, I've got good news," said Summer. "Gordon hired your friend to help me settle Harper's estate."

Theodosia stared at Summer, not quite understanding her meaning at first. Then she did a double take. "My friend . . . you mean Jory Davis?"

"Exactly," grinned Summer. "Gordon figured it was better to just plunge ahead."

"He's probably right," said Theodosia, wondering if Jory was suddenly out of the picture now as far as helping her investigate the members of the English Breakfast Club. *Of course he was. Lawyers upheld strict protocols on confidentiality when it came to clients. They were kind of like ministers that way. Well, highly paid ministers, anyway.*

"Anyway," continued Summer, "it feels like a huge weight's been lifted from my shoulders. I haven't had a chance to meet with Mr. Davis yet, but we chatted on the phone less than an hour ago."

"Good," said Theodosia. "Great." Somehow her inner enthusiasm didn't match the heartiness of her words. *Jory Davis pulled in to work for Summer. Was there something fishy going on?*

"Anyway, I'm thrilled," said Summer. "I've been getting all sorts of conflicting advice and now I feel like I've got someone whose loyalty is to *my* team."

Theodosia stared at Summer. "Conflicting advice from . . ."

"Oh you know," said Summer, rolling her eyes. The *boys.* The so-called English Breakfast Club."

"I take it they all have their own ideas about things?" said Theodosia.

Summer shifted in her chair. "Do they ever! Close the

store, expand the store, sell off everything, donate it to the Heritage Society . . . you name it, they've suggested it."

"Interesting," said Theodosia.

"Not really," said Summer. "More like confusing. But hey, that's all behind me now." She smiled brightly, then paused as a cacophony of loud voices suddenly erupted from the tea room out front. "Theodosia," said Summer, "from the sound of things, I'd say you better get out there!"

Delaine threw back her head and uttered a low, throaty laugh. The camera was focused squarely on her and she was clearly reveling in the attention.

"She's completely over the top," Drayton whispered in Theodosia's ear. "She's gone from playing Scarlet O'Hara to Blanche duBois to Joan Crawford in *Mommy Dearest*!"

Theodosia patted Drayton's arm. "Don't worry," she told him. "If it's too weird, they won't use it. The footage will end up on the proverbial cutting room floor."

"Promise me?" he asked. "Cross your heart and hope to *die*?"

"Drayton, really," Theodosia assured him. "This is for local midday TV. The last thing Channel Eight wants is something that strays even slightly beyond the bounds of middle-of-the-road. Besides, we've got bigger things to worry about."

"Like what?" Drayton glanced at her sharply.

Theodosia put a hand on his sleeve and tugged him out of range of all cameras and microphones. "For one thing, Gordon Sargent just hired Jory Davis to represent Summer Sullivan."

Drayton's bushy eyebrows flew up in surprise. "For what reason?"

"Supposedly to help settle Harper Fisk's estate."

"Which is soon to become *her* estate," said Drayton.

"I believe that's the general idea."

"You don't think she's trying to cut the Heritage Society out of their just due, do you?"

"I have no idea," said Theodosia. "All I know is she's tired of getting conflicting advice from the various members of the English Breakfast Club."

"Hmm." Drayton scratched his chin thoughtfully, pondering the situation. "The fact that she's gone ahead and hired Jory. Do you see this as a problem?"

"Nooo . . . not really," said Theodosia slowly. "I mean, I *guess* not. I guess I've assumed all along that the will would eventually be pried out of that old hard drive."

"And that most everything really *was* left to Summer," finished Drayton. "With just a few of Harper's personal things going to the Heritage Society."

"Right," said Theodosia.

"So what are you worried about? Certainly not a rush to judgment," Drayton said.

Theodosia shook her head. "Jory wouldn't do that. He wouldn't strong-arm everything through just because Summer was a paying client."

Would he? No, I'm sure he wouldn't.

"Tell you what, Drayton," said Theodosia. "Jory and I are supposed to go for a sail tonight. I'll talk to him. Bring it up in a fairly subtle way."

"Excellent," nodded Drayton. "Put our concerns to rest."

Theodosia nodded. If only putting their concerns to rest were that easy.

"Theodosia, can we *please* have you in this shot?" Amy Chancellor raised her voice in a loud appeal. It was obvious that, after her little taping session with Delaine, she was experiencing a slow meltdown.

Hustling over to stand behind the counter with Haley, Theodosia tried to ignore Amy Chancellor's histrionics. Despite everything, taping was proceeding very well. *And why not,* decided Theodosia. *Throw together a room full of colorful characters and you get a blend that's akin to a good low-country gumbo. Rich, sometimes quirky, decidedly peppery.*

"Here's what I have in mind," said Amy, fanning herself with one of the tea shop's take-out menus. "While you and Haley assemble tea baskets, I want you to talk in a general way about tea. You know, the popularity of tea, the significance of tea shops today, that sort of thing." Amy wrinkled her nose and peered at Theodosia. "You think you can improvise for thirty or forty seconds? Enough so I can put together a couple fifteen-second promos?"

Theodosia nodded. Of course. And what was there to improvise? She'd simply deliver her standard pitch on tea. The same one she gave when she hosted a tea tasting, or pitched a new client on the idea of hiring the Indigo Tea Shop to cater their bridal shower tea or garden tea. It was during these little talks that she spoke with a heartfelt enthusiasm for the gentle art of tea that was driven by both passion and pleasure. And it was the reason the Indigo Tea Shop, barely a couple years old, was such a rousing success.

"Haley, keep your hands away from your face," coached Amy. "And focus only on the tea baskets. Don't keep looking over at Drayton."

"He's making me giggle," said Haley.

Amy spun on her squatty little heels and flashed Drayton

a disparaging look. A look that clearly communicated, *Don't screw up my shot, buster.*

Chastised, Drayton busied himself pouring tea for his guests from the Lady Goodwood Inn as well as the remaining guests who, still fascinated with the goings-on, stayed glued in their seats.

CHAPTER 18

✖✖✖

𝒲ATER LAPPED GENTLY against the silvered wooden pilings and halyards clinked against aluminum masts as Theodosia and Jory picked their way down the long pier. It was a perfect night to sail, Theodosia decided. Low sun dancing off waves lent a golden glow to everything. And with the wind at about six knots, there'd be a nice little chop on the water once they got out into Charleston Harbor.

Jory's sailboat, *Rubicon*, was moored in Slip 112, about halfway down the main pier, then out on one of the less stable auxiliary piers. As they picked their way along, hauling life jackets and a wicker picnic basket, Theodosia was surprised at how many boats were still tied up here on this perfect sailing evening. J-24s, Columbias, San Joses, even a few Santanas.

"What I was thinking," said Jory as he grabbed Theodosia's elbow to help her step down onto the bobbing auxiliary pier, "was that we'd head out into the harbor, turn south, and make a run down to Folly Beach."

Folly Beach was a summer playground that sported a six-mile beach, dozens of resorts, and a thousand-foot fishing pier. The pier was replete with tackle shops, snack bars, game arcades, and restaurants, and was a nostalgic, slightly gaudy throwback to an earlier era when pavilions and board-walks were considered the height of fun.

"You're thinking about that little oyster shack down there, aren't you," said Theodosia. "What's the name again? Finnegan's? Florian's?"

"Flagherty's," said Jory with a crooked grin. Jory was an oyster lover of the first magnitude. Raw oysters, fried oysters, oysters Rockefeller, oysters Florentine, you name it, Jory snarfed the little critters with great relish.

"Right," said Theodosia. "I remember they serve those homemade . . ." Her voice suddenly trailed off and the smile slipped from her face. For there, sitting before them in the water, listing very badly and half filled with green seawater, was Jory's sailboat!

"Jory, it's half sunk!" cried Theodosia. She dropped her duffel bag, grabbed at one of the lines, and leaned precariously toward the boat. She was about to leap on board when Jory clamped a hand on her shoulder.

"Hold on!" he warned. "Let's check this out first. If the plug's been pulled, the boat's not stable. You could plunge all the way to the bottom."

Color drained from Theodosia's face. It was deep here. And dangerous, littered with all sorts of harbor debris. "Holy smokes," she said. "You're right."

Jory was looking decidedly grim. "Who would do this?" he fumed, dropping life jackets and picnic basket in a heap. He took a couple steps, whirled about in frustration, then stared back toward the clubhouse. "The caretakers are sup-posed to watch out for things like this," he fretted. "That's what we pay *dock fees* for. So this kind of thing *won't* happen."

"Maybe there's something wrong with the boat?" suggested Theodosia. "What if it's sprung a leak or the bilge pump somehow reversed itself?" Neither were particularly convincing arguments and Theodosia knew it. She was just trying to impart a little hope and smooth Jory's ruffled feathers.

"I don't think so," Jory stormed. "This looks intentional. In fact, it looks like somebody was attempting to scuttle the whole darn thing!"

Theodosia stared at Jory's beautiful boat. What had been a sleek, well-maintained J-24 now looked like a soggy wreck. Riding dangerously low in the water, the boat was canted at a forty-five-degree angle with foamy green water sloshing around inside its cockpit. She hated to think what things looked like below deck. The two small bunks were probably water-logged and ruined.

Jory was obviously thinking the same thing as he kicked off his deck shoes and peeled off his polo shirt.

"You're going aboard?" she asked.

"Sure am."

"But you're not going below, are you?" asked Theodosia, knowing full well that was *exactly* what he intended to do.

Stepping nimbly onto the floundering boat, Jory balanced himself carefully, then reached a hand down into the water and searched for the hatch. "Darn," said Jory. "The lock's busted."

Theodosia frowned. A broken lock meant someone had, indeed, smashed their way in and intentionally vandalized the boat. "Be careful," she cautioned Jory as he pulled at the submerged hatch.

There was a *whoosh* as the hatch door flew open and water from the deck drained into the lower compartment.

"How does it look?" Theodosia called to him.

"Flooded," said Jory. He climbed down two steps, hesitated a moment, then disappeared down the companionway.

"Be careful," yelled Theodosia.

She stood on the dock, hoping Jory would reappear in a matter of seconds. When her Tag Heur watch told her it had been a good minute and a half, she decided to take matters into her own hands. Moving carefully, she stepped from the dock onto the flooded deck of the *Rubicon*.

Kneeling now, she peered down the companionway. "Jory?" she called.

Jory's head popped up inches from hers. "Whoa!" he exclaimed. "I didn't know you were there. You scared me half to death!"

Theodosia put a hand to her heart. She hadn't been expecting Jory to pop up beside her like a manic gopher, either. "Sorry," she told him.

Still crouched on her hands and knees, she backed up so Jory could scramble his way out.

"Well, what's the verdict?" she asked him.

Jory reached down and grabbed at the left leg of his cotton shorts. Twisting the fabric, he wrung out a steady stream of water. "This was no accident," he told her. "Some kids probably came on board and pulled the plug."

"You're sure?"

Jory bobbed his head in disgust. "Trashing a guy's sailboat, that's gotta be a real thrill."

"Jory," said Theodosia gently, "what if this wasn't random?"

His startled dark eyes met hers. They were both silent for a few moments, listening to the ripple and snap of nylon flags overhead and the squeak of wooden boats against pilings. "What are you talking about?" Jory finally asked.

Theodosia hated to verbalize it, but knew she had to. "Jory, what if this is all related? What if this has something to do with your representing Summer Sullivan?"

Seconds passed as they stared at each other.

"Explain," said Jory.

Theodosia stood up on the still-listing boat, her T-shirt and shorts also soaked. "What if this was intended as some kind of message? You know, a not-so-subtle warning to back off."

Jory squinted at her then swiped the back of his hand across his chin. "To back off," he repeated. He stepped from the boat onto the dock, then reached back to give Theodosia an assist. When they were both back on stabler footing, he peered at her with curiosity. "Okay, Sherlock," he said in a manner that was not unkind, "since you've obviously got a theory percolating away, why don't you lay it out for me. Exactly *who* do you think wants me to back off?"

Theodosia took a deep breath. "The English Breakfast Club?"

"You really believe that?" asked Jory, looking slightly stunned.

"Yes. No." Theodosia raised her hands in a gesture of appeal, then let them fall to her side. "I don't know. Oh Jory . . ." She took a step toward him. "I'm *so* sorry about your boat."

He put his arms around her, and pulled her close. "Yeah, me too."

"I know you can get it pumped out," said Theodosia. "And if there's any kind of bash below the water line . . . well, you'll be able to get it patched, right?"

Jory gave a weak smile even as he gazed sadly at his boat.

"Oh, I expect that in a city whose residents own more than thirty thousand boats, we'll find *someone* who can salvage the *Rubicon*." He sighed deeply, then gave a rueful chuckle. "Sorry about tonight's sail, kiddo. Looks like you'll have to settle for a rain check."

"Not a problem," she told him. "You know that." She turned in his arms and gazed back at the clubhouse. "For now, let's just go back to the clubhouse and report this, okay?"

"Sure," he said. "I guess. Better phone my insurance agent, too."

"Who's your insurance agent?"

"Guy who works at the law firm."

"At least that part's easy," said Theodosia.

Jory leaned down to gather up the life vests and the picnic basket. "Are you kidding?" he said. "*Nothing's* ever easy."

The phone was ringing as Theodosia turned the key in her lock. Tossing down her duffel bag, she ran for the wall phone in the kitchen, snatched the receiver from its hook. "Hello?" she said breathlessly.

"Theodosia, hello," came a friendly voice. "It's Naomi Morison. How've you been?"

Naomi Morison from the Charleston Foundation. Oh boy. Probably wants to know why I'm dragging my feet.

"Good. Great. How about you?" said Theodosia. *Should I tell Naomi that within the last few days I stumbled upon a dead body and found out my friend's sister might be a kleptomaniac? Or that tonight we discovered my boyfriend's boat had been trashed? No, probably not. Interesting stuff, but probably not subject matter fit for friendly banter.*

"I'm wondering," said Naomi, "if you've been able to plow through that pile of grant requests yet."

Theodosia peered through the doorway at the stack of grant requests that now sat center stage on her dining room table. *Tell Naomi the truth? Tell a little white lie? Ah, the lies have it.*

Theodosia crossed her fingers and grimaced. "Sure have," she said with forced enthusiasm. *I'll finish them tonight. I really will. I promise.*

"Wonderful," enthused Naomi. "I knew I could count on you. So I can expect to get your preliminary recommendations on—"

"Monday," finished Theodosia, even as a little voice inside her wondered just how she was going to sandwich in those grant requests in addition to everything else she had to do at the tea shop and for Delaine's Fashion Bash. *And by the way, just what the heck am I going to do about Professor Gibbon's grant request? Toss the old fellow out because he could be a suspect? That isn't exactly fair, is it?*

"You've got my fax number and e-mail, right?" said Naomi. "At the foundation?"

"I sure do," said Theodosia.

"Monday then," said Naomi hopefully. "I'll look for your recommendations on Monday."

Standing in the kitchen, her shoes squishing on the floor, Theodosia reached down to pat Earl Grey, who'd padded over to meet her. But the dog just sniffed at the puddle of water she'd deposited, then turned tail and loped back into the living room.

Probably worried about getting blamed for the puddle, thought Theodosia. *Lots of dogs, Earl Grey being one of them, seem to be hypersensitive about being blamed for things. Chalk it up to doggy paranoia.*

Theodosia had just slipped into a cotton robe when the phone shrilled again. This time she picked up in the bedroom.

"Hello?"

"Theo, it's Drayton. You'll never guess what happened."

She cinched the robe tightly about her waist. "I'll bite. What happened, Drayton?"

"Professor Gibbon just called."

Speak of the devil.

"What's he up to?" asked Theodosia.

"Get this," exclaimed Drayton. "He claims to have just discovered a copy of Harper Fisk's will!"

"Are you serious? That's what I'd call amazingly convenient," said Theodosia.

"Ain't it just," said Drayton.

"Did he say where he found this mysterious copy? Or did a little bird just happen to drop it down his chimney?"

"Oh, he had an answer for that," said Drayton.

"I'll bet he did," said Theodosia.

"Professor Gibbon claims he stumbled upon a copy of the will just this evening. Said it was at the bottom of a pile of papers he had on his desk. Gibbon told me it had slipped his mind entirely, but that Harper Fisk had given him a copy. You know, to sign as a witness."

Theodosia considered this. "Well, I suppose his explanation *sounds* plausible."

"But you're not buying it entirely," said Drayton. "Right?" From the tone of Drayton's voice, he wasn't either.

Theodosia sat down on the edge of her bed, rubbed her bare feet across the silkiness of her Aubusson carpet. "I'm not sure *what* to believe anymore." She paused. "Did Professor Gibbon offer to share the contents of this will with us?" asked Theodosia.

"He said he believed the most appropriate venue would be via a legal forum."

"He actually used those words? Proper venue? Legal forum?"

"He did," said Drayton. "And, Theodosia, I must tell you, the old fellow seemed rather breathless and elated about the whole thing."

"Which would lead one to believe that—"

"He's a beneficiary," finished Drayton.

"Like I said before, it's all very convenient," said Theodosia.

"Entirely too pat," agreed Drayton.

"I have some strange news of my own," offered Theodosia. "When Jory and I showed up at the yacht club for our sail, we found his boat trashed."

"You're kidding!"

"Well, maybe not completely trashed, but vandalized anyway. Some jerk must have climbed on board and pulled the master plug. The boat was half sunk in the water."

"Awful, just awful," commiserated Drayton. "And such a lovely, sleek little yacht, too. Jory must have been awfully upset."

"He was, believe me. We went back to the clubhouse and spoke with the caretaker, but the guy claimed not to have seen or heard anything."

"Did you believe him?" asked Drayton.

"He seemed sincere," said Theodosia. "And the man's been working as a custodian at the yacht club for more than ten years, so I don't think he suddenly decided to launch a personal vendetta against Jory."

"Sure are strange goings-on around the neighborhood," said Drayton. "Be sure to lock your door and instruct that dog of yours to remain on guard."

"Don't worry," Theodosia assured him. "I will."

CHAPTER 19

✦✦✦

ALTHOUGH THEODOSIA HAD inadvertently spilled tea on her fair share of towels, napkins, and tablecloths, she'd never gone so far as to throw caution to the wind and submerge an entire article in a vat of tea. This, she was quickly learning, might have been a huge mistake on her part. For the dusky pink hue that resulted from immersing a piece of linen in a bath of hibiscus tea was truly spectacular.

Besides herself, there were four other women gathered at March Forth this Friday morning. And of course, there was Hillary Retton from Popple Hill Design, who was leading the seminar, and Lawrence March, the shop's venerable proprietor.

"Theodosia," said Hillary Retton, "since you're our resident tea expert, I'll pose this question to you. If you want to dye a piece of lace a light ochre color, what kind of tea would you use?" Hillary Retton smiled a wide smile. With her short, spiky hair and sleek, polished look, she looked just as youthful and energetic as her business partner, Marianne Petigru.

Theodosia thought for a minute. *Ochre color? Must be a Keeman or an oolong, right?*

"How about oolong?" proposed Theodosia.

Hillary Retton bobbed her head with approval. "Very good. Now if you're looking for a subtle yellow, you'd want to use chamomile tea. And if your heart's desire is a lovely mint green, try dyeing your fabric in gunpowder green tea. But remember, you're always going to get variations in color. Swishing your fabric in the tea will help produce a smooth textured finish, but the dye coverage is never going to be perfectly even. Of course, if you really *want* a mottled effect, just soak your fabric in the tea bath instead of moving it around."

Theodosia was trying to absorb all of Hillary's ideas, but they were coming at her fast and furious. She was learning that tea dyeing was an easy and inexpensive way to give fabrics a muted, antiqued look. But tea dyeing really worked only on natural fibers. Cotton, silk, linen, and some woolens were perfect, but polyester was a no-no. The dye simply wouldn't take.

Pulling fabric from a vat of Darjeeling, Hillary showed off a garment that had begun its life as a white lace blouse. Now it was a dusky, soft coffee brown, the rich color of café au lait. Theodosia could easily picture that elegant blouse paired with a long velvet skirt in a warm terra cotta color.

Wiping her hands on a towel, Theodosia ambled over to where Lawrence March was perched on his oversized library table.

"This was a marvelous idea," she told him.

"Ah, you're having fun," he chuckled. "Wonderful. Glad

to hear it." He peered at her through slightly tinted wire-rimmed glasses. "Hillary is a love, isn't she? So talented and wildly creative. You should see her work sometime. Her decorating skills are quite prodigious."

"Actually, I *have* seen some of her work," said Theodosia. "She and her partner Marianne worked on the Featherbed House. And I believe they redid one of Timothy Neville's front parlors."

"Yes, dear old Timothy," said Lawrence March. "I imagine that albatross of a house needs some tweaking now and then."

"You know," said Theodosia, "Drayton got an interesting phone call from Professor Gibbon last night."

Lawrence March picked up his cup of tea and took a sip. Theodosia had the distinct feeling he seemed to know what was coming.

"Professor Gibbon claims to have found a copy of Harper Fisk's will," Theodosia said in a low voice.

"Does he now," said Lawrence March. "Good for him, I guess."

"Apparently there was some dispute over what was left to Summer Sullivan, versus the Heritage Society and certain members of the English Breakfast Club," continued Theodosia.

Lawrence March gazed out across his store. "My dear Miss Browning, I could care less if Harper Fisk left the whole shooting match to a bunch of flat earth cult members who run around with tinfoil on their heads. The fact of the matter is, the will simply doesn't interest me."

Staring at Lawrence March, Theodosia could almost believe him. After all, of all the English Breakfast Club members, Lawrence March was the one who'd expressed not the slightest bit of interest in the will, and had even abstained from attending Harper Fisk's funeral. Lawrence March obviously marched to his own drummer.

"Anyway," said Theodosia, "we really won't know anything until next week. Apparently that's when Professor Gibbon is going to get together with Summer Sullivan and her attorney."

Theodosia kept her eyes on Lawrence March. There was no indication that he even knew who Summer's attorney even was. *Good. I hereby decree that Lawrence March's name be stricken from the current list of suspects concerning Harper Fisk's death. Whew.*

"Mr. March, may I use your phone to call the tea shop?" asked Theodosia. "I left my cell phone out in my Jeep, and I want to check with Drayton and Haley. Fridays aren't usually too hectic, but you never know."

Lawrence March hopped to his feet. "Certainly, dear girl. In fact, follow me and I'll make you comfortable in my office. It's small, but highly serviceable, I assure you."

Lawrence March was quite correct. Instead of the jumbled, cluttered little office one might expect of someone who owns an antique shop, this office was businesslike, bordering on tidy. Pushed up against one wall, a large wooden desk held a phone, fax, and orderly stacks of papers. The four-drawer file set against the other wall must have contained the rest of Lawrence March's paperwork. On the wall was a nice collection of framed prints, maps, and photos.

Making herself comfortable in Lawrence March's bright purple ergonomically correct chair, Theodosia picked up the receiver. As she began to punch in numbers, she glanced about at the walls.

A map depicting a number of shipwrecks in Charleston Harbor caught her eye.

Shipwrecks. Interesting.

Quietly, Theodosia slid the phone back into its cradle and stood up to investigate. Yes, it was, indeed, a map. But not a historical map, as she'd initially thought. Besides the usual "X marks the spot" notations on various shipwrecks, this map was topographical. It indicated water depths as well as underwater shelves and channels. There was also a legend printed at the bottom: *Data compiled by the Academy of Maritime Sciences.* And the map was fairly recent. Printed in 2002.

So Lawrence March does have an interest in shipwrecks. Or else why would this map be hanging here?

One more tidbit to relate to Drayton, Theodosia told herself as she turned her attention back to Lawrence March's desk. Sitting down again, she reached for the phone. And found herself staring straight at an old photo of Lawrence March.

Her curiosity once again roused, Theodosia studied the old black-and-white photo. In a shot that had to be at least fifty years old, Lawrence March was posed in old-fashioned knit swim trunks at the edge of an Olympic-sized swimming pool. Positioned next to the photo, also enclosed by the frame, was a coppery-looking medal. The cardboard photo mat had been cut in a circle to accommodate the trinket. Intrigued, Theodosia squinted at the medal.

Nineteen fifty-three Intercollegiate Swim Champ.

Swim champ! Theodosia frowned. *Lawrence March had been a star swimmer.*

She let this idea percolate in her brain for a few moments.

Was he still a strong swimmer?

She decided that if he was, there were a number of possible implications.

Lawrence March is interested in shipwrecks. And ship-wrecks often yield treasure. Okay, I know that Harper Fisk was a treasure hunter. So does this point to the possibility that Lawrence March might have been the second passenger in Harper Fisk's boat?

Had Harper Fisk been seriously on to something? And had Lawrence March, on the pretext of helping him, conked Harper Fisk on the head? He could have then stolen his maps, scuttled the boat, and swum back to shore.

Or had Lawrence March tossed Harper Fisk out of the boat then made his way to Sullivan's Island, where the boat was subsequently discovered?

Nice old Lawrence March, who still mourned a wife who died of pancreatic cancer? Nice old Lawrence March who drank tea?

Yeah. Maybe. I suppose.

Could he have somehow fudged up Harper Fisk's computer, too?

Theodosia glanced around the office. No computer in sight.

"Theodosia," said Lawrence March, standing in the doorway. "You make your call?"

She popped up from his chair as if the cushions were spring-loaded. "Sure did. Thanks a bunch," Theodosia said in her chirpiest voice.

Lawrence March focused a thin smile on her, and Theodosia wondered if he could tell by the light on the extension out in the shop that she hadn't been on the line long enough to actually make a call.

Theodosia smiled back at him. He gave her nothing.

Oh well.

Theodosia turned, snatched her purse from his desk, and slung it over her shoulder. Deciding the smartest thing to do was head back to the Indigo Tea Shop, she hustled out of Lawrence March's office. But not before she caught a glimpse of a laptop computer tucked in next to his set of file drawers.

CHAPTER 20

THE INDIGO TEA Shop was fairly jumping when Theodosia returned. Two of the colorful horse-drawn jitneys that ferried tourists through the cobbled and tree-bowered streets of the historic district had clip-clopped their way to the front door and disgorged a huge number of thirsty, eager customers.

"How was your tea-dyeing lesson?" asked Drayton, who barely waited for an answer before he thrust an apron into Theodosia's hands and announced, "Good thing you're back, we're absolutely bonkers!"

Theodosia immediately threw herself into action. One of the realities of running a tea room was that, while everything might appear calm and relaxing for the customer, there was a huge amount of kinetic energy generated behind the scenes. There was always fresh tea to be brewed, sugar bowls and creamers to be refilled, crusts to be sliced from sandwiches, three-level tea trays to be artfully arranged, and fresh-baked scones that needed a final dusting of powdered sugar. After all, when you ran a tea shop, quality was essential and presentation was everything.

"Brooke dropped off those oyster pendants," said Drayton as he fussed at the counter, arranging three small Japanese teapots on a black lacquer tray. "She can't make it to Fashion Bash tomorrow and was wondering if you could come up with some sort of creative way to display them?"

Theodosia fretted as she prepared two cups of iced tea for takeout. "Are you serious? We don't even have all our *own* tea baskets put together yet. And can you believe Fashion Bash happens *tomorrow*? Where on earth did the week go?"

Carefully pouring steaming water into the tiny teapots, Drayton nodded in agreement. "I know exactly how you feel. I've got to orchestrate another tea tasting, then hustle my old bones over to the Heritage Society after lunch to pick up the script Delaine left for me. Seems she doesn't own a computer, so she typed everything out at the Heritage Society."

"Delaine wrote the narration for tomorrow's show?" asked Theodosia.

"I'm afraid so," sighed Drayton. "Which means the script is likely to be a bit florid and flowery."

"Delaine always *did* want to be a romance writer," chuckled Theodosia. "Any thoughts on a rewrite?"

Drayton fluttered a hand to his chest and projected a look of sublime mock surprise. "*Moi?* Fiddle with someone's carefully penned prose?" He smiled to himself as he set a half-dozen tiny glazed Japanese teacups on the tray. Their cobalt blue, celadon green, and reddish-amber glazes glinted enticingly. "There," he announced. "Pretty teacups and delicious teas."

Theodosia peered at this lovely piece of handiwork. "Which Japanese green teas are you brewing?" she asked.

"I've paired a nice bright Sencha with a slightly smoky Genmaicha, then added a Bancha blend accented with citrus flowers," Drayton told her. "Should make for an interesting tea sampler, don't you think?"

"Drayton," said Theodosia, "it's beyond interesting, it's *perfect*." And Theodosia meant those words with all her heart. When it came to blending tea or creating a tea-tasting experience, Drayton seemed to possess an unerring instinct. And whether a customer was a longtime tea lover or a tea initiate, Drayton always seemed to intuitively choose the exact teas that made their tea drinking both pleasurable and memorable.

Drayton ducked his head, obviously pleased by Theodosia's compliment. "Thank you kindly, ma'am."

Theodosia was on her hands and knees, searching through the bottom cupboard, when Haley came swinging out of the kitchen, laden down with a large silver tray. Pausing in midstride at the sight of Theodosia half crouched on the floor, she asked, "What on earth are you doing down *there*?"

"Looking for those tea candles in the tiny blue and white porcelain containers," Theodosia told her.

Haley switched her tray from one hip to the other, kicked out her right foot to indicate the cupboard closest to her. "This cupboard," she told Theodosia. "They're in there."

Theodosia retrieved the ceramics in a second.

"I need to display those silver oyster pendants Brooke brought over," explained Theodosia, "and I thought these might work." Theodosia set a box of Chinese blue and white porcelain containers on the counter.

"You're going to put the oyster pendants on top of the candles?" said Haley, clearly confused.

"No," explained Theodosia. "I was going to put a tiny

piece of moss atop each candle, then nestle the silver pendant on top of that."

"Oh cool," said Haley. "I get it. The container looks like a miniature porcelain jewelry box, then when you remove the pendant, you still have the candle. Works for me."

"Good. I was afraid you wouldn't approve," said Theodosia with a quick grin.

"Awright, smarty," said Haley, "see if you get lunch today."

"What's on the menu?" asked Theodosia.

"While you were playing lady bountiful and dyeing snippets of lace and velvet in simmering vats of tea, I was sweating over a cold refrigerator," announced Haley, tipping her tray slightly for Theodosia to see. "Ta da!"

"Oh my goodness," exclaimed Theodosia. "Country pâté?"

"You got it," said Haley. "Served with a cup of chilled asparagus soup."

"Heavenly," said Theodosia.

"That's what I thought," said Haley, looking pleased.

"Can I help you serve?" asked Theodosia.

Haley gazed out across the tea room. Her first course of lemon scones had been eagerly consumed and Drayton was busy removing the used plates. It would appear that the soup and pâté were ready to be served.

"Let's do it," said Haley.

At one-thirty Delaine's sister, Nadine, suddenly walked into the Indigo Tea Shop, turning up like the proverbial bad penny.

Haley glanced up from where she was ringing change at the old brass cash register. "Uh, hi there, Nadine," she said somewhat awkwardly.

Nadine flashed a hundred-watt smile that also dripped with condescension. "Hello, dear."

"Something I can do for you?" Haley asked. One eyebrow rose slightly and quivered with disapproval. It was a little trick she'd learned from Drayton.

"I'd like to speak with your employer," said Nadine. Shifting a straw bag embroidered with flowers and palm trees to her other arm, she gazed toward an empty table. "I shall sit down and wait for her," announced Nadine. "Could you please bring me a cup of tea?"

"Any particular kind?" asked Haley grudgingly.

"Surprise me," said Nadine in a flat tone.

"Theodosia!" Haley lost no time in scrambling back to Theodosia's office. "Delaine's sister is here. She wants to talk to you."

Theodosia, who'd been going over revisions to her web site, rose in her chair in surprise. "Nadine's here? Now?"

"Yup," said Haley. "Acting like the queen of the May, too. Like nothing ever happened."

"Maybe it didn't," said Theodosia.

Haley twisted the lower half of her face into a wry grin. "Yeah right."

"Nadine," said Theodosia, joining Delaine's sister at the little table. "This is a surprise."

"Hello, Theodosia," said Nadine, her voice dripping with honey. "So *wonderful* to see you again."

"Can I get you something?" Theodosia asked. "A cup of tea? A scone?"

"Your girl was going to bring me a cup of tea," said Nadine. "Lord knows where she's run off to."

"She's right here," snapped Haley, setting the tea down in front of Nadine. "Care for lemon? Or sugar?"

"Nothing, thank you," said Nadine as Haley flounced off.

She took a quick sip of tea, then focused large, liquid eyes on Theodosia.

"Theodosia, Delaine and I are *desperately* in need of your help."

Oh Lord, thought Theodosia, feeling a slight prickle of panic. *What's this going to be about?*

"Nadine," she said. "What's wrong?"

Placing both hands flat on the table, Nadine cocked her head to one side in a piteous gesture. *"Everything!"*

"Tell me," urged Theodosia. If this was about the shoplifting charge, maybe she could call Detective Tidwell and somehow convince him to pull some strings.

"Lillian Lee Burton is a no-show," moaned Nadine.

Theodosia stared at her. *Who on earth is Lillian Lee Burton? And what's this about a no-show?*

Nadine continued with her cryptic delivery. "Lillian Lee was a size *ten*."

Theodosia was beginning to get an inkling of what this conversation was really about. "She was a size ten," Theodosia repeated.

"Yes," said Nadine. "Lord knows, *I'd* wear the shantung silk top and slacks, but I'm an *eight*. Plus I'm already modeling the power suit and the floral slip dress."

Tension that had gripped Theodosia's chest suddenly released. "This is about the fashion show tomorrow," she said.

Nadine sipped at her tea. "Yes. Of course. What did you think it was?"

"Nadine, exactly what is it you want?" asked Theodosia. "Why are you *here*?"

Nadine gazed up with a hurt expression. Obviously, she wasn't used to having questions fired at her point blank. "To implore your *help,* of course," replied Nadine. "Delaine was *positive* you'd want to pinch-hit for Lillian Lee. I mean, you two *are* best friends."

Are Delaine and I best friends? wondered Theodosia. *Hmm, the jury might still be out on that one. And after sending her sister in on this little reconnaissance caper, the jury might be out for quite some time.*

"Delaine wants me to model an outfit in tomorrow's show," said Theodosia. It was a statement, not a question.

"Yes," gasped Nadine, as though her request had been a deep, dark secret, and the fact that Theodosia now understood it was a huge relief to her.

Model a dress, thought Theodosia. *Finish the tea baskets, package Brooke's oyster pendants, finish up here at the tea shop, huddle with Drayton and tell him about Lawrence March, help decorate tomorrow morning. Got a lot on my plate.*

"Since tomorrow's Fashion Bash *is* a fund-raiser for the Heritage Society, Delaine was positive you'd want first crack at modeling," said Nadine, suddenly smiling brightly.

"All right," said Theodosia reluctantly. "Tell her I'll do it."

"You can tell her yourself," chirped Nadine. "She wants you to stop by the store for a fitting."

"Right now?" sighed Theodosia. *It would have to be now.*

"Oh, absolutely," said Nadine. "In fact, it's quite imperative. You see, that particular outfit hasn't even been *accessorized* yet. I do hope this isn't inconvenient for you."

Theodosia glanced about the tea shop. Only three tables were occupied right now and the customers all seemed settled in with tea and afternoon treats. "Let me run back to the kitchen and check with Haley," Theodosia told Nadine.

"Of course, dear," said Nadine sweetly. "I'll be waiting."

"Go," Haley told her. "It's not that busy. I can handle things."

"Okay," said Theodosia slowly. "But maybe I'll wait until Drayton returns. It feels like I've been leaving you in the lurch all week long."

"Not a problem," said Haley. "Besides, you've had a lot on your mind."

"We all have," said Theodosia.

Gathering up her long white apron, Haley wiped bits of dough from her hands. "Can you believe it's only been a week since we discovered Harper Fisk's body? Since *you* discovered it."

"And we haven't come any closer to figuring out what happened to the poor man," said Theodosia. "I feel awful about that."

"Good heavens, Theo," said Haley. "It's not that you haven't *tried*. It's just that . . . well, maybe this is one mystery that will remain unsolved."

"Not if I can help it," said Theodosia as she pushed her way back through the green velvet curtain into the tea room. She was resolved to keep at this, no matter how long it took.

"Nadine," said Theodosia.

Nadine had abandoned her place at the table and was now standing in front of the counter, admiring Brooke Carter Crocket's silver oyster pendants. Theodosia had laid all the handmade silver pieces out on a piece of indigo blue tissue paper, until she could run next door to Floradora and cadge a bit of moss from Hattie Boatwright.

"These necklaces are *beautiful,*" Nadine crooned. "So whimsical and delightful."

"Yes, aren't they?" said Theodosia in a matter-of-fact voice. "Tell Delaine I'll be over in a half hour, will you?"

Nadine turned sad eyes on Theodosia. "You can't come right *now*?"

I'll be a half hour at the most," said Theodosia, grasping Nadine's elbow and walking her to the door. "And tell your sister I'm delighted to help."

"You're delighted, *really*?" asked Nadine.

"Absolutely," said Theodosia, thrusting a hand behind her back and crossing her fingers.

"I thought she'd *never* leave," moaned Haley. "Plus she's always so snotty to me. Of course she gets this phony attitude of sweetness and honey whenever you show up," complained Haley.

"I know she does," said Theodosia. "Don't worry about it. She's going back to New York on Monday."

"Well, good riddance," fumed Haley. She stared down at the counter. "What the . . . ?" she began

Something wrong?" asked Theodosia.

"Didn't Brooke bring over four pendants?" asked Haley.

"Four. Yes, that's right."

"Well, there's only three here now."

"You're kidding," said Theodosia.

The two women stared at each other.

"She wouldn't dare . . ." began Theodosia.

"I think she *did* dare," said Haley, her eyes widening in alarm.

"Oh no," said Theodosia, pawing through the tissue paper and sliding around the blue and white ceramic jars that sat atop the counter. But Haley was right. There were only three pendants on the counter now.

"Can you believe the *nerve* of that woman?" wailed Haley. "I've got half a mind to march over to Delaine's store and rummage through Nadine's purse."

"Unfortunately, the law won't allow you to do that," said Theodosia.

"What if I phone Detective Tidwell and ask him to come over here?" Haley shook her head angrily. "Whew! And I don't even *like* the man!"

"What unfortunate devil is bearing the brunt of your wrath now, Miss Parker?" asked Drayton as he came up behind them. He'd obviously walked down the back alley, then slipped in the back door that led through Theodosia's office.

"We think Delaine's sister just stole one of Brooke's pendants," said Theodosia.

Drayton's lined face crumpled into a look of concern. "Oh no," he said. "Are you quite positive?"

"Nadine was standing right here and now one of the pendants is missing," said Haley. "That's pretty cut and dried in my book."

Drayton glanced at Theodosia. "Theo?" he said, cocking his head at her.

"It doesn't look good," Theodosia admitted.

An hour later, when all the customers had departed and Haley was busy sweeping the floor, Theodosia and Drayton continued to ponder what Drayton had now dubbed *The Case of the Missing Mollusk.*

"Do you really think she made off with it?" asked Drayton.

"Probably," admitted Theodosia. "Or maybe she just decided to borrow it."

"Either way, it's a good thing she's going home soon," said Drayton. "This could lead to some very sticky problems."

"Did you pick up tomorrow's script?" asked Theodosia, eager to change the subject. What with all the excitement, she'd almost forgotten why Drayton went dashing off to the Heritage Society.

"I got the script plus something even better," said Drayton with a twinkle in his gray eyes.

"What's that?" asked Theodosia.

Drayton dug in the pocket of his tan slacks for a moment then, with a flourish, held up an old brass key.

"A key," said Theodosia. "Don't tell me the Heritage Society finally changed their outmoded locks."

"No, no, no," said Drayton. "Timothy's far too parsimonious for that. But I'll tell you something, Theodosia. This isn't just *any* key I have clutched in my hand. This happens to be the key to Harper Fisk's house!"

"No!" said Theodosia, her face suddenly breaking into a delighted grin.

"Yes!" said Drayton, pleased he'd been able to get such a rise out of her.

"How on earth did you get it?" asked Theodosia in a hushed voice.

"You're not going to believe this," said Drayton, "but the circumstances were incredibly simple if not downright fortuitous. Timothy Neville has actually had this key in his possession for several years."

"Whoa. Explain please," urged Theodosia.

"Judas Priest," said Drayton with a crooked smile.

"Drayton!" said Theodosia, lifting an eyebrow.

"No, no," said Drayton. "Harper Fisk had a *cat*. An old orange tabby cat by the name of Judas Priest. The cat's been dead almost a year now, but apparently Harper Fisk had given this house key to Timothy so he could run down the block and feed Judas Priest whenever Harper was out of town."

Theodosia gazed at Drayton in utter disbelief. It was hard to imagine Timothy Neville, the very patrician-looking, somewhat cranky director of the Heritage Society, creeping into someone's home bearing a can of Fancy Feast.

"So how did you get the key from Timothy?" asked Theodosia.

"I happened to mention to Timothy that Harper Fisk's will seemed to be unequivocally locked in a frozen hard-drive."

"And . . ."

"Timothy, good man that he is, fumbled around in his desk for a few minutes and produced said key," finished Drayton.

"Just like that? He didn't have a problem with your entering Harper Fisk's house?"

"Apparently not. Timothy was quite cognizant of Harper's intentions to will some of his antiques to the Heritage Society, so he probably just assumed that same information could be gleaned from papers stored in Harper Fisk's house." Drayton paused. "And since Timothy had already been granted access, I'm sure he viewed that as tacit approval for me to go ahead in."

"And it is, isn't it?" said Theodosia hopefully, almost gleefully.

Drayton rolled his eyes. "Darned if I know, but I'm not about to telephone the Heritage Society's high-priced attorneys and run it by them. It's been my sad experience that attorneys *always* say no."

Theodosia thought about Jory Davis. What would *his* approval rating be if he knew they were seriously considering a look-see inside Harper Fisk's house? As Summer Sullivan's attorney of record, he'd say *absolutely not, stay out.* Let this play out in legal proceedings. So . . . was she going to run this by him? Nope. No way.

"I've got lots to tell you, Drayton," said Theodosia.

"About Lawrence March and the maps in his office and . . ." She stopped and grinned at him crazily. "But first, we better decide if we're really going to use that key tonight."

"Absolutely we are," said Drayton. "We owe it to Harper."

"Good. What time then?"

Drayton considered this. "Let's say nine o'clock. We'll meet in Saint Philips Cemetery by the veep's grave," said Drayton, referring to the grave of John C. Calhoun, former statesman and vice president of the United States. "Then we'll cut through Gateway Walk and pop out on Archdale Street."

Theodosia gave a shiver. Gateway Walk was a tree-shrouded pathway that would take them on a ramble through four different churchyards filled with old marble tombstones. A little creepy, to be sure, but a good way to cut through the neighborhood if you didn't want to be seen.

"You're on," she told him.

CHAPTER 21

*T*ENDRILS OF FOG swirled around giant live oaks and crumbling gravestones as Theodosia hurried along the uneven cobblestone walk. An unexpected pocket of cooler air had pushed down from the north and collided with the warm air that hung over Charleston. The ensuing fog muffled footsteps, formed eerie halos around old-fashioned street lamps, and lent a spooky, soft focus quality to just about everything else.

"Psst, over here," came a whispered voice.

Theodosia relaxed. *Drayton's already here, waiting for me. Bless him.*

"Hey, Drayton," she called. Tension had been building up inside her, and Theodosia was surprised at how relieved she was to hear the sound of his voice.

"Shhh." Drayton emerged from behind the Calhoun monument with a finger to his mouth. "There are still a few people around," he told her.

"On Gateway Walk?" she asked.

He nodded. "I think the Library Society must be holding some sort of event tonight."

They strode briskly down the walk together, past the handsome old stone building of the Charleston Library Society, where light spilled out from stained glass windows, across King Street, and once again, through a fog-shrouded graveyard, this one snugging up against Saint John's Church.

Turning down Archdale, it was only a matter of minutes before they found themselves on Lenwood, right behind Marianne Petigru's enormous house.

Drayton dug in his pocket for the key as Theodosia gazed at the slightly Gothic-looking carriage house that Harper Fisk had called home for the past two decades. Standing on the front stoop, she noted that the dark, arched windows and slightly peaked roof of the two-story stone structure looked more forboding than welcoming.

"Creepy," mused Theodosia. "The place looks like a Hansel and Gretel cottage."

"It *does* look spooky," admitted Drayton. He peered sharply at Theodosia. "Tell me you're not nervous."

"Not a bit," she said, mustering every ounce of bravado. "How about you?"

Drayton's hands trembled as he pulled open the screen door and inserted the key in the lock. "Steady as a rock," he told her, then paused just before he turned the key. "You know, one of us has to go in and poke around, and one of us should probably stay outside and keep watch."

Theodosia thought about this. Drayton had a good point. "You go in then, and I'll stay out here," Theodosia offered, although she would have given her eye teeth to go in and snoop around.

"You're sure?" asked Drayton.

Theodosia nodded. "Besides, Timothy gave the key to you. You're the one who's got permission. Sort of."

"Sort of," echoed Drayton as he finally turned the key in the lock. He had to struggle with it a moment and almost force the lock open. "Sticks," he told her.

Then the door swung open on creaking hinges and darkness yawned.

Theodosia handed Drayton her flashlight, a little Maglite she kept in case of power outages. "Take this. And try to turn on as few lights as possible. We don't want to alert the neighbors." She thought of Marianne Petigru in the big house out front. It wouldn't do to have her thinking they were breaking and entering.

"Right," said Drayton as he slipped inside the carriage house and pushed the door closed behind him.

Standing on the front porch in the dark, keeping a look-out, suddenly felt awkward to Theodosia. *This looks a little too suspicious. Somebody who's gung ho about participating in their neighborhood watch group might spot me and report me in a heartbeat.*

Stepping off the porch, Theodosia followed an over-grown brick path around toward the rear of Harper Fisk's carriage house. Even in the darkness, she could see heroic stands of oleander and hydrangea, as well as clumps of Japanese maple and red banana.

Pretty. Reminds me a little bit of Gordon Sargent's patio garden.

Theodosia sighed as she ran a hand along the rough back of an ornate wrought iron bench nestled in a grove of dog-wood. Earlier today, she'd gone over to Cotton Duck for her last-minute fitting for tomorrow's fashion show. After much fussing and fidgeting, Delaine had finally settled on a pink jersey sundress with grosgrain ribbon details. The dress had looked sleek and polished when she tried it on, and even though the color wasn't lavender per se, Delaine had admitted that the color was at least in the *family*.

A waning moon peeked out from between clouds, and silver light trickled down to illuminate even more of Harper Fisk's side garden. English daisies and loquat looked darkly gilded in the low light, and Theodosia wondered what would happen to them. Who would tend this garden now that Harper Fisk was no more?

A sudden muffled *thunk* from deep inside the house startled her.

"What the . . . ?"

Before Theodosia could react to the sound, there was a sharp crack as the screen door flew open and banged against the front of the house. Then came the sound of leather slapping the pavement. Someone was running away. Running hard.

Drayton? The notion puzzled her for a split second.

No way. Can't be Drayton. Even if something scared him to death, he'd never just cut and run and leave me here by my lonesome.

Then who?

Fear for Drayton's safety made Theodosia bold as she sprinted back down the path toward the front door. Leaping up onto the stoop, she was startled to find the front door standing open. Hesitantly, Theodosia stumbled into the dark mustiness of Harper Fisk's house, calling Drayton's name loudly.

Theodosia padded through a small parlor where the dark outlines of furniture loomed large, started into the second room of the railroad-style house. A soft groan brought her up short. As her eyes quickly grew accustomed to the darkness,

Theodosia saw that Drayton was sitting on the floor directly in front of her, clutching his head with both hands.

She dropped swiftly to her knees. "Drayton! Are you all right? What happened?" Fighting to keep panic and hysteria from her voice, Theodosia feared that Drayton might be seriously injured.

Drayton's hands continued to rub slowly at the back of his head. "My head," he moaned. "Some idiot jumped me from behind and split my poor head open."

"Oh Drayton, let me see!" Theodosia cried.

She sprang to her feet, fumbled along a wall, searching for a light switch. She sent two small oil paintings crashing to the floor before she found one.

As warm, yellow light flooded the room, Theodosia knelt down to take a careful look at Drayton's head. Blood matted his hair, but she could see immediately that he'd been fortunate. No real damage had been done. Drayton had been lucky, if you could call it that, in that he'd received a glancing blow from his assailant rather than a direct hit. His scalp wound was more abrasion than cut. Nothing deep, certainly no split tissue that would require staples or stitches.

"How bad?" asked Drayton.

"Not bad at all," said Theodosia, exhaling slowly. "A cut is all."

Drayton grimaced at her touch. "I always knew this hard head would serve me well someday." There was a faint tinge of humor in his voice.

"I want to get a towel, though," said Theodosia. "Wipe away some of this blood and make absolutely sure. Head wounds can be deceptive."

"You'll get no argument from me," croaked Drayton.

Figuring *what the heck* about remaining low-profile, Theodosia turned on lights as she went, finally making her way through a small dining room that seemed to function more as a study, and into Harper Fisk's small, neat kitchen. She pulled open a number of drawers before she located a stack of clean, white kitchen towels. Then, turning on the tap, she ran a towel under cold water.

Drayton had pulled himself into a chair by the time she returned. He held her broken flashlight in his hand.

"Do you feel dizzy?" Theodosia asked, hovering over him and daubing gently at his cut head.

"No, just stupid," replied Drayton. "I feel like the proverbial fly who waltzed blissfully into the spider's web."

"Hey," argued Theodosia, "we had no idea someone else would be sneaking around inside." It was true. The notion had never occurred to her. Now, however, as she stood next to Drayton watching the white terry cloth towel slowly turn a brilliant red, she marveled at how blithely unprepared they'd been. She should have figured that if she and Drayton were willing to practically *break in* in order to search the premises, maybe someone else, someone fairly unsavory (like Harper Fisk's murderer?), might *also* come prowling around as well.

Suddenly aware of how vulnerable they both still were, Theodosia declared, "We've got to get out of here. Immediately." It was entirely possible that their nasty intruder might come back, or a neighbor who overheard the disturbance might have phoned the police. Theodosia really didn't want to deal with either scenario.

"I agree," said Drayton. He put his hands on the arms of the chair, started to push himself up.

"Think you can walk?" asked Theodosia. Leaning forward, she stretched an arm around Drayton's waist and helped pull him slowly to his feet.

"I'm good, I'm good," protested Drayton as he hobbled

toward the front door. "You go back and turn off all the lights."

"Right," said Theodosia. She flew back into the kitchen, checked to make sure everything was in place, and flipped off the light. The bloodied towel would go home with them.

Passing back through the dining room with its walls lined with bookcases, Theodosia couldn't help but notice how much Harper Fisk's home resembled Drayton's home. Harper Fisk had been a book lover, too. And a bit of a scholar. He had used his dining room table as an extension of his office. A case in point, the battered old dining table was still littered with open books that depicted sketches of various Civil War uniforms. A notebook with blue-lined pages was filled with cramped handwriting. There were even a few battlefield relics scattered about. Two Civil War medals, their yellow ribbons long since disintegrated. A rusty metal piece from an old bayonet. A handful of old uniform buttons.

Fascinated, Theodosia reached down and picked up one of the buttons. Holding it to the light, she saw it had a dirty, faded gilt finish with a barely legible scroll work design. Theodosia studied the button for a moment then turned it over. On its back were engraved the words *Scovill Mfg. Co.*

One hundred and thirty years had passed since the Civil War ended inside a small farmhouse at Appomattox, Virginia. But fascination still burned brightly for this chapter of American history that had touched so many lives.

"Theodosia, are you coming?" Drayton's voice, though still sounding shaken, was nevertheless insistent.

"Be there in a second," she called back. Hesitating for a moment, Theodosia slid the button into the side pocket of her khaki slacks. She wasn't *stealing* it, she just wanted a little more time to study it. When she was finished, she's simply slip it back with the other buttons, whether the collection ended up at the Heritage Society, with Summer Sullivan, or with one of the members of the English Breakfast Club.

As Theodosia flipped off the dining room's overhead chandelier, she wondered fleetingly if the three factions would end up in a heated dispute.

Or maybe that's going to depend on just how much Harper Fisk's treasures are worth.

Theodosia slid a cup of steaming tea in front of Drayton. "You really deserve this," she told him.

He inhaled deeply, then smiled. "It's Sree Sibbari, isn't it?"

Theodosia nodded. "Anybody who got clunked on the head as hard as you did deserves a cup of sixty-dollar-a-pound tea."

Indeed, tea from the Sree Sibbari estate in India was somewhat costly. But this big-leafed Assam tea yielded an aroma that was full-bodied and rich, yet uniquely fruity and pungent. In other words, worth every penny.

While Theodosia had been hustling about in her kitchen, brewing tea and defrosting a plate of lemon bars, she'd been recounting her visit to March Forth this morning and, specifically, what she'd observed in Lawrence March's office.

Drayton hadn't been shocked, but he hadn't been pleased either. Now, as they both sipped tea and munched lemon bars, their conversation seemed to migrate toward a kind of unofficial review of their list of suspects.

"You know," said Drayton, brushing a spate of crumbs from his upper lip, "it seems to me Summer Sullivan has the most to gain from all of this."

"That's what I've been thinking, too," said Theodosia. She genuinely wanted to like Summer and felt a kinship for her as a fellow small-business owner. Yet, she was increasingly unsure of the girl's veracity.

"On the other hand," said Drayton, "Lawrence March could be playing us like a fish. *Who me? I'm not a bit interested in what happens. I don't give a darn about Harper's will.*" Drayton looked grim. "You know, Lawrence March *is* an amateur actor in Charleston's Little Theater."

"I still don't believe Harper was killed because of what he was going to leave behind," said Theodosia. "I think he was killed because he *knew* something. Or he'd *found* something."

"Back to the treasure theory?" said Drayton.

"Yes," said Theodosia. "Which is why I think we need to scrutinize everyone regarding motive."

"What was Buddy Clark's motive?" asked Drayton.

"Money," said Theodosia immediately. "The old guy is broke. He tried to sell some of his Japanese art and now he's trying to rezone his house so it can be turned into a B and B."

"You don't think old Buddy was simply bit with the innkeeping bug?" asked Drayton with a slight smile.

"No, I don't," said Theodosia. "It's just too hard to launch a business like that at his age."

"I'll have you know Buddy Clark is barely five years older than I am," huffed Drayton. Even though he was still feeling subdued, he managed to muster a modicum of indignation.

"You're different," said Theodosia, patting Drayton's hand gently. "You're . . . I don't know . . . you've got a young mind and a flexible attitude."

"Thank you kindly for your sublime vote of confidence," remarked Drayton. "I shall be sure to send a missive to that effect to the good folks at AARP."

Theodosia poured out a little more tea for the two of them. "Getting back to our list," she said, "Professor Gibbon figures prominently, as well."

"Because he's trying to get a grant," said Drayton.

"Because he's trying to get a grant for an underwater *excavation*," said Theodosia. "And the way his grant application is worded, it would appear he's already *discovered* what it is he wants to excavate."

"Could be unrelated to anything Harper Fisk discovered. If he ever really found something in the first place," said Drayton.

"Could be," said Theodosia, but she didn't sound convinced. "Plus Professor Gibbon claims to have found that copy of Harper Fisk's will."

"Maybe it's the genuine article," said Drayton. "Harper makes out his will, passes along a copy to Professor Gibbon to witness and sign, then Gibbon forgets all about it."

"Do people really do that?" asked Theodosia. "Just forget about something like that?"

"I do," replied Drayton. "I have trouble remembering what I ate for breakfast last Tuesday," he said, yawning loudly. "Oh, excuse *me!*" he apologized.

"No," said Theodosia, "I'm the one who should be apologizing. I've been rattling on about suspects and motives when you should be home in bed popping Tylenol gel caps and relaxing with an ice pack on your poor noggin." She stood up. "Come on, Drayton, I'll drive you home."

Drayton clambered to his feet, somewhat unsteadily. "It's only a few blocks," he mumbled. "I'm sure I can manage—"

Drayton cut short his sentence as the telephone rang.

"It's no trouble," said Theodosia as she reached for the kitchen wall phone. "Hello?" she said into the receiver.

Listening for a few minutes, Theodosia nodded, then hung up the phone.

"That was Earl Jeffries at Renaissance Computer," she told Drayton. "He apologized about calling so late, but said he's got the hard drive working again."

"You mean Harper Fisk's computer?" asked Drayton.

"Earl figured out the glitch then backed everything up on a Syquest. We can take a look at it first thing Monday."

"So it doesn't matter that we didn't turn up a copy of Harper's will tonight," said Drayton, giving Theodosia a downcast look. "I got smacked on the head for nothing."

Theodosia thought about this for a moment. "Actually, I think we found out quite a lot tonight." She gazed at Drayton, whose eyelids were definitely drooping. "But we can hash all that out tomorrow. Right now, we're going to get you home."

He sighed. "If you insist."

"I do," said Theodosia. "And Drayton . . ." He'd already started for the door. Now he hesitated and turned back toward her. "You do *not* have to stand up and play master of ceremonies at Fashion Bash tomorrow. I'm certain Delaine can handle it herself. Or worst-case scenario, I'll be your stand-in."

"She'll be awfully disappointed if I don't show up . . ."

"Wait and see how you feel," advised Theodosia. "You never know."

"You'd really pinch-hit if I couldn't make it?" he asked hopefully.

Theodosia's eyes were filled with warmth. "In a heartbeat."

*   *   *

About to climb into bed, Theodosia was haphazardly folding her T-shirt and slacks when a tiny *ping* sounded against the wooden floor.

She looked down and squinted. The button she'd taken from the dining room table at Harper Fisk's house had fallen out of her pocket and gone spinning across the carpet onto the wooden floor.

Theodosia snatched it up, then studied it for a few seconds.

Is this little thing worth anything? Seems like Civil War relics, no matter how small, are still awfully popular. Hmm, only one way to find out.

It was amazing how many Internet sites existed that dealt in Civil War relics. There was the Blue and the Gray Trader, Bull Run Relics & Remains, Colonel McCullin's War Relics, and perhaps fifty more sites, all of them interested in the business of buying and selling tiny pieces of history.

Theodosia clicked on Colonel McCullins War Relics and was amazed at the depth and breadth of offerings. There were pistols, rifles, bayonets, medals, minnie balls, paper documents, coins, uniforms, and wouldn't you know it, buttons for sale.

Buttons. Here they are. Okay, let's check this puppy out.

There were more varieties of buttons than Theodosia had ever thought possible. Union and Confederate. Silver, pewter, and brass. Buttons for officers' uniforms, buttons for enlisted men. Theodosia had to skim down a long chart before she finally found a photo that corresponded to the uniform button she'd picked up at Harper Fisk's.

Touching an index finger to the screen, she followed the chart across. Yes, this was the correct button. Scovill Mfg. Co, made of tin with a gilt wash, asking price was . . . *oh, my goodness! Four hundred dollars?*

She shook her head. *Can't be. That must say forty dollars, right?*

Wrong. The asking price was clearly listed at four hundred dollars.

And that's just for one Civil War uniform button. Imagine stumbling across an entire cache of them! Or better yet, real Civil War–era gold coins!

Undiscovered treasure was still out there, that was for sure. Every few months there was an article in a South Carolina or Georgia or Virginia newspaper that told how some good old boy went out exploring with a metal detector and located a nice chunk of bayonet or a handful of coins.

Is this why Harper Fisk was killed? Because the old fellow really had stumbled upon Civil War treasure? Or at least Civil War valuables?

Deep in her heart Theodosia felt that was exactly what happened. But the problem still remained . . . how to find Harper Fisk's killer.

CHAPTER 22

WHITE LINEN TABLECLOTHS crisscrossed with lavender ribbons fluttered in the gentle morning breeze. Tiny white lights strung from sun-dappled palmetto trees glowed festively overhead. Centerpiece topiary trees of purple lavender and white tea roses decorated each table. And large Oriental rugs in cinnamon and blue tones had been laid down the center aisle between tables to impart an elegant touch and form a genteel catwalk for the Fashion Bash models.

Theodosia and Haley arrived at Gordon Sargent's Garden Gate Restaurant around 9:30 A.M., laden with tea baskets for the silent auction and bearing giant trays heaped with lavender-infused goodies. Within seconds, Delaine pounced on the two women like a hungry duck scrabbling for beetles.

"Did you bring the lavender scones?" Delaine demanded. "And what about the lavender cookies?"

"It was a stretch, but everything came out of the oven just this morning," said Haley. Flipping back one corner of a yellow-checked tea towel, she revealed a large basket filled with scones. Plump and golden, they nestled together enticingly, exuding a faint aroma of lavender with almond undertones.

"Fabulous," declared Delaine. Gussied up in a white halter dress with a plunging neckline and lace skirt, she had a manic, bright-eyed quality about her. Theodosia decided that Delaine was nervous and on edge, and seemed to be holding her breath, as if awaiting some sort of catastrophe.

How could there be another catastrophe after last night? Theodosia wondered. Her heart still weighed heavy for Drayton, who showed up twenty minutes later looking tired and subdued and sporting a white bandage at the back of his head, a nasty reminder of their misadventure at Harper Fisk's house.

"Hey," said Haley as she busily arranged tea baskets on one of the side tables. "What's with the bandage, Drayton?"

"Oh," said Drayton, self-consciously putting a hand to his head. "Silly me. It seems I had an unfortunate hit-and-run with a closet door."

Haley shook her head. "Ye gads, what a klutz."

"Haley!" said Theodosia, somewhat horrified by the young woman's comment and blasé attitude. She was sure that if Haley knew the true circumstances concerning Drayton's injury, she'd be offering sympathy instead of criticism.

But Drayton, ever the good-natured soul, took matters into his own hands. "That's right, Haley," he called from across the patio, "let's just call Drayton a piñata and give him a good bash, shall we? Really have at it."

"Hey, you're the one who smacked into the closet door, not me," said Haley. "And you're the . . ." She stopped midsentence as Theodosia put a hand on her shoulder.

"Let it go," said Theodosia in a low voice.

Haley whirled to face her. There was something in the *tone* of Theodosia's voice that stopped her short. "I was just kidding," Haley explained, her face suddenly crumpling with worry that she'd gone too far.

"I know you were," said Theodosia gently. *I'll tell Haley what happened last night, but just not right now. Too many folks milling about.*

"Shouldn't you be thinking about changing into your outfit pretty soon?" asked Theodosia. "Remember, you've still got to submit yourself to Delaine's mandatory hair and makeup routine." She peeked at her watch. "And the fashion show's scheduled to begin in about forty-five minutes."

In fact, a few early-bird guests had already arrived and were casting interested glances toward the auction tables that held the tea baskets, silver oyster pendants, and Popple Hill gift certificates.

"Oh, gosh yes," said Haley. "But what about you, Theodosia? You're in the show, too."

"I'll finish arranging things for the silent auction, then I'll be in later," Theodosia told her. Gordon Sargent had generously given up his outer office, private office, and private bathroom for use as changing rooms and hair and makeup salons. Drayton had dubbed that area the "eye of the hurricane" and right now it overflowed with racks of clothes and teemed with a bevy of highly excited amateur models, as well as two frantic hairdressers and a makeup artist.

"Theodosia!" called Gordon Sargent from across the patio. "I've got the rest of the items for your silent auction." He staggered toward her carrying a huge plastic basket piled high with what appeared to be dried flowers, reeds, and driftwood arrangements.

"These must be the beach harvest arrangements donated

by Celerie Stuart," said Theodosia. She'd heard so much about them, now she was anxious to get a good look at them.

Gordon set the basket down carefully, mindful of dried branches and pieces of driftwood that arced out in artful sweeps. "Celerie dropped these off early this morning," he said. "Sorry, but I just now remembered them. I've been so busy seeing to the food."

"No apology necessary," said Theodosia, smiling at him. "In fact, you've positively outdone yourself. The patio looks gorgeous and you've been more than generous in working with us on the menu."

Gordon Sargent grinned back at her. "You mean trying to appease Delaine on the menu," he said. "Do you know I had to talk her out of lavender leek soup and lavender-mustard crusted tenderloins? We would have been way over budget. To say nothing of being over-lavendered."

"I know Delaine hasn't been easy," offered Theodosia. "But she's got a lot on her mind." In fact, Theodosia figured that Delaine was extra-hyper today because she'd brought Nadine along. Haley had confided earlier that Delaine was still letting her sister *model,* for goodness' sake.

"Let's see," said Gordon, "in the last twenty-four hours I've had to locate lavender candles, install a bamboo arch complete with grape vines, and rustle up five more sets of wrought iron tables and chairs."

"Gee," said Theodosia, "and the only last-minute chore we had to do was bake lavender scones and cookies. Oh, and Drayton had to whip up his lavender and Earl Grey summer blend for the iced tea."

"Which has been properly brewed and is right now chilling," said Gordon. He wangled a finger in Theodosia's face. "I think you got off easy."

"Say now," said Drayton, coming up behind them. "That samovar over there is an awfully handsome piece."

The three of them turned to look at the large silver samovar that rested on a serving cart draped with a white linen tablecloth. Gordon had positioned the samovar against the far wall of the patio, where it would serve as a focal point, but still be out of the way.

Gordon smiled, pleased that Theodosia and Drayton were so appreciative of his efforts. "Thank you, Drayton. Coming from a fellow restaurateur, that means a lot to me."

"Oh, Drayton!" called Delaine. She suddenly appeared in the doorway of Gordon's office looking somewhat perplexed. "There seem to be some impromptu *changes* in the fashion show script."

"Exit, stage left," Gordon Sargent muttered under his breath, and was gone in a flash. Probably, Theodosia decided, Gordon was heading for the kitchen, where Delaine wasn't likely to follow.

"Did *you* make these unauthorized changes?" Delaine asked as she thrust the pages of the script at Drayton and tapped a toe, waiting for an answer.

"Since I authored these scant few changes, I'd say they *were* authorized," said Drayton, trying his best to be playful.

Already in a state of excitation, Delaine was not amused.

"It's extremely important that descriptions of the various outfits are read *verbatim*," Delaine told him. "Women, especially fashion-focused women, are very particular about *details*."

"Don't you think most people are coming to have a good time?" asked Theodosia. "The food, the fashion, the silent auction, and being with friends are all important elements, like ingredients in a recipe. But it's the overall feeling of fun and *enjoyment* for the event that people will take away with them."

Delaine stared at Theodosia for a few seconds. "As you wish," she said, fanning herself with a hanky. "Right now I'm far too overwhelmed with last-minute details to put up any kind of argument against the two of you."

"Then stop being overwhelmed," urged Theodosia. "Decide *not* to sweat the small stuff and just try to have fun. Savor the day, moment by moment. After all, it was *your* hard work that pulled this all together."

"People will look back at Fashion Bash with *very* fond memories," said Drayton. "I know your fashion shows are always crowd pleasers."

Delaine nodded imperceptibly.

"And I took a peak at some of the tea sandwiches Gordon's staff has prepared," continued Drayton. "They're utterly scrumptious. The Indigo Tea Shop couldn't have done better."

"Really?" asked Delaine, still looking nervous and hungering for reassurance.

"Truly," said Theodosia. "Please relax, Delaine. Everything's going to come off without a hitch."

"Except, perhaps, for your assistant over there," noted Drayton. He'd been watching Janine, who seemed to be running around like a chicken with its head cut off.

"Delaine, we *really* need you in the fitting room!" pleaded Janine, whose face was glowing so red she looked like she was ready to blow a gasket.

"Is there a *problema*?" asked Delaine innocently.

"Kitty Carsdale *refuses* to wear pajama pants . . . she claims they make her hips look enormous . . . we can't seem to find even *one* straw handbag, and Carol Britton just flew back from Tokyo and her feet are so swollen her shoes won't fit," said Janine. "Oh, and quite a few of our models are vehemently objecting to the lipstick color," added Janine.

"Did you explain that this is a *lavender* and lace–themed luncheon?" asked Delaine.

Janine tugged at Delaine's arm. "Of course I did. But perhaps *you* could reemphasize that point?"

"All right," sighed Delaine. "Ta," she said, waving nervously to Theodosia and Drayton.

Relieved that the issue of the script changes had been unceremoniously dropped, Drayton waved back at her. "Ta."

Drayton was rehearsing his narration and Theodosia had almost finished laying out the beach harvest arrangements when Haley suddenly came charging out of the dressing area, looking ferociously unhappy and tugging wildly at her dress.

"Look at this, Theo!" wailed Haley. "My dress doesn't fit!"

"What's wrong?" asked Theodosia, even though Haley looked quite adorable in her form-fitting white chiffon dress with its tiny ruffled bodice.

"It just seems so much *tighter* than when I had my fitting at Cotton Duck!" complained Haley. "I can barely breathe. Do you think I gained *weight*?"

"No I don't," said Theodosia, "but if you're really unhappy, let's go see if there's something else you can wear." Taking Haley's arm, Theodosia guided her back to the makeshift fitting room.

"Delaine," said Theodosia, stepping inside to find dozens of models in various stages of dress and a general air of bedlam. "Is there an alternate outfit Haley can wear? She thinks the fit is all wrong."

"It's way too tight," added Haley unhappily.

Delaine smiled brightly. "That's because the dress *is* tighter."

"What?" said Haley, looking frantically between Theodosia and Delaine.

"That's what a fitting is all about," Delaine explained in a none-too-tactful manner. "Making a garment *fit*. I had Janine take in the bodice and waist a notch." Delaine reached out and fussed with the scoop-neck bodice of Haley's dress. "You don't want to just *slop* down the runway, do you dear?"

"But I can't *breathe*," complained Haley.

"Shush," said Delaine. "This dress is a *privilege* to wear. Plus it's *haute couture*, so it's *supposed* to feel tight and uncomfortable. Now here are your matching sandals, Haley. Kindly slip out of those old shoes and slide into these." Delaine continued to fuss with the front of Haley's dress, pulling it down an extra inch as Haley struggled into the shoes Delaine had given her. "And please try to smile," Delaine told her. "Modeling is supposed to look *effortless*."

With a wan smile pasted across her face, Haley teetered a couple steps in her strappy high-heeled sandals.

"No, no, no," said Delaine. A tiny frown line had insinuated itself between her delicately waxed brows. Obviously these *amateur* models were severely testing her patience.

"You don't want to *gawk* down the runway all pigeon-toed," Delaine admonished her. "You must *glide*. Imagine yourself a ballerina, a *première danseuse* executing an elegant *jeté*."

"I think it's all a bunch of *crappé*," Haley confided to Theodosia once Delaine was out of earshot. "This dress is way too frilly and frou-frou for me. Just not my persona."

Theodosia thought Haley looked very polished and grown-up in the dress, but she also knew Haley preferred wearing comfortable little stretchy T-shirts paired with cropped pants or long, flowing skirts. The fact that Haley's long, straight hair had also been lacquered into an upswept, updated bullet-shaped beehive by Mr. Delacroix of Haute Hair Creations also didn't help matters.

Soft jazz flooded the courtyard and Theodosia marveled at what a lovely day it had turned out to be. The combination of sunshine and overhead leafed-out trees created a lovely dappled lighting effect, the humidity had somehow (glory be!) dissipated, and palmettos waved their lacy fronds in the gentle breeze. Over by a brick wall smothered with a tangle of vines bearing red and purple grapes, bees buzzed happily. And guests had been arriving in droves.

"Do you need any help?"

Theodosia, who'd just finished tying tiny silver spoons to the tea baskets, whirled about to see who'd just spoken to her.

A petite woman, dressed in blindingly white T-shirt, slacks, and sandals, and sporting a mass of blond curls, smiled winningly at her. "I'm Celerie Stuart," said the woman, sticking out her hand in a friendly, forthright gesture.

Theodosia grasped Celerie's hand. "Yes, of course. Please tell me my display has done justice to your marvelous beach harvest creations." She fingered a swag made from bittersweet, cattails, and yarrow, arranged over a knot of dried seaweed. Slender branches of driftwood curled upward, and a gauzy lavender ribbon was tied at the bottom.

Suddenly, Celerie Stuart's beach harvest swags and wreaths reminded Theodosia of the day they'd found Harper Fisk's boat marooned on the beach at Sullivan's Island. And triggered within her feelings of both sadness and helplessness. She'd promised Drayton they'd get to the bottom of Harper Fisk's death and they hadn't even come close. All they'd really done was uncover clue after useless clue that didn't seem to point to anything conclusive. *It's got to be someone who went out with Harper Fisk in that little boat,* Theodosia decided, in what she hoped was either genuine intuition or a flash of psychic insight.

Theodosia had to force herself back to the here and now. "Your pieces are lovely," she told Celerie. *Maybe when I've got some time, I could incorporate some of these design ideas into displays for my T-Bath products.*

"Oh, they're the simplest little things to pull together," said Celerie Stuart, as if she was reading Theodosia's mind. "Just come beach walking with me some morning and I'll give you a few pointers. You have to get there early, though, almost before the sun comes up. That's when all the good stuff drifts in on the tide."

"I'd like that," said Theodosia.

"You know who's a confirmed beach walker?" said Celerie. "Our genial host over there."

Theodosia stared across the patio where models were mingling with guests and Gordon Sargent chatted animatedly with two women who were wearing large straw hats bedecked with colorful flowers. "Gordon Sargent?" said Theodosia. "Really?"

"At least I've seen him wandering Folly Beach a few times," said Celerie.

And I thought Gordon Sargent said he worked fourteen-hour days. Oh well . . .

"Ladies! Ladies! May I *please* have your attention?" The jazz ended abruptly as Drayton's amplified voice rang out across the courtyard. "If you'll all take your places, please." There was a buzz of excitement and a scraping of metal chairs against bricks as the guests rushed to sit down. "And yes," Drayton continued, "there are place cards for everyone. If someone needs help, one of our volunteers will quickly be around to assist."

And then, after Drayton's warm welcome and a short preamble, the show was off and running.

Ba-dum, ba-dum.

The insistent, hard-edged beat of rock music throbbed loudly throughout the courtyard. And like peacocks strutting their finery, the models began their stilted parade down the runway.

Ba-dum, ba-dum.

Drayton's well-modulated voice began a gentle, running patter. After introducing each model, he then described her outfit in careful detail. Waiters wearing white jackets and black slacks slipped in among the tables, pouring both hot tea and iced tea and serving the lavender-infused scones, Devonshire cream, and DuBose Bees honey.

Watching from the sidelines, Theodosia had to admit it: Delaine's recruits looked good. Darned good.

Angie Congdon of the Featherbed House, looking extremely *haute couture* in an off-the-shoulder ruffled blouse and matching skirt, did a very credible strut, then executed a perfect end-of-runway pause and turn. A sort of fashion show bump-and-grind.

Two more models fluttered down the runway, looking all the world like butterflies in their frothy outfits. Then it was Haley's turn.

Managing to look both fresh-faced and sophisticated, Haley in her chiffon dress and high-heeled sandals elicited an appreciative round of applause from the audience. And when Haley paused and twirled at the end of the carpet, she even managed to look a trifle bored and scowly—à la a real

New York model. Probably due to her enforced corsetry, Theodosia figured.

Knowing her turn would be coming up in another ten minutes or so, Theodosia decided it was high time she ducked into the changing room and got dressed.

I must be the last one to get ready, she thought guiltily as she hustled into Gordon's suite of offices, which were by now completely deserted. *Even the hair and makeup people are outside watching the show.*

Theodosia shucked out of her sundress and quickly pulled on the lavender shantung silk tank top and slacks she'd been fitted for yesterday afternoon. Luckily, the beleaguered Janine hadn't found time to take *her* outfit in. It still offered breathing room.

Checking herself in the temporary three-way mirror that had been set up in the outside office, Theodosia fluffed up her already humidity-enhanced hair, and grabbed a neutral-colored lipstick. Applying it quickly, she also daubed a little powder across her face as a final touch-up.

There. That'll have to do. Don't want to look like too much of a poser.

Glancing at a copy of the models' lineup that was posted on the wall, Theodosia noted that her entrance would come at about the halfway point.

Wow, even the models that come after me are already dressed, coifed, and made up, and are outside watching the show from the sidelines. Well, if you can't beat 'em, join 'em . . .

Stepping out of the makeshift dressing room, Theodosia hesitated as she passed in front of a Chinese screen that had been set up just outside the door to Gordon Sargent's office. An intense, whispered conversation was taking place on the other side of that screen. An *angry* conversation.

What's going on? A fight?

Yes. And she recognized the voices. *Delaine and Nadine!*
Theodosia thought with a start. Hesitantly, she peered
around the corner.

Grasping her sister roughly by the elbow, Delaine spoke
to her in an angry hiss: "I can't believe you'd do this to
me . . . today of all days!"

Theodosia couldn't quite make out all of Delaine's
words. But it was obvious from the look on Delaine's face
that she was furious with Nadine.

Theodosia stood there uncomfortably for a few seconds,
wondering what to do. Then, when she saw tears streaming
down Delaine's face, her curiosity and sympathetic nature
got the best of her.

"Delaine, are you okay?" Theodosia asked, not wanting
to butt in but feeling she had to do *something.*

Startled, Delaine whirled to face Theodosia. "I am definitely *not* okay," she whispered. "Do you know about my
sister's nasty little secret?" she asked, swallowing hard and
suddenly mustering her full anger. "She *steals* things! She's
a *kleptomaniac.*"

"Delaine . . ." began Theodosia, worried now that Delaine's voice might inadvertently carry to the far side of the
patio where the Fashion Bash audience, all two hundred of
them, were watching the show. "This probably isn't the time
or . . ."

But Delaine wasn't about to be deterred. "My *sister* has
a rather serious problem she refuses to *admit* to." Delaine
was wound up now. Her eyes gleamed with fury and her
voice trembled with anger. "Do you know she's even been
arrested? And given court-mandated *counseling*? And she
still won't deal with her problem. To her it's just a lark!"
Tears coursed down cheeks that were flushed pink. "And

now look what she's done!" Delaine suddenly thrust out her hand.

Theodosia peered down at dozens of small sparkling objects clutched in Delaine's hand, what she thought must be a handful of coins. But gazing at them more carefully, she saw they weren't coins at all. They were buttons.

Oh, my goodness. They're Civil War uniform buttons. Just like the ones that were sitting on Harper Fisk's dining room table. Same as the ones I saw selling for three and four hundred dollars apiece on the Internet last night. Only these are all spiffed up and shiny.

Theodosia stared at the antique buttons, glistening and glinting in the sunlight. *Where did they . . . ?*

And then the realization struck her. Nadine must have stolen them!

But from where? From Gordon Sargent's office?

Confused, Theodosia stared down at the handful of antique Civil War uniform buttons. *So Gordon Sargent is also a collector.*

As if reading her mind, Delaine hissed: "My sister *stole* these from Gordon's office! Can you believe it?"

Theodosia turned to stare at Nadine. *It's all true. Nadine is a kleptomaniac.*

Nadine rolled her eyes and pulled her mouth into a harsh snarl. "Oh *please*. Once again my dear sister chooses to make mountains out of molehills. I was merely *looking* at the silly things. They're a mildly interesting collectible."

"You see?" an exasperated Delaine said to Theodosia. "She won't even admit her guilt. It's a *sickness* with her."

Delaine plucked at Theodosia's sleeve. "Put them back, will you?" she asked.

Reacting to Delaine's plaintive request, Theodosia cupped her hands and held them out.

"Please," said Delaine, her eyes pleading, "put them *back,* Theo. I'm *begging* you." Delaine poured the buttons into Theodosia's waiting hands.

"Okay," said Theodosia, deciding she'd better make it quick. "But you two get out of here, okay? Go mingle with the rest of the models or something."

Delaine and Nadine scurried off as Theodosia stepped quickly through the outer office and into Gordon Sargent's private office.

The place still looked like a wreck. An empty metal garment rack was pushed up against the wall, shoes and shoe boxes were scattered across the floor, a heap of chiffon scarves was piled on Gordon Sargent's desk.

Okay, thought Theodosia. *The trick is to return these buttons and get the heck out of here.*

She glanced around the office again. No display cases, no leather-bound cache boxes sitting atop his desk.

Where did Nadine snatch these from? Theodosia wondered as she glanced about hurriedly.

Desk. Had to come from one of his desk drawers.

Crossing to his desk quickly, Theodosia slipped into Gordon Sargent's chair and pulled open the top drawer.

A jumble of pens, markers, business cards, and embossed Garden Gate matchbooks met her eyes. *Nope. Try again.*

As she searched, Theodosia was acutely aware of the constant *thump-thump* of the rock music, could envision a bevy of proper Charleston ladies striding boldly down the Oriental carpet runway, swinging their hips in time to the throbbing beat.

The second desk drawer held only Charleston phone directories, the yellow pages and the white pages.

But in the third drawer, the bottom drawer, three black velvet boxes sat atop a black ledger.

Theodosia pulled one of the boxes out, hoping it might be the box that had contained the buttons. Flipping open the lid, she saw it wasn't. In fact, this box held a dozen large silver coins.

Frowning, Theodosia picked up one of the oversized coins and studied it. A Spanish cross and the words *Felize V* were engraved on one side. On the other side was the date sixteen forty-two.

Sixteen forty-two. Twenty-eight years before the original Charleston, or Charles Town Landing, was colonized. These Spanish coins must have come from . . . what? . . . a Spanish galleon?

Theodosia tossed the coin back into the box and snapped the lid shut. It looked like Gordon Sargent must have done a little treasure hunting on his own. The question was . . . was it really on his own?

Theodosia was beginning to get a very bad feeling. A nervous, restless vibe was suddenly telling her that the relationship between Gordon Sargent and his erstwhile girlfriend, Summer Sullivan, might not be based entirely on romantic feelings. In fact, she was suddenly very sure that Gordon Sargent had used Summer to get to Harper Fisk's notes.

Plucking a second black velvet box from Gordon's bottom drawer, Theodosia opened it, found it empty, quickly dumped the brass buttons inside. Placing the box inside the drawer, she was about to close the drawer when the black ledger caught her eye.

Take time to look? Or get the heck out of here and call the police?

Against her better judgment, Theodosia pulled the ledger out and quickly flipped it open. She pawed through several pages until the realization struck that she was staring at handwriting that looked awfully familiar.

Yes, I've seen it before. But where? Oh cripes! Last night at Harper Fisk's house! In a different ledger sitting on his dining room table.

Did Gordon Sargent steal this stuff from Harper Fisk? Worse yet, did he kill the old man for his treasure maps?

"Looking for something?"

Oh no!

Theodosia whirled about to find Gordon Sargent standing a few feet behind her. His dark eyes shone with a hard, sinister light. As he took a step closer, his presence seemed large and threatening. She hadn't realized how powerfully built Gordon Sargent was until just this moment.

"Delaine's sister . . . was, uh, looking at your Civil War buttons," stammered Theodosia.

"Was she now," said Gordon Sargent, his voice edged with flint.

"I was returning them for her," said Theodosia, moving two steps away from Gordon Sargent. She threw him a loopy, goofy grin, the kind of grin she'd seen Delaine manage a thousand times.

Maybe I can bluff my way out.

"No harm done, I hope." Theodosia took another step toward the office door, wondered if she could somehow get a jump on Gordon. Could dash outside and then scream bloody murder for help.

Just five more steps to the door, another dozen to the outside patio.

Theodosia saw the look of intensity on Gordon Sargent's face and decided she better get out of there quick. She bolted left, tried to scramble her way around Gordon Sargent, just like one of the Citadel's champion quarterbacks. Her initial burst of speed carried to the first doorway, where her fingers scrabbled for purchase on the door jam, and she tried to push off hard, to propel herself through to the outer office.

She was fast, but she wasn't fast enough.

One of Gordon Sargent's big hands wound around Theodosia's neck from behind. His other hand closed over her nose and mouth, roughly jerking her back a step and completely cutting off her air supply.

Terrified, Theodosia kicked out at him, aiming for his shins and instep.

"Settle down," he snarled, snapping her head back hard. "Stop kicking!" He moved his hand down a half inch so she could breathe through her nose.

Theodosia sucked in air and the burning in her chest subsided as Gordon pulled her backward toward his desk.

"You going to be a good girl?" he asked. He relaxed his grip just enough so she could give a small nod. "Good," he purred. "Excellent." As his hand came away from her mouth, she snapped it opened, prepared to scream. But her efforts were immediately stifled as he stuffed a silk scarf into her mouth. Just as quickly, another scarf went across her mouth and eyes, securing her gag and cutting off her vision. Then Gordon spun her around like a top and cinched her hands behind her back.

"Now *march*," ordered Gordon Sargent, giving her a rough shove.

Blindly, Theodosia was propelled forward even as Gordon Sargent maintained a viselike grip on her neck and shoulders.

Just where am I supposed to march to? she wondered. *Outside? Is he foolhardy enough to try to pass this off as some kind of practical joke?*

But Gordon Sargent had other plans. As they reached his

outer office, he spun Theodosia to the right and pushed her up against a wall. She sensed him fumbling for something nearby, then felt a *whoosh* of air on her face. An unexpectedly sharp shove in the middle of her back knocked her off balance and sent her flying.

Unable to put her hands in front of her to break her fall, Theodosia stumbled forward, anticipating a nasty crash landing.

Whoosh . . . crack.

She landed. Not on the hard floor but on something that felt like a hard cushion.

What?

She turned her head slowly, felt more than heard something *crackly.*

Got to get his darn blindfold off.

Working her head against the hard, crackly cushion, Theodosia managed to dislodge the scarf that covered her eyes and mouth.

She was in a dim closet, lying on top of something. She stared down at the diamond-shaped label that lay directly beneath her: BOYD BROTHERS PAPER PRODUCTS.

She'd landed on a case of paper towels. Not the nice squishy kind that came in rolls, but the kind that came in packs of five thousand and loaded into wall dispensers.

Lucky break, Theodosia told herself. *I could have landed badly and broken my nose. Or smashed my front teeth.*

Fear prodded her to her feet. Okay, now what?

Gotta get this stupid scarf out of my mouth!

Working her tongue and kneeling down to use the corner of the case of paper towels, Theodosia managed to ease the scarf out of her mouth.

Aaargh! Now that she was able to finally take a deep

breath, Theodosia felt hard, hot anger bubble up from deep inside.

Gordon Sargent, that two-faced jerk! He must have ingratiated himself with Summer Sullivan and found out about Harper's most recent find. Then, when he'd won Summer's confidence, he set out to con Harper Fisk out of his maps. Only whatever trick or con game he'd run obviously hadn't worked. Because he'd ended up killing the old man.

Gordon Sargent killed Harper Fisk!

The reality of that knowledge struck her like a bolt of lightning.

And he'll come back and kill me soon as he gets the chance.

Working her hands frantically, Theodosia fought to release herself from her bonds. She pulled, tugged, then picked at the knots until her wrists were raw and her hands cramped up painfully. No way was she making any progress. Delaine's silk scarves were worse than duct tape, they were like some terrible torture device from the Inquisition.

Theodosia tried yelling. She stood at the door and screamed bloody murder for somebody to come let her out. She screamed for Drayton, for Haley, for *anybody* to free her from this awful closet.

But the music continued to thump away incessantly. Loud music, something by the Rolling Stones or The Who. Music that completely drowned out her frantic cries for help.

Panic was building fast and the intense heat within the tiny closet made her feel miserably disoriented.

Theodosia closed her eyes, trying to slow her respiration and willing herself to relax. But when she opened her eyes, tiny bright specs of light danced dangerously at the outside of her vision.

If I faint, she worried, *I won't be able to defend myself when Gordon comes back. And he will come back.*

That fear propelled her to action. Desperately searching the dim closet, her hands still tied behind her back, Theodosia looked for a weapon, a way out, anything.

And saw . . .

A mop?

What could she possibly do with the long-handled mop that was propped in the corner?

To start with, I'd like to mop the floor with Gordon Sargent, she thought angrily. Turning her back to the mop, Theodosia eased herself in close to it, then grasped it with her hands.

Okay, I'm holding a stupid mop behind my back. Now what?

She fumbled with the mop, hefted it, balanced it tentatively. Tried to get a nice firm grip right in the center of the shaft.

Staring at the walls of her makeshift prison, Theodosia blinked. She thought for a moment, trying to recall something Gordon Sargeant had said. Or maybe it was something she'd seen . . .

Sidestepping away from the closet door, Theodosia approached the opposite wall. *Is this an outside wall?* she wondered. Outside wall, outside chance.

Still holding the mop behind her, she tapped gingerly at the wall.

Thunk thunk. The wall was solid, all right. Solid wood.

But hadn't Gordon Sargeant said something about a . . .

Theodosia repositioned herself and aimed the pointed end of the mop more toward the center of the wall. With as much play as she could get from the scarves that held her tightly, she thumped at the wall a second time.

Thwap. This time she heard a different sound. A softer, almost *hollow* sound.

Theodosia considered this.

Hadn't Gordon Sargeant said something about interior walls being moved? That his old office used to be against this wall? That it used to have a window?

She closed her eyes, trying to recall an image she'd seen. Masses of ivy curling in front of . . . what? Wooden shutters?

Was this where the window had been? And if so, in the hurry and flurry of remodeling, had it just been covered over with something akin to plasterboard?

Plasterboard. That's a lot easier to crack through than solid wood.

Theodosia shook her head like an angry bulldog. Her brows knit together determinedly. This was definitely worth a shot, she decided.

Grasping the mop in both hands, Theodosia fixed in her mind what should be the midway point of the wall. Then she lunged forward.

Driving sideways, knees pumping, arms and shoulders steeled, she tried to put every ounce of body weight behind her effort.

Crack!

A crack like a rifle shot sounded, then immediately on the heels of that sound came shattering glass.

Theodosia was instantly jubilant. She'd rammed the darn mop through what must have been plasterboard and an old window!

And as fully half the shaft of the mop disappeared through the hole, there ensued yet another loud noise! A tremendous *clang*!

Carried by the momentum of the mop bursting through

the wall, Theodosia bumped hard against the wall, stumbled, then fell to her knees. At the same instant, she heard a faint chorus of shrieks and screams rise up, human noise this time. And she wondered, *What on earth did I do?*

Ripping the mop handle back through the hole she'd just created, Theodosia pressed an eye to the newly punched hole and stared out. The fashion show audience had risen en masse to their feet and seemed to be staring down at something.

What the . . . ?

Casting a glance downward, Theodosia was shocked and delighted to see an ocean of iced tea washing across the patio!

Holy smokes, I dumped over the samovar!

Now Theodosia pressed her mouth to the hole. "Drayton!" she screamed frantically, finally managing to make herself heard over the din of the crowd. "Get me out of here! And call the police!"

CHAPTER 23

"*TEA DYEING,*" *CHUCKLED* Drayton. "A novel technique to be sure, and really quite effective."

"Are you insane?" shrilled Delaine. "Do you know the entire fashion show ground to a screeching halt when that iced tea came sloshing across the courtyard like a giant tsunami wave?"

"Do you know that Theodosia was almost killed?" yelled Haley, hopping up and down and forcing herself in Delaine's face.

"Do you people *always* carry on like this?" asked Detective Tidwell, standing off to one side, eyeing an enormous tray of tea sandwiches.

"I'm afraid we do," said Delaine, fluttering her lashes at him.

"By the way, Detective Tidwell," said Drayton, "you don't just show up routinely on all 9-1-1 calls, do you?"

Tidwell offered them a slow smile. "Only when I've had a suspect under observation for quite some time," he replied.

"You've been watching Gordon Sargent?" asked Theodosia.

Well, this was news.

Tidwell nodded even as he pulled his cell phone from his belt, punched in digits with his giant fingers. "Gordon Sargent first popped up on the U.S. Coast Guard's radar screen several months ago. He'd been spotted checking out underwater archaeological sites that were under federal jurisdiction, particularly one near Patriots Point. The *Sea Witch*, a ship that was supposedly one of the blockade-running ships during the Civil War, went down with a load of Confederate gold but had only recently been located. Anyway, the Coast Guard tried to keep an eye on Gordon Sargent when he was on the water, and Charleston PD loaned me out to see if I could come up with anything on the home front. Unfortunately, we didn't realize until too late that Sargent had been getting his "inside" information by pilfering Harper Fisk's maps." Tidwell held the phone to his ear, listened for a moment, nodded. "Go ahead and process him," he growled into the phone. "But do it exactly by the book. We don't want this bird scooting on any technicalities." Tidwell punched a final button to hang up.

"So it was Gordon Sargent all along," said Theodosia. "I wish you'd told us."

"Ah, Miss Browning," said Tidwell, "we weren't *entirely* sure."

"And then when Harper Fisk's body turned up last week?" said Theodosia.

"We still didn't have any hard evidence," said Tidwell. "Sargent played it pretty close to the vest. We also think he trashed your friend's boat in an attempt to shift suspicion to the members of the so-called English Breakfast Club," continued Tidwell. "He knew you were looking at them hard, so he decided to help things along, give you a little push." Tidwell's gaze wandered to Drayton. "Sorry we weren't completely on our toes, Drayton. I know Fisk was a friend."

Drayton just nodded.

"So the English Breakfast Club really is just the English Breakfast Club," said Haley. "No sinister motives after all."

"Just a bunch of old farts with their own personal problems," sniffed Drayton. "Buddy Clark's got money problems and rowdy neighbors, Professor Gibbon is a tired old academic scratching around for a grant."

"What about Lawrence March?" asked Haley.

"Another old curmudgeon," said Drayton. "Albeit a nice one."

"Do you think Professor Gibbon really *does* have a copy of Harper's will?" asked Theodosia.

"Maybe," said Drayton tiredly. "Probably. Does it really matter any more? Now that the files on the hard drive have been recovered?"

"Not really," murmured Theodosia. She peered at Detective Tidwell as he jotted something on a clipboard, then handed it off to a uniformed officer. "What about Summer Sullivan? Was she involved?"

"Not that we can see," said Tidwell. "She was duped, same as Fisk. Although somewhere during his boat trip with Gordon Sargent, Harper Fisk probably came to realize he'd been conned and that Gordon Sargent meant to harm him."

"Too bad Harper even got in the boat with Sargent," said Drayton sadly.

"We won't know how Sargent pulled that off unless he comes completely clean," said Tidwell. "But thanks to all of you, we'll begin to methodically build a case against him." He searched their faces. "Any other questions?"

"Just one," said Theodosia. "Are you retiring?"

"Me? *Retire?*" Tidwell threw back his head and un-leashed a burst of hearty laughter. "That is *not* in my near fu-ture, I assure you. However, I'll be the first to admit that our police force is plagued with, shall we say, a few highly ter-ritorial players who probably need to be reassigned. But me retire? Hardly, dear lady." Tidwell's bulk was still jiggling with genuine merriment as he shook hands all around. "I'm off," he told them. "Call me if you come up with anything else."

Then they were left alone. The four of them, staring at each other.

"What now?" asked Haley.

"What are we going to do about the fashion show?" wailed Delaine. There was a loud buzzing on the other side of the Chinese screen, where the audience and models were still gathered. "Our audience shelled out sixty dollars for what was supposed to be a bang-up event. What are they going to think?"

"They'll think they got a bang-up event," said Drayton. "Complete with police, handcuffs, and screaming sirens."

"Will you *please* be serious, Drayton," hissed Delaine.

"I am," said Drayton. "Which is why I announced to them earlier that there was going to be a fifteen-minute intermission."

"Did they believe you?" asked Delaine, glancing at her jewel-encrusted Chopard. "It's been almost half an hour!"

Drayton shrugged. "Nobody's walked out yet."

"Probably because they haven't been served lunch yet," said Haley with a mischievous grin.

Delaine continued to daub at her eyes with a hanky as tears trickled down her cheeks.

Theodosia peered at Delaine carefully. *Are those croco-dile tears? No, they actually appear quite genuine. Poor De-*

laine, she worked so hard to pull this off. Now the show is half-wrecked, her audience is over there milling about uncertainly.

"You know," said Theodosia slowly, "I'm a firm believer in the old adage, the show must go on." She turned to Drayton. "What do you think, Drayton, still feeling game?"

He mopped his brow with a hanky and tugged at his bow tie, which had been knocked slightly askew in all the commotion. "Why not?" he said with more than a little bit of enthusiasm. "Let me go forth and attempt a bit more damage control."

With spring in his step and resolution in his attitude, Drayton strode to the podium, and stepped confidently up to the microphone. Holding up his hands, he once again gained the attention of the audience. "Ladies, my very profound apologies. We experienced a bit of an impromptu disaster, which has since been resolved by our own Miss Theodosia Browning. But I guarantee you, this fine luncheon and rather fanciful fashion show shall not miss a beat." Drayton signaled the waiters who were by now standing by, bearing giant silver trays of tea sandwiches and slices of quiche. "Our lavender and lace tea is going to proceed as scheduled. And as you enjoy your exquisite luncheon, our very comely models shall continue to dazzle you with a splendid array of summer fashions from Charleston's own unique boutique, the Cotton Duck."

There was delighted applause all around, and an appreciative chorus of ooh's and ah's as the food was set on the tables. Then Drayton signaled for the music to resume and quickly crossed the courtyard to rejoin Theodosia, Delaine, and Haley.

"Haley," he asked, "think you have the energy to sashay down the runway one more time?"

Haley lifted her right leg in a sharp kick that sent one of her high-heeled sandals flying across the patio. Lifting her other leg, she sent the second shoe flying into a potted palm. "Now I'm ready," she proclaimed.

"Delaine?" said Theodosia. "Ready to walk the runway?"

"We're really going to finish the show?" Delaine asked hopefully.

"Of course we're going to finish the show," Theodosia said as she slung her arms around Drayton's and Haley's shoulders and pulled them close to her. "Let's do it!" she urged.

Drayton linked his right arm around Delaine's shoulders and pulled her in line with the three of them. "Buck up, will you?" he said encouragingly. "After all, Fashion Bash is *your* show."

"But Theodosia turned out to be the star," said Delaine, grateful tears glistening in her eyes.

"Star investigator, anyway," pronounced Drayton. "On that we all agree."

Then the four of them, arms linked together, walked Wizard-of-Oz-style down the Oriental carpet to the delighted applause of the audience.

RECIPES FROM
THE INDIGO TEA SHOP

Haley's Sweet Potato Muffins

1/2 cup butter or margarine, softened
1 1/4 cups sugar
2 eggs
1 1/4 cups mashed cooked sweet potatoes
1/3 cup milk
1 1/2 cups all-purpose flour
2 tsp. baking powder
1/4 tsp. salt
1 tsp. ground cinnamon
1/4 tsp. ground nutmeg
1/2 cup raisins
1/4 cup chopped pecans
2 Tbsp. sugar
1/4 tsp. ground cinnamon

Cream butter then gradually add in 1 1/4 cups sugar, beating at medium speed. Add eggs, one at a time. Stir in sweet potatoes and milk.

Combine flour, baking powder, salt, 1 tsp. cinnamon, and 1/4 tsp. nutmeg; add to creamed mixture and stir until moistened. Stir in raisins and pecans. Spoon into greased muffins pans, filling about two-thirds full. Combine 2 Tbsp. sugar and 1/4 tsp. cinnamon, and sprinkle over batter. Bake at 400 degrees for approximately 25 minutes. Yield 2 dozen.

Blackberry Cobbler

1 cup all-purpose flour
1/4 tsp. salt
2 Tbsp. plus 2 tsp. vegetable oil
3 Tbsp. cold water
2 Tbsp. cornstarch
1/2 cup unsweetened orange juice, divided
8 cups fresh blackberries
2/3 cups sugar
1/4 tsp. ground cinnamon
1/4 tsp. ground nutmeg
1/4 tsp. ground cloves
Vegetable cooking spray

Combine flour and salt in a small bowl and stir well. Combine oil and water in a small bowl and stir well. Pour oil mixture into flour mixture and stir with a fork until dry ingredients are moistenend. Shape into a ball, cover, and chill.

Combine cornstarch with 1/4 cup orange juice and set aside. Combine remaining 1/4 cup orange juice, blackberries, sugar, cinnamon, nutmeg, and cloves in a heavy sauce pan. Stir and bring to a boil, reduce heat, and simmer 8 minutes, stirring occasionally. Stir in cornstarch and orange juice mixture. Return to a boil and cook 1 minute, stirring constantly until mixture is thick and bubbly. Remove from heat and pour into a 10x6x2-inch baking dish coated with cooking spray.

Roll dough to 1/8-inch thicknesss on lightly

floured surface. Cut into 1/2-inch strips and arrange over blackberry mixture in a lattice design. Bake at 425 degrees for 30 to 35 minutes. Yields 8 servings.

Chilled Peach Soup

4 ripe peaches
1/2 cup dry white wine
1 1/2 cup low-fat buttermilk
1/4 cup orange juice
2 Tbsp. honey
Salt

Peel and pit the peaches, then cut into chunks, removing bits of red flesh. Combine peaches and wine in blender or food processor and puree until smooth. Combine puree with buttermilk, orange juice, honey, and dash of salt. Cover and refrigerate at least 4 hours. Makes 6 servings.

Ginger-Pear Scones

2 cups all-purpose flour
1 cup sugar
1 tsp. baking powder
1 tsp. ground ginger
1/2 tsp. baking soda
1/2 tsp. salt
1/2 cup butter, cut into small chunks
3/4 cup pears, diced and dried
1/3 cup chopped candied ginger
2/3 cup buttermilk
1 egg, beaten, for tops

In large bowl mix flour, sugar, baking powder, ground ginger, baking soda, and salt. Cut in butter until mixture is crumbly. Mix in the pears and candied ginger. Mix in buttermilk just to blend. Gather mixture into a ball and gently knead on lightly floured surface. Pat or roll out 3/4 inch thick. Cut out 12 circles with a 2 1/2-inch or 3-inch cutter, rerolling scraps as necessary. Place on baking sheet and brush tops with beaten egg, then sprinkle with sugar. Bake at 425 degrees for 12 to 15 minutes until lightly browned and springy to touch.

Miniature Almond Cakes

1 cup blanched almonds
1 1/3 cups sugar
1 cup all-purpose flour
3 egg whites

Pulse almonds in food processor until finely ground. Add sugar and flour, process until blended. Blend in the egg whites. With floured hands, shape mixture into 24 balls and place 2 inches apart on greased cookie sheets. Bake at 325 degrees for 28 minutes, or until almond cakes are crisp on the outside and soft on the inside. Cool almond cakes on racks.

Tea-Bone Sauce

3/4 cup boiling water
2 tsp. loose green tea or 2 green tea bags
3 Tbsp. minced green onions
2 Tbsp. extra virgin olive oil

1 Tbsp. fresh lemon juice
1 Tbsp. soy sauce
2 tsp. honey
1 tsp. minced fresh-peeled ginger
1/4 tsp. minced and seeded chili pepper
1/8 tsp. salt
3 cloves garlic, minced

Combine boiling water and tea in bowl; cover and steep for 3 minutes. Strain tea into another bowl or remove tea bags. Add remaining ingredients, stir, then cover and chill for about 30 minutes. Brush sauce on steak or chops before grilling and or use as a dipping sauce.

Planked Fish

Drill several holes in a 1-inch thick cedar plank or purchase a "grilling plank" from a gourmet shop. Allow plank to soak in water for 1 hour.

Season a 3-pound salmon fillet with salt and pepper and place on top of plank.

Mix together the following ingredients:

2 small Vidalia onions, thinly sliced
3 garlic cloves, minced
2 green onions, finely chopped
2 Tbsp. fresh rosemary, chopped
2 Tbsp. rice wine vinegar
2 Tbsp olive oil

Spoon mixture over fish and place plank on grill. Cover and cook over medium-high heat until fish flakes with a fork, about 20 minutes. Garnish with lemon wedges. Serves 6.

Tea Dyeing

Boil 4 cups of water for each yard of fabric you want to dye. When water comes to a boil, add 2 tea bags for each cup of water. Allow tea to steep for about 5 minutes. Remove tea bags and soak your fabric in the pot of tea. Swish fabric around if you want to achieve even coloration, move it less often for a more mottled effect. Depending on your tea and your fabric, you might need to soak for an hour or as long as overnight. Once fabric is slightly darker than you want, remove fabric and rinse under cool water. Color will be lost by doing this, but you can always resoak if you want to darken it. Now toss your fabric into the dryer and tumble dry on a high heat setting to set the color.

Dyeing Tips

* Tea dyeing works only with natural fibers—cotton, silk, linen, and wool.
* It's a good idea to test a small piece of fabric first.
* Peppermint tea yields pale yellow.
* Orange spice tea yields beige-tan.
* Hibiscus tea yields pink.
* Orange pekoe tea yields orange.
* All tea-dyed fabrics will fade with time.
* If you don't like the color, wash your fabric out with bleach.

Teatime Entertaining Ideas

Going out to a tea room is always a special event,
but it's also fun to invite friends into your home
for tea, treats, and good conversation.

Pick a theme and let your imagination soar.

If your garden is blooming, stage an outdoor Rose
Tea. Scatter rose petals across white linen tablecloths,
use rose-themed dishes, add bouquets of fresh flowers. Serve almond cakes, tartlets filled with fresh
berries, and green tea sorbet. Rose hips or hibiscus tea
would be delicious. If the day is warm, add a crystal
pitcher of orange-lemon iced tea.

A mystery book discussion or tales of family "skele-
tons in the attic" can kick off a Ghost Story Tea. Serve
pumpkin bread with cream cheese, apple or prune
tarts, chocolate chestnut torte. A full-bodied Assam
would be highly complementary.

Tiny teacups are the rule for a Tea Taster's Tea. Serve
tiny sandwich wedges, teenier slices of cake and sweets.
Serve a "flight" of Keemun, Yunnan, and Puerh black
teas. Or indulge in fruitier teas like jasmine, mango, and
Indian spice.

If your high tea includes flouncy hats, a silver tea
service, and white gloves, chances are it's a Great
Gatsby Tea. Pristine linen napkins, your best china,

and flickering candles make the table luxe. Lobster or shrimp salad is wonderfully indulgent, as are blinis spread with caviar and sour cream. Earl Grey would be highly appropriate.

Invite your musically inclined friends to perform or play a CD to set the mood for a Chamber Music Tea. Sensuality rules with brioche, chocolate cake flavored with a hint of jasmine, and Darjeeling, the champagne of teas.

Jasmine
Moon Murder

The traditional Ghost Crawl in Charleston's Jasmine Cemetery is an annual autumn event. Under a full moon, amateur actors attired in Civil War–era costumes reenact historic scenes with a flourish of pageantry and pomp. But as stage lights flicker and dim and actors appear and disappear among ghostly gravestones, something goes terribly wrong. Dr. Jasper Davis, Jory Davis's uncle, clutches his chest in pain and collapses. Even though the paramedics arrive moments later, Theodosia soon learns that their heroic efforts were in vain. For nothing could have revived Jory's uncle from a mysterious and toxic dose of fentanyl!

**Be sure to read all the books in the
Tea Shop Mystery series by Laura Childs.**

Death by Darjeeling

*Meet Theodosia Browning, owner of Charleston's beloved
Indigo Tea Shop. Patrons love her blend of delicious tea
tastings and Southern hospitality. And Theo enjoys the full-
bodied flavor of a town steeped in history—and mystery!*

"A delightful book!"   —*Tea—a Magazine*

"Murder suits her (Laura Childs) to a Tea."
                                              —*St. Paul Pioneer Press*

"Tea lovers, mystery lovers, this is for you."
                                       —Susan Wittig Albert,
                        author of the best-selling China Bayles series

"The well-drawn plot includes an intriguing amateur sleuth,
and the likeable cast of characters makes *Death by Darjeeling* a wonderful reading exprience."

                                              —www.bookreview.com

"Gives the reader a sense of traveling through the streets and
environs of the beautiful, historic city of Charleston."
                                              —*Lakeshore Weekly News*

"We are treated to a behind-the-scenes look at running a tea
shop, as well as solid tea information."

                                              —www.theteashop.com

"A good beginning to a new culinary series that will quickly
become a favorite of readers."   —*The Mystery Reader*

"Tea lovers in particular will enjoy the arcane world of tea. But these details merely add depth and flavor to the story, never distracting from the likeable characters or the nicely crafted plot." —MysteriousStrands.com

"Any fan of Agatha Christie would enjoy this as well."
—*Tea Time Worldwide*, Online Newsletter

"If you devoured Nancy Drew and Trixie Belden, this new (Tea Shop) series is right up your alley."
—*The Goose Creek (SC) Gazette*

Named #1 Paperback Bestseller by the Independent Mystery Booksellers' Association

Received the "2001 New Discovery Award" from the Literary Guild's Mystery Book Club

Named to "Mystery Hotlist" by Overbooked.com

Book choice for Yahoo.com's Mystery Book Discussion

Book choice for the Food and Friends Book Club at MysteryLovers.com

"Highly Recommended" by the Ladies Tea Guild

Named "Book of Choice" by the Red Hat Society

Gunpowder Green

Theodosia finds herself in hot water again when an antique pistol misfires during a sailboat race in Charleston Harbor.

"A charming mystery . . . as brisk and refreshing as any brew! —*Romantic Times Magazine*

"Brilliantly weaving suspense and tea knowledge, this is a true gem." —*In the Library Reviews*

Shades of Earl Grey

Earl Grey, Theodosia's lovable mixed-breed Dalbrador, helps bring a cat burglar to justice.

Chosen an "Editor's Monthly Alternate" by the Literary Guild's Mystery Book Club

#2 on the Paperback Bestseller List of the Independent Mystery Booksellers' Association

"Highly Recommended" by the Red Hat Society

A "Featured Selection" of the Ladies Tea Guild

"A heart-stopping opening scene."   —*St. Paul Pioneer Press*

"Delicious cozy."   —BooksnBites.com

"Once again, the reader experiences the scents, atmosphere, and elegance of Charleston."   —*Lakeshore Weekly News*

"The great attraction of Laura Childs's tea mysteries is their coziness, but they go beyond that; they're like comfort food with a criminal element."   —*Tea A Magazine*

"A galaxy of well developed characters."
                                —*The Drood Review of Mystery*

"A delightful mystery full of all the things cozy fans look for."   —*The Mystery Reader*

"The Indigo Tea Shop mysteries are a tasty travelogy of gorgeous Charleston."   —MysteryLovers.com

"*Shades of Earl Grey* is another winner!"—Ladies Tea Guild

PHOTO FINISHED
The second book in the Scrapbooking Mystery series.

What could be more fun than an all-night crop at Carmela's scrapbooking shop? As ideas on rubber stamping, hand-tinting photos, and decorating album covers are shared, scrapbookers also help themselves to hurricane rum drinks, jambalaya, and homemade praline pie. Spirits run high and the soft New Orleans night buzzes with excitement. But when Bartholomew Hayward, the shady antique dealer from next door, is found sprawled in the back alley with scissors jammed in his neck, it looks like the work of a very crafty killer!